Kate scowled
at the bottom

Adam stood and wa... ribbons of her cloak.

'Let me do that,' he said gently. Their hands met and he forgot this morning's anger.

'Do you remember the first time we met and I helped you tie some ribbons? I thought you were a Gorgon but then I discovered you were Tom's sister.' He put his hands on her shoulders. 'You don't look like your brother, Kate, but last night when you were laughing I could see Tom in you.' He smiled ruefully. 'We really shouldn't fight. I promised your brother that I would make sure you were safe. Don't condemn me for taking that promise seriously.'

Katharine dropped her eyes. 'I'll try not to. I know you mean well—I'm just not used to obeying orders!'

'Is that what they sound like? I'm sorry. Let's make a bargain. I will try to sound less peremptory if you will make an effort to meet me halfway when I am doing my best to look after you. Agreed?'

Dear Reader

The Duchess of Richmond's ball, in Brussels on June 15th 1815, was one of the great dramatic occasions in history. But what makes the ball noteworthy isn't the brilliance of the guest list—it is the poignancy of what happened in the three days that followed.

The young men who danced so light-heartedly in their uniforms of scarlet, blue, green and gold on the night of June 15th, dazzling the beau monde with their gaiety and charm, left the ballroom, some of them still in their dress uniforms, to ride straight into one of the hardest-fought battles in European history—the battle of Waterloo. By 18th June the Duke of Wellington had triumphed over Napoleon Bonaparte. But the cost in lives was huge, and many of those young men were never to return.

Firm friends Adam Calthorpe, Ivo Trenchard and their commanding officer Colonel Ancroft do survive the battlefield, to return to London Society's opulent drawing rooms. Three soldiers, skilled at war but not nearly as adept as they think when it comes to the ways of women. How will they fare? I hope you enjoy *Lord Calthorpe's Promise*, which is the first of three linked books.

Sylvia Andrew

LORD CALTHORPE'S PROMISE

Sylvia Andrew

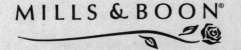

MILLS & BOON®

First published in Great Britain 2002
Harlequin Mills & Boon Limited,
Eton House, 18-24 Paradise Road, Richmond, Surrey TW9 1SR

© Sylvia Andrew 2002

ISBN 0 263 83124 8

Set in Times Roman 10½ on 12¼ pt.
04-0602-75592

Printed and bound in Spain
by Litografia Rosés S.A., Barcelona

Sylvia Andrew taught modern languages for a number of years, ultimately becoming Vice-Principal of a sixth-form college. She lives in Somerset with two cats, a dog, and a husband who has a very necessary sense of humour, and a stern approach to punctuation. Sylvia has one daughter living in London, and they share a lively interest in the theatre. She describes herself as an 'unrepentant romantic'.

Chapter One

June 1815

Adam Calthorpe stood in the doorway of the Duchess of Richmond's ballroom and surveyed the scene. The Duchess had spared no effort to make this ball one of the season's outstanding events, and it looked as if she had been successful in spite of considerable competition. Ever since the Duke of Wellington, Commander-in-Chief of the Allied armies, had made the Belgian capital his headquarters, pleasure seekers from all over Europe had been gathering to enjoy the brilliant social life to be found there, and for weeks Brussels had been a whirl of parties, concerts, dances, picnics, musical rides and a host of other entertainments. Adam wondered briefly how long it would last...

With an effort he dismissed all thought of the worrying news coming in from the French border. Time for that later. He and the others were here to spread confidence, to reassure. He looked down the ballroom, and smiled. Everything seemed to be as usual in the Duchess's ballroom. Tom Payne was galloping down the country dance set with more enthusiasm than grace, Ivo Trenchard was leaning over the beautiful wife of a Belgian diplomat as if she were the only woman in the world for him. As she was, thought Adam cynically, for the next half-hour. They were all, so to speak, on duty—detailed to represent the Duke's staff at the ball—and were all wearing full dress uniforms. It was a very hot evening. Adam felt uncomfortable enough in his high stock and black cravat, his scarlet and gold lace, Tom's face was shining with his exertions, but Ivo looked as cool and controlled as ever in his magnificent Hussar uniform. All the same, that fur-trimmed pelisse must be unbearably warm. Even as Adam looked, Ivo offered his arm to the lady and they walked out through the long windows into the garden…

'Lord Calthorpe!'

Adam turned. An elderly lady in a blaze of diamonds caught his arm anxiously. Adam took the clawlike hand and kissed it. As he straightened up he smiled reassuringly. 'How may I help you, Countess Karnska?'

'The Duke. He is not here?'

'Not yet, Countess. But you know how much his Grace likes dancing. He'll be here presently.'

'But what does it mean that he is late? Is it true what they are saying? That Bonaparte has crossed the Belgian border? Is the Duke aware of this? Should we leave Brussels while we can?'

Mentally cursing the busybodies who ferreted out the latest news from the frontier and spread it among the anxious populace, Adam smiled again and said, 'You may be sure, Countess, that the Duke is fully aware of the situation. But there is really no cause for alarm, I assure you. Brussels is in no danger.'

'It's all very well to say so, *milor'*.' The Countess had been joined by her son, a florid gentleman in a puce coat. 'But Bonaparte is a genius. A genius! And, as far as I know, the Duke of Wellington has not yet ever faced him in battle. How can you be so sure?'

'Comte, Napoleon Bonaparte may be the genius you say he is, but I fancy the Duke has his measure. You and your mother should forget Bonaparte and enjoy the ball. The Duke has everything in hand. Now, may I fetch you some wine, Countess? You will see his Grace very soon, I promise you. He is merely dining late.'

Adam fetched some wine for the two guests, and then made his escape. He hoped he knew his duty, but enough was enough. The air in the ballroom was stifling, and the thought of even two minutes of reassuring yet another aristocratic visitor, who had come to enjoy the brilliant social life in Brussels and had stayed to regret it, appalled him. In the past hour he had had a dozen such conversations and for the moment he was tired of concealing his own anxieties.

He saw that Ivo and his lady had returned to the ballroom and decided to have some air himself. But even out in the garden at ten o'clock at night it was still very warm, with not the slightest hint of a breeze. Adam stood watching the dancers for a while through the wide glass doors. It was a splendid sight, dominated by the scarlet and gold of uniforms, the ladies in their light muslins and silks fluttering like moths around them. But the laughter was more highly pitched than was normal, and more than a few of the faces round the ballroom were anxious.

For all his reassuring words to the Countess, Adam knew the situation to be even more disquieting than they suspected. News of Bonaparte's sudden advance against the Prussians had come late to the Allied head-quarters, and, far from dining late, the Duke and his aides were closeted in the Richmonds' library, conning maps and writing sheaf after sheaf of new orders. Soon Adam and others like him would be galloping to de-liver them all over the Belgian countryside, wherever the Allied troops were encamped. It looked as if Bo-ney might have stolen a march after all on the Allied Commander-in-Chief...

Oddly, Adam had no doubt of the outcome. After seven years of campaigning with Wellington he had absolute confidence in the Duke's ability to get the better of his enemy. But the battle ahead was going to be a tough one, of that he was equally certain. He sighed. It would probably be his last. The Army had been good to him—promotion had come quickly, and at thirty he was on the Duke's own staff, seconded from his regiment with the acting rank of Major. But once this campaign was over, he must think seriously of going back to England. Inheriting his uncle's estate had been an unexpected piece of good fortune, but it also brought its duties. The estate was large and had been neglected—it would need a great deal of his at-tention. And it was time he set about finding a suitable bride...

It was certain to feel strange at first, after ten years of marching, fighting and bivouacking all over West-ern Europe. Ten years ago it had been perfectly in order for a young man with no hint of future riches, no prospect of a title and estates in England, to take a commission in the British Army. Ten years ago he had had two lusty cousins between him and the handsome estate near Bath which was now his. It was ironic that Adam had survived ten years of some of the toughest fighting in Europe, while his cousins had both died in the pursuit of pleasure at home—one in a brawl outside a tavern in London and the other on the hunting field. Quite unforeseen, Adam had come into a title, as well as a substantial fortune. He owed it to his family to return to England and to look after the inheritance which had so unexpectedly come his way. The excitement of life in the Army, the cameraderie, the fights, the celebrations—one last great battle, and then they would be over.

He turned towards the ballroom again, but stopped short when he caught sight of a young couple coming his way. They were a handsome pair—the lad's distinctive uniform of the Blues was a wonderful foil for the girl's white dress and guinea-gold hair. They paused in the doorway… Adam drew a sharp breath and his heart gave a thump. *Julia!* What in the name of all the gods was Julia doing here? For a moment he couldn't think—he was transported back ten years to a glade in the woods which surrounded the Redshaws' estate…

He had a vivid picture of himself at twenty, just down from Oxford and passionately in love with Julia Redshaw. He had met her often in the woods which separated her home from his, the secrecy of their meetings adding to the romance of their affair. It had all been touchingly innocent. But the day came when he had kissed her, kissed her with all the ardour of a lover… They had drawn back from each other, gazing in wonder, mixed with a touch of fear, he remembered. The whirlwind they had raised between them had astonished them both.

It wasn't surprising that his voice had been a touch unsteady as he said, 'I…I shouldn't have done that. I'm sorry, Julia.'

Julia's eyes had sparkled blue fire at him. 'Don't you dare say you're sorry, Adam Calthorpe!' she had said. 'How could anyone be sorry about a…a kiss like that? To know that we love each other like that? I'm not sorry! Kiss me again, Adam!'

Adam smiled. At twenty he had been so serious, such an idealist! He remembered feeling slightly shocked, saying, 'N…No. Not again. Not before you'll say that you'll marry me.'

That was when disillusionment had set in. Julia's eyes had widened and their sparkle diminished. '*Marry* you? Why?'

'Well, of course we must marry! It's what we've always wanted…isn't it? I know I fell in love with you the minute we met. Are you saying you don't love me after all?'

'No, no! I do, I do!' She had flung her arms round his neck. 'You know I do!'

How hard it had been to ignore those arms! But he had put her gently aside. 'Well, then…?'

'But marriage is something different. I couldn't possibly marry *you*, Adam. What on earth should we live on? No, no, when I get married it will be to someone rich!'

The memory of his disbelief was still surprisingly

strong. But he hadn't been able to move her. She had remained as affectionate as ever but adamant. Julia Redshaw was determined to marry into a fortune, and though she loved Adam Calthorpe as much as it was in her to love anyone, she was not going to change her mind. She would not even promise to wait. In one short summer Adam Calthorpe lost his love and his ideals, and grew up. He refused to stay and watch while the love of his life pursued her goal of marrying a wealthy man. Instead, he had persuaded his uncle to buy him a commission in the Army, and had left England. It had been his good fortune that the regiment he had chosen eventually turned into one of the crack fighting machines in the Peninsula...

He stole another glance at the girl in the doorway. How stupid of him! This couldn't possibly be Julia. This girl was hardly more than seventeen, and Julia was only three years younger than he. Julia would be twenty-seven now, certainly a married woman, no doubt a *wealthily* married woman. He shook his head, impatient with his own folly. How odd that the sight of guinea-gold hair, a tumble of curls over a heart-shaped face, still had the power to disorient him! He would have sworn he had forgotten Julia Redshaw. Certainly, for the past six or seven years, he had seldom given a thought to the girl whose rejection had first sent him into his present career.

He smiled wryly. How oddly it had all turned out! Would it have made a difference if Julia and her father had known that Adam would one day step into his uncle Calthorpe's title and riches? Hardly! Time waited for no one, and ten years would have been a long time for a girl of seventeen to wait! He himself had changed in those years. He was no longer the hot-headed romantic who had joined the Army in despair when Julia Redshaw had rejected him. He had since enjoyed several quite lively affairs, with no thought of marriage on either side. And now, at thirty, he was all set to look for a wife with whom he hoped to enjoy a more mature relationship, with less passion and more sense! There would be affection, he hoped, and respect, but not the headlong folly of that first love. Julia Redshaw would remain in the past and he would find a modest, well-bred girl to take her place—in his life, if not in his affections.

He watched the golden-haired girl floating away on the arm of her partner, and felt a last momentary pang. Then he shook his head and made for the ballroom again.

He was met at the door by Lieutenant Tom Payne. The country dances were finished and Tom was alight with excitement.

'I say, sir, isn't this a splendid do? What a send-off for the troops, aye!'

Adam smiled. It was impossible not to smile at Tom. Six feet tall, fair hair that was usually falling over one eye, fresh-faced and full of enthusiasm, he reminded Adam of a large puppy and aroused in him the same amused affection, tempered with respect for his qualities as a fighting man. Tom had been a member of Adam's company ever since Spain, and his devotion to Adam was second only to his devotion to life in the Army generally.

Adam asked, 'Any news, yet?'

'No, I've just been to enquire. The Beau is still

stuck in his papers with De Lacey and the others. Lord, I wish they'd get on with it.'

'"The Beau" is no way to refer to our revered Commander-in-Chief, you graceless young dog! How ready are you to ride off when the orders do appear? I can see you're dressed as unsuitably as I am for a swift ride through the night.'

'It won't take me long to change, I promise you. What about you, sir?'

'It might take me a fraction longer, but I'll manage. I wish the Duke had chosen someone else to do his entertaining for him, I can't say I've enjoyed it.' There was a short silence as they paused to regard the dancers circling round.

Then Tom Payne said, 'I know I have to leave the Army after this is all over. But I'm not looking forward to it. It'll all seem a bit tame after Spain and now here. Y'can't hunt and shoot all the time, and what else is there at home?'

'You and the Army might have been made for each other, I agree. But your grandfather's death was bound to put an end to it all, Tom.'

'That's true! I should have gone back months ago. There's the estate, and there's my sister, too. Heaven knows what would happen to her if I left her to herself. What she needs is a husband, of course.'

Adam laughed. 'That's a coincidence! I have just been deciding that I need to settle down and look for a wife!'

'You're not thinking of leaving the Army, are you sir?' Tom's face was a picture of astonishment. 'Not when you don't *have* to?'

'But I do have to. You're not the only one with

responsibilities, Lieutenant! And I'm a good bit older than you. No, we shall have one last glorious fling, and then we shall both knuckle down to a sober, industrious life at home!' He laughed at the expression of disgust on Tom's face. 'It won't be so bad. And you know, Tom, once we've settled Napoleon Bonaparte once and for all, life in the Army in peacetime could get very dull.'

'There'll always be a fight somewhere, sir! You know I'm not very good with words, but I've never been as happy as I am now. I've never fitted in anywhere as well as I fit in here.'

Adam looked at his junior. Tom was right. By temperament and character he was an ideal soldier. Whether he would have reached the top was more questionable. He was a man of action, not of thought. In battle there was no better fighter, no one more daring, or more loyal. But inactivity bored him, and when he was bored he tended to get into mischief. During quieter periods in Portugal and Spain, Adam had more than once been forced to defend Lieutenant Payne against a charge of misconduct—usually successfully, for everyone liked Tom. What would happen when he was forced to lead the quieter life of a country gentleman? The high spirits and daring, which made him such a brilliant soldier, might well turn to recklessness. Or would he move to London, where he would find even more dangerous adventures? From what Adam knew of his family, there was no one to check him. The two Paynes, brother and sister, were alone in the world. He was so deep in thought that he did not at first hear Tom's hesitant voice.

'Sir…sir!'

'Tom?'

'Sir, are you definitely leaving the Army?'

'Quite certainly.'

'Sir, may I ask something? If you don't like it, you only have to say no…'

Adam knew that pleading tone. Tom was about to ask something outrageous. 'Out with it!' he said with a resigned smile. But even he was not prepared for quite how outrageous Tom's request would be.

'Sir, if you liked the idea…I mean, if you are really looking for a wife… Would you…would you consider my little sister? I'd like nothing better for her than to marry you.'

Adam was speechless with astonishment. 'Tom! Are you out of your mind?'

Tom's desperation gave him the courage to pursue his goal. 'Oh, I realise that you would need to meet her before you considered such a thing. But… but…if…if you liked each other… And you did say that you wanted to marry… And as sisters go, she's not at all bad. She's fun to be with, and she is very good-tempered and…and patient. Usually. She's had a rough time these past years with my grandfather being ill, and me away in Spain. And she *needs* someone—someone like you, to look after her!'

'I thought that was to be your job,' said Adam sternly.

'Well, I will. But she must marry some time!' When Adam continued to regard him in the severest disapproval Tom went on, 'She's a very pretty little thing, too. And…and very understanding. Tolerant.' He stopped and looked at Adam with the air of a starved puppy looking for a bone. Adam began to be amused at his persistence.

'What is this, Tom? Why are you so keen to marry your sister off?'

'Well, I thought…I thought that if I could find someone I could trust to look after her I might be able to think of the Army again…'

'The idea is absurd! Give it up!' Adam started to walk back to the ballroom. 'Come on! It's time we reported for duty.'

'Well, would you think about coming down to Herriards? Just to meet her?'

'I'll agree to that. Not with the idea of meeting your sister with an eye to marriage, Tom—but I'd be pleased to visit you once we're back in England. Come!' Tom looked crestfallen, but obeyed the dismissal in Adam's voice. Together they walked briskly through the ballroom and up the stairs to the small 'den' which had been allotted to the Duke's staff.

Here they found several others, waiting for orders. Any minute now they would be given their assignments, to ride into the night with new commands for the regiments stationed in the countryside round the Belgian capital. Adam hoped he'd be given a chance to change out of his full dress uniform before leaving. White breeches, gold lace and silken sashes did not stand up well to the sort of hard riding which would be expected of him. His regiment was stationed almost as far from Brussels as it was possible to be.

He turned as Ivo Trenchard came in, resplendent in his pelisse and fur. 'You look warm, Ivo!'

'It must be the hottest night yet! But that's not it, my dear boy. If I look a trifle flushed, it's through hard work. I've been reassuring all the ladies that Boney ain't going to capture the lot of them and haul 'em all off to Paris.'

'I'm sure you reassured them every one... splendidly,' drawled Adam. 'Madame de Menkelen seemed particularly impressed. But does she realise that Bonaparte might not be the only danger she faces?'

There was a shout of laughter. Captain Lord Trenchard was Brussels's worst flirt. His exploits with the ladies—who were most of them, it has to be said, only too willing—were legendary. Adam knew him for a cool, resourceful fighter, and a ruthless opponent in the field, but no one observing his indolent figure and lazy charm at work in the drawing rooms of Society would have suspected as much. He had a number of advantages, of course. He was not only rich and related to half the top families in England, but was tall, with dark brown hair, sparkling blue eyes and a slow smile which wrought havoc among the female population wherever he happened to be. Perhaps it was this ease of conquest which had made him somewhat cynical, certainly in his attitude to the fair sex. Be he never so charming, no woman had as yet managed to hold his attention for long, and the matchmaking mamas of Brussels had long regarded him as a hopeless case. But though Adam might deplore Ivo Trenchard's more outrageous affairs, the two men were good friends. Adam found it significant that the men in Ivo Trenchard's company had enormous respect and trust in him as a leader.

'How is it that you're still with us, young Tom?' Trenchard asked now. 'I thought you had decided to leave us to fight without you? Or have you changed your mind?'

The Lieutenant coloured up. 'It wasn't because I was tired of fighting,' he began defensively. 'I wish I needn't leave at all—' He stopped. Adam intervened.

'Leave the poor fellow alone, Ivo! He really ought to be in England at this moment, but he decided to postpone his departure from the Army when he heard about Boney's escape. Wasn't sure we could finish this job without him, were you, Tom?'

The ready colour surged once more in Tom Payne's cheeks. He ignored Adam's teasing words and said, 'But this is going to be the greatest fight ever! Boney has never faced the Duke directly before! He's bound to lose, of course, but think of the challenge! I couldn't have missed a battle like this. I think I'll just slip downstairs to see if anything has cropped up. We can't have to wait much longer. Excuse me.' He gave a slight salute and hurried out.

The two older men smiled at the Lieutenant's eagerness. 'All the same, Adam,' Ivo said, 'the boy is right. It's going to be a battle between Titans. Let's hope we survive to tell the tale afterwards.'

'We shall, Ivo, we shall. Only the good die young. But I hope Tom manages to keep a cool head. He's apt to let his enthusiasm run away with him, and take unnecessary risks.'

'While you, as we all know, stand back and let others do the dangerous work?' said Ivo with a mocking smile.

'I don't lose my head, Ivo! I'm too old for that. But Tom... The trouble is that he's so sick at the thought of leaving the Army that he might well decide to go out in a blaze of glory.'

'Why *is* he leaving? Or am I being indiscreet?'

'Not at all, it's very straightforward—I'm surprised he hasn't told you. Tom and his sister were brought up by their grandfather. They haven't any other close relations. The grandfather died last year, and Tom really has no choice but to go back to England and look after his sister and what, from all accounts, is a substantial estate. But he put off leaving when the news came through that Napoleon had slipped the leash on Elba and was marching through France, ready for another campaign.'

'What about the sister?'

'There's a governess or companion—something like that. She's looking after the girl until Tom gets back.'

'Let's hope he does…'

Adam frowned. 'Amen to that! The Payne estate is entailed. If Tom dies without an heir it goes to a distant cousin. I wonder what would happen to his sister then?'

'If she has half of Tom's looks and charm she will probably marry some local squire and be perfectly happy,' said Ivo with a cynical smile. He stretched himself and yawned. 'Lord, where the devil are those orders?'

In fact, it was half an hour before Tom returned. His eager informality had vanished, for he accompanied Colonel Ancroft, the commanding officer of their group. But underneath Tom's rigidly correct manner Adam could see that the young man was still ablaze with excitement.

'Well, gentlemen, it looks as if we shall all be in

action tomorrow. The last checks are being made and as soon as the orders are brought you will be dispersing at speed. Meanwhile, shall we drink to Boney's downfall? Tom?'

Tom went over to the corner table and poured out some wine. He served them all round, and they solemnly toasted the King, each other, and lastly, but most heartily, they drank to death and destruction to Napoleon and his troops. Then Colonel Ancroft nodded and they sat down. There was a moment's pause, while they all tried to think of something to break the silence. Their commanding officer had an air of authority which came from more than his rank. Adam knew him to be not more than five or six years older than he was himself, but the Colonel's coal-black hair had silver wings at the temples, and under the severity of his gaze was a hint of pain, disciplined, suppressed, but there. He was generally held to be a cold man. He was certainly austere. Though he had the trust of all the men under him, and was known to be absolutely fair and impartial, it was not easy to like him. It certainly wasn't easy to make light conversation with him. But Adam had known him for a long time, and, acquainted as he was with some of the Colonel's history, he understood and respected the other man's reserve. However, perhaps because of the tensions of the night, their commanding officer seemed to be in a talkative mood.

'So, what are you all planning to do with yourselves after this is over? I hear you're leaving the Army, Tom? Reluctantly, I gather.'

'Sir.'

'You too, Adam?'

'I'm afraid so, sir.'

'Are you taking part in this wholesale exodus, Ivo? There'll be one or two sighs of relief among the husbands in Europe if you do!'

They laughed, Ivo as well. Then he looked down into his glass and said, 'To be honest, I don't know. sir. I have one or two bits of unfinished business in England. It's time I put things right with my father, for a start.'

'That's good! Lord Veryan will be pleased to see you again.'

'You think so? When I last saw him he was shouting that he never wished to set eyes on such a villainous, unnatural monster again.'

'I shouldn't let that deter you. People often say things in a rage that they don't really mean.' Colonel Ancroft stopped short. 'And do things, too,' he added, almost to himself. The curious little silence that followed was broken by the arrival of one of the Duke's aides. He had a sheaf of papers in his hand which he handed to the Colonel, who read them through, then gave them out. Most of the men were to rejoin their own regiments carrying the orders with them.

'The news is as bad as it can be, gentlemen. Napoleon has attacked the Prussians in force, and it seems likely that they will not be able to hold. To save Brussels we must concentrate our forces at Nivelles— these are the orders. God speed to you all!'

Ivo was the first to go, bound for Ninhove where the bulk of the English Cavalry could be found. Tom was given the task Adam had expected for himself, sent off to Ath to deliver the orders for the Light Divisions. His turn came immediately after.

'Wait outside, Lieutenant. Major Calthorpe will join you in a moment.'

Adam waited while his superior fidgeted with some papers. 'I've given you the hardest assignment, Adam. You're to deal with the Belgians—the King's generals can be touchy if they think their royal prerogative is being undermined. Tact and charm are needed, but above all they must move quickly!' The Colonel looked up with a gleam of humour in his hard grey eyes. 'I'd have sent Trenchard, but since his escapade with the Comtesse Leiken he's *persona non grata* at the court. But you have plenty of tact—you can deal with them. Get them to accept the Duke's commands—we can't afford debate, they're damned urgent.'

'Sir!'

'And, Adam—!'

'Sir?'

'You and young Payne will ride together for some of the way. Do what you can to calm him down. He's in too much of a death-or-glory mood.'

Adam gave a nod of understanding, saluted and left.

He found Tom outside, practically hopping with impatience. Together they set off to the west.

For a while they rode in silence, concentrating on getting out of Brussels as expeditiously as possible. But then they dropped the pace to a trot to allow their mounts time to recover. The cooler air outside the capital seemed to have a sobering effect on Tom. He said eventually, 'I'm not altogether a selfish villain, sir.'

Adam looked in surprise at him. 'I never thought you were. What is on your mind, Tom?'

'Asking you to consider my sister. It's not only that

I want to be free to rejoin the Army. But...but if any-thing happened to me—I know it's unlikely, but it could happen—she'd be left without protection from my cousins.'

'She would need protection? From members of your own family? Surely not!'

'Sir, she's by way of being a bit of an heiress. If anything happened to me, she'd be even more of one. The Payne estate is entailed on a distant cousin, but not any of the money. Henry Payne would have the house and lands, but not much to support them. I...my grandfather never trusted him and nor do I. And he has a son of my age—single and free to marry some-one like Kate. I knew him at Eton—he's a bit of a worm.'

'Whew!' Adam felt growing anger at the extent of Tom's irresponsiblity. 'In that case, why the devil did you risk staying on for this battle? You'd better make damned sure you come through it, my boy!' He stopped before he said something he might regret.

Tom was suffering from a belated attack of con-science. 'Kate always said I laughed too much and thought too little. I'll go back to England as soon as the Army releases me. But if anything should happen to me, sir, would you...?' He turned a worried face to Adam. 'Please! If she was married to you, she'd be safe.'

Adam said in exasperation, 'I can't promise to marry your sister—apart from anything else, she may not want to marry me! Have you thought of that? But I'll make sure she's looked after. And now we must push on. I turn off at the next crossroads.'

They rode on again at speed, pausing only briefly

where their ways parted. Adam wanted to urge Tom to caution, but found he couldn't. That was no way to send a serving soldier into battle. So he merely nodded and called 'Good luck!' as he turned on to the road to Braine le Comte.

Behind them, on the other side of Brussels, the Prussians were fighting a losing battle against the massed forces of the French. It would soon not be enough for Wellington's troops to wait at Nivelles. Before morning the Army would be ordered to Quatre Bras to meet Napoleon, and the final battle would be fought outside a small, as yet unheard-of village called Waterloo.

Chapter Two

July 1815

Katharine Payne stood at the window of her sitting room, a letter loosely held in her hand. The room had been hers ever since her grandfather had decided that she was old enough to leave the nursery and have her own set of rooms on the first floor. Till now, even in her most difficult or tempestuous moments, she had found calm and consolation in the view over the garden and beyond to the Hampshire countryside. But today she was blind to the flower beds, bright in the colours of high summer, the beautiful specimen trees, planted by her great-great-grandfather, the wide lawns, vividly green after a recent shower.

Tom was dead. Killed in action.

She had been told several weeks ago, of course. But throughout all the dreadful formalities, the visits from the family lawyers and all the rest, she had lived in a daze, still half expecting Tom to come bursting in through her door, his handsome face alight with laughter, mocking her for having fallen for one of his tricks.

Now this letter had brought the bitter truth home to
her at last. Tom would not come back. Not ever…
The letter fluttered to the floor as she hid her face in
her hands.

'Katharine! My dear!'

Katharine straightened up at the sound of Tilly's
voice.

'It's all right, Tilly,' she said, turning round. 'I'm
not about to break down.'

'It might do you good if you did,' said Miss Tillyard
gruffly. 'You can't go on as you are, Katharine.'

'No, I know. I must pull myself together and make
some plans.'

'That's not what I meant! But I agree you need to
think of the future.' She came over and picked up the
letter lying on the floor. 'Is this what has upset you?'

'Yes. It's from one of Tom's friends in the Army.
A Major Calthorpe—Lord Calthorpe. I've heard Tom
talk about him. It is…it is very kind. He obviously
liked Tom a great deal.'

'Was Lord Calthorpe with your brother when…?'

'No, but he has spoken to someone who was. He
tells me that Tom…died bravely.' She paused. Then
she went on, 'Lord Calthorpe saw Tom for the last
time on the evening before Waterloo. They talked of
me…' Her voice died again, and again she rallied. 'He
is coming back to England for a short while and would
like to call here. He knows I have no one else and
offers to help me in any way he can. It's a very kind
letter.'

Katharine's voice broke again, but Miss Tillyard resisted the temptation to put her arm round the girl. She
knew her pupil of old. When Katharine Payne was

hurting, any attempt to comfort her would be instantly rejected—she would regard accepting it as a sign of weakness. So Miss Tillyard kept her distance and asked instead, 'When will you see him?'

'I shan't see him at all. I don't want to see anyone.'

'But you ought—'

'It's very kind of Lord Calthorpe, but what could he do?'

'Katharine, he has taken the trouble to write. You ought to see him.'

'No, Tilly! No! I couldn't bear it. I shall write to thank him for the offer, of course.'

'Don't put him off completely, my dear. You might find you need his help in the future. Why not say that you would see him in a few weeks, when you are feeling better?'

'He wouldn't be able to come. From what Lord Calthorpe says, he is still on the Duke of Wellington's staff, and on duty with the Duke in France. And I really can't imagine what help a perfect stranger could give me. But if you think it is more polite, I'll do as you say.' Katharine turned back to her contemplation of the view. There was silence in the room.

Then Miss Tillyard asked quietly, 'When is your uncle due to arrive?'

'Any day now.'

'Have your guardians decided what is to happen to you?'

'General Armitage told me to wait till after my uncle has taken over here at Herriards. Sir James, of course, agreed with him.' She added with a touch of bitterness, 'I think those two old men are hoping that

Uncle Henry will offer me a home. They wouldn't know what to do with me otherwise.'

'The system of entailing property is a monstrous one!' Miss Tillyard said with uncharacteristic heat. 'You're the one who has really looked after the Herriards estate, Katharine—not just while your grandfather was ill, but for all the time your brother was away in the Army.' She stopped and thought. 'And now that I consider it, you were the one who saw to the estate when your brother *was* here, as well! All Tom ever thought about was the Army and how soon he could get back to it. And now, just because you are a female, you are effectively homeless, and Herriards is to go to someone who has never taken the slightest interest in it! It isn't right!'

Katharine gave a rueful smile. 'It's not exactly Uncle Henry's fault that he hasn't ever been here. My grandfather wouldn't let him come!'

'And why was that, pray?'

'I never knew. Uncle Henry isn't really my uncle. He's a distant sort of cousin, so Tom and I never had much to do with him. I think there was bad blood between the two branches of the family. Grandfather always called him ''that villain Henry''.'

'And look what has happened! Herriards now belongs to this same Henry Payne, simply because he is next in the male line after Tom. It is all his—farms, lands and this house as well.'

Katharine's face closed up. 'Yes. I've lost my home, as well as my brother,' she said. She spoke in such a detached tone that only someone who knew her as well as her former governess did could detect the heartache behind those briefly spoken words.

There was a pause, then Miss Tillyard said briskly, 'We must look on the bright side, Katharine. You know very little about Mr Henry Payne. I doubt he is the villain your grandfather called him. You told me that he has a family—a son and a daughter about your age. They could be ideal companions for you. You've lacked company of your own age for years.'

'I never wanted it. You were company enough for me, Tilly.'

'An old governess!'

'And now a friend,' said Katharine with a look of affection. 'I cannot say how grateful I am that you came back to live with me after Grandfather died. I know how much you love your little house in the village.'

'It's still there,' said Miss Tillyard. 'And, as soon as Mr Payne and his family come, I shall move back into it. You won't need me then—and your uncle won't thank me for staying. Now, why don't you write that letter to Lord Calthorpe? Are you sure you don't want him to come?'

'Quite sure. I already have two guardians to tell me what to do. I don't need advice from another elderly gentleman, however kind he may be.'

'Katharine! Lord Calthorpe is a serving officer. He can't be all that old!'

'He's on the Duke's staff. You noticed that he was not in action with Tom during the battle? He was probably safely back at headquarters. Tom used to call staff officers a lot of old women—and that was when he was being polite! No, I don't want some bewhiskered Army Major coming here to tell me how my brother died. And I certainly can't imagine that I would ever need any help from him.'

A week later Katharine sat in the saloon with Miss Tillyard. Both ladies were listening with an air of determined calm for sounds of arrival. Mr Henry Payne had announced his intention of coming that afternoon to take up his position as owner of Herriards. A crunching of gravel on the drive, sounds of bustle in the hall, then the door of the saloon opened and a large gentleman strode confidently in, brushing the housekeeper aside as he did so. Katharine was fascinated to see that his eyes were blue like Tom's, that his colour was high, as Tom's had been, and that his hair, though touched with grey, still had traces of Tom's reddish-gold. But his features were coarser, harder, in spite of his broad smile.

'No need to announce me! I'm not a guest.' He came over and took her hands in his. 'And here is little Katharine! My dear, I am delighted to meet you at last!' Then his face grew solemn and he added heavily, 'Though, of course, the circumstances are very sad for you. Indeed, for us all, for us all. How are you, my dear?'

'I am well, Uncle Henry, thank you. But where is Mrs Payne? Is she not with you?'

'Your Aunt Ellen and the children are arriving tomorrow. They can hardly wait to see their new home, but they couldn't leave Cheltenham when I did.' He looked inquiringly at Miss Tillyard. 'And this is?'

'This is my former governess and a dear friend, Miss Emily Tillyard. Mr Payne, Tilly.'

Henry Payne's smile diminished. He gave the brief-

est of nods in reply to Miss Tillyard's curtsy and said,
'Your governess, eh? Aren't you a little old for gov-
ernesses?'

'You mistake me, Uncle. Tilly isn't my governess
any more, she came back to live with me when Grandfather died.'

'Ah! Your companion! Well, there'll be no need for
that now, my dear. Miss Tillyard will be free to look
for another post as soon as your aunt arrives. Which
is tomorrow.' He beamed at them both as if he had
conferred the greatest of favours. He added, 'Sit down,
sit down, my dear! There's no need to stand on ceremony with me. You, too, Miss…er, Tilson—unless
you wish to go to your own quarters, of course. To
pack.'

Katharine was outraged. Annoyance at the insult to
Tilly was added to strong resentment at being invited
to sit down in what had been till now her own home.
But a warning glance from Tilly restrained her from
responding too hastily. After a pause she managed to
say calmly, 'Miss Tillyard has no need to find another
post, Uncle Henry. She is a friend, not a paid servant,
and has a home of her own in Herriard Stoke.'

Henry Payne was not listening. He walked round
the room, examining the pictures and ornaments on
display with a proprietorial air. At length he turned
and said, 'You know, there's some damned valuable
stuff here. Mrs Payne will be delighted. As soon as
she is here tomorrow you must show us both round
the rest of the house. I shall leave it to her to choose
rooms for the children and herself. But don't worry,
Katharine, my dear. If you wish to stay with us, I'm

sure we can find room for you, never fear! Somewhere.'

After this experience with her uncle, Katharine was
better prepared for making Mrs Payne's acquaintance.
That lady arrived the next day in a showy barouche,
her daughter at her side. They were attended by several grooms dressed in elaborate livery.

Feeling in need of some moral support, Katharine
had persuaded Tilly to delay her departure for Herriard
Stoke until after Mrs Payne's arrival, and they now
both waited a little behind Henry Payne on the steps
at the front of the house.

The carriage came to a halt, the grooms came round
to the doors, and Mrs Henry Payne descended. Rather
stout, of not more than average height, she was an
impressive figure all the same. She wore a striped silk
jacket over an elaborately ruched and padded robe of
bright blue silk. Both garments were obviously new.
Two of the largest feathers Katharine had ever seen
curled round the brim of her matching bonnet. She
paused before coming up the steps. A pair of rather
hard blue eyes surveyed Herriards's graceful frontage,
its wide flight of steps leading to the door, its beautifully proportioned windows to either side, its handsome balustrading.

Mrs Payne frowned. In a tone of deep disapproval
she said, 'Henry! I hadn't realised the place was so
small! We shall have to extend, of course!'

'Whatever you say, my love. There'll be time for
all sorts of plans later. Come! You must meet your
niece. This is Katharine.'

As Katharine curtsied, Mrs Payne gave a little laugh

and said, '*Katharine?* Oh dear, we can't have that! That's my daughter's name. You will have to be Kate. *This* is Catherine!' She turned and beckoned her daughter forward. Catherine Payne was in white with more frills and ribbons than good taste would have thought necessary. But her face and figure could not be faulted. She was small, but perfectly proportioned, with large blue eyes, a rose and ivory complexion and guinea-gold curls clustered round her heart-shaped face. The Payne looks in enchantingly miniature form. She gave Katharine a delightful smile as she curtsied. Katharine feeling rather like an elephant beside Miss Payne's dainty grace, responded politely, and presented Miss Tillyard.

The Paynes gave the slightest of nods in Tilly's direction and swept into the entrance hall. 'Ah! Now something could be made of this!' exclaimed Mrs Payne, looking at the branching staircase and the white and gold coffered ceiling. 'It needs refurbishing, of course. It has been sadly neglected, but, yes, it has possibilities.' She turned to Katharine. 'I should like to see the bedchambers, Kate, before our belongings are brought in.'

'Of course. Shall I send for the housekeeper, ma'am?' Katharine asked coolly.

Mrs Payne replied with a smile, 'It is surely for *me* to send for the housekeeper, my dear? But it is an excellent idea.' She turned to a manservant who was waiting in the hall. 'You! Fellow! Fetch— What is the woman's name, Kate?'

'Mrs Jarnes, ma'am.'

'Fetch Jarnes!' The servant paused and looked at Katharine, who nodded.

'I expect she is upstairs, Charles,' she said quietly. 'Ask her to come down to meet her new mistress.'

Mrs Payne pursed her lips. 'As to "new mistress," we shall have to see,' she said. 'I hope I may be allowed to decide for myself what servants I hire. However, for the moment… I'd like you to come with us to look at the rooms, Kate. It would be easier to discuss the changes I shall make. After I have settled on bedchambers for my family, I suppose we shall have to find one for you. I understand from your uncle that we are all the family you now possess?'

'Yes,' Katherine replied. 'But…' She hesitated. She was not at all sure that she wanted to stay with Henry Payne and his wife, but it might seem discourteous to say so at this early stage.

Her aunt pursed her lips again. 'That is most unfortunate. We shall have to see what can be done. Your companion will be leaving, of course. *Her* room will definitely be required. What arrangements have you made for her departure?'

'Miss Tillyard is returning to her own home today, ma'am.'

'Good! Well, where are these rooms?'

Tilly went off to put her things together and Katharine was left to escort Mrs Payne round the house.

The following hour was one which Katharine would have been glad to forget. Herriards was not a large mansion; it was a comfortable, beautifully built family home. Succeeding generations had added their own touches to the house, but on the whole it was a harmonious collection of ideas and tastes. But it failed to meet with Mrs Payne's notions of what was due to her newly elevated status. She stared, criticised, planned to knock down walls, throw up screens, add doors or windows until Katharine was ready to scream. Nothing met with her approval until they came to Katharine's own rooms.

'Now this is a very pleasant suite,' she said as they entered, gazing round. Katharine was surprised and pleased. She had chosen the decoration schemes herself and the rooms were simply, but very prettily, furnished. She would not have thought they would appeal to Mrs Payne's taste.

'The prospect from the windows is extensive,' pronounced her aunt, 'and though the bedchamber is on the small side, the sitting room is quite large. Catherine will like these.'

'Catherine, ma'am?'

'Of course, they will need redecoration before they are fit for my daughter. The furnishing is sadly simple. But with curtains and a few extra draperies in the modern style, I fancy she will do very well here. Those bookcases would be taken out, of course, and room made for a larger dressing table and clothes chests.'

Katharine was stunned into silence, but Mrs Jarnes said, 'Beggin' your pardon, ma'am, these are Miss Katharine's rooms. This Miss Katharine.'

The cold blue eyes surveyed Mrs Jarnes. 'I think you mean they *were* Miss Kate's, Jarnes. Things have now changed. From now on, it is my daughter who will be known as ''Miss Catherine''. And she will have these rooms. Miss *Kate* will be accommodated elsewhere. The changeover will take place after the weekend.'

'But—'

Katharine intervened before the housekeeper could say any more. 'Mrs Payne is quite right, Mrs Jarnes. Herriards has new owners, who wish to make their own arrangements. We must fit in with their plans. As best we can.' She turned to her aunt and said firmly, 'These are the last rooms on this floor, Aunt Ellen, so I hope you will excuse me. I...I have promised Miss Tillyard that I will help her with her removal to Herriard Stoke.'

'Oh! Well, I suppose I shall have to,' her aunt said ungraciously. 'I had thought... Still, we have done quite a lot, and I suppose I am a little fatigued. Jarnes, I should like some tea. Bring it to the saloon in ten minutes, if you please.' She swept out, leaving Katharine and the housekeeper standing in the middle of the room. Mrs Jarnes shook her head.

'Don't say it, Jarnesy!' Katharine said. 'It won't help, and it may make matters worse. You must consider your own future.' Then, as the housekeeper turned reluctantly away, Katharine added under her breath, 'As I shall certainly have to consider mine.'

That evening at table Uncle Henry talked of the changes he intended to make on the estate. He talked glibly of yields and planning, of new methods and latest trends, but Katharine found him unconvincing. By dint of careful questions she found that her uncle had, in fact, had very little experience of running any kind of estate, and it seemed to her that his theme was exploitation, rather than development. The Paynes had apparently chosen to get rid of their own small inheritance some years before, and had since been living in style on the proceeds in Cheltenham. They were all full of ideas of what they intended to do with the new-found wealth and status which had come to them through Tom Payne's unexpected death.

'And that reminds me, Kate, my dear,' said her uncle. 'I intend to drive to Basingstoke tomorrow to see the lawyers. I noticed you had taken the phaeton out this afternoon to convey your governess to Herriard Stoke. I dare say it hadn't occurred to you to ask my permission. But in future I should like you to do so before you take any of the carriages out. That goes for the horses, too.'

'But the phaeton is mine, sir. For my own use. So are some of the horses.'

'That may have been true in the past, Kate. But as we keep saying, my dear, things have changed.'

'Not everything. The horses—'

'I will not be interrupted or contradicted at my own table, Kate! Not another word!'

'But—'

'Not one other word, Kate!' Uncle Henry still smiled, but the table fell silent. 'Once I have talked to the lawyers we shall see what can be done about your future. I will be as considerate as I can. But until then I do not wish to hear any discussion of the matter. Meanwhile, I hope you will do as I wish.' He looked round the table. 'We will now talk of something else.'

If I had a nobler nature, thought Katharine, I should make a better effort to prepare Uncle Henry for the shock which is waiting for him in Basingstoke, however richly he might deserve it. But, too heartsick and too weary to try, she listened in silence as Aunt Ellen talked of the bedchambers and how she proposed to allot them. And when, after debating which room could best be spared, her aunt finally decided to give her a small room on the upper floor, last used by a visiting maidservant, Katharine still said nothing. Neither the size nor the location of the room was of any consequence. She would not use it for long. To stay any length of time at Herriards under her uncle's regime was clearly out of the question.

Having come to this conclusion Katharine made up her mind to consult her guardians about a move as soon as possible. Indeed, she would have gone to see them the very next day if Uncle Henry had not already announced his intention of going into Basingstoke himself. But the thought of travelling to Basingstoke and back with her uncle was so unattractive that she decided to postpone her own visit till the day after. It seemed a harmless enough decision, but, if she had known what distress it would cause her in the weeks to come, she would have travelled in his company even if it had been twice as disagreeable.

At the time she congratulated herself on her foresight. The journey back from Basingstoke would have been highly uncomfortable. Uncle Henry was in a vile mood when he returned from his session with the lawyers who acted for the Payne estate. His horses showed signs of rough treatment as he drove up; he bellowed at the groom as he got down, and he roughly pushed aside the servant who opened the door and threw his hat and cane into the unfortunate man's face. Then he shut himself in the library and only reappeared when summoned to the dinner table.

Even though Katharine had a pretty good idea what had caused such ill humour in her uncle, she was astonished at the change in him. His air of beaming, self-confident benevolence had quite gone. Instead he ate in silence, drinking heavily and beating an impatient tattoo on the table when his glass was empty. Except for a brooding look in her direction from time to time, he ignored the rest of the family. She looked round. At the other end of the table her aunt, seemingly unaffected by her husband's behaviour, was deep in conversation with her son and daughter, who were seated on either side of her. Walter Payne, Uncle Henry's son and heir, had only arrived that afternoon and this was Katharine's first opportunity to study him. Though he had given her a charming smile when his mother had introduced them, had kissed her hand and declared himself enchanted to meet her, his attention had soon been caught by something else, and from then on he had hardly spoken to her. She had the distinct impression that he had taken stock of his homeless Cousin Kate and dismissed her as unworthy of further consideration.

Walter was tall, like his father, though less heavily built, and he too had the Payne blue eyes, rich gold curls and fresh complexion. Katharine felt strangely puzzled as she looked at him. He was like, and yet not like, Tom. He had something of the same looks, the same readiness to laugh, the same charm, but, though she couldn't quite put her finger on it, there was a difference. Tom had been carelessly transparent, everything on show, nothing disguised or held back. He might infuriate you, annoy you, upset you with his lack of tact, but you always knew where you were with Tom. Walter Payne's manner was altogether more consciously charming, more carefully designed. For all his apparent frankness, she had a feeling that there was more to him than he allowed the world to see.

She was startled out of her deliberations when Henry Payne suddenly roused himself and snapped, 'Walter! Why do you neglect your cousin in this cavalier fashion? She'll think you a boor!' As Katharine turned to look at him, surprised at his tone, he added with an attempt at geniality, 'We can't have Kate thinking you don't know how to behave, my boy.'

Father and son looked at one another in silence for a moment, then Walter shrugged his shoulders and said in a neutral tone, 'I'm sorry, sir. I wasn't aware I was misbehaving.' He turned to Katharine with a smile. 'Have I been rude, Cousin Kate? You must forgive me—I've been hearing all about Herriards from my sister and mother. They are full of plans for improvements to the house—though for my part I think it is perfect as it is. You will be sad indeed to leave it, I think.'

'Yes, I am,' said Katharine. 'I have lived here all my life. Anywhere else will seem strange at first.'

Catherine Payne turned at this. 'All your life? All the time?' Katharine nodded. 'But you must have been to London!'

'No, I've never been away from Herriards.'

Aunt Ellen's voice was heavy with disapproval as she asked, 'Do you mean to say that your grandfather made no arrangements for you to be introduced to Society? I am astonished.'

'I believe he had it in mind just before he was taken ill for the first time. There never seemed to be an opportunity after that.' Katharine spoke stiffly, resenting this criticism of her beloved grandfather.

'He should have made one! For look at the fix you are in now! At eighteen, as Miss Payne of Herriards, I daresay you might have made a very good sort of match. But at—what are you? Twenty-three?'

'Twenty-one, ma'am.'

'Really? Only twenty-one? I am surprised. But now that you are older, and Miss Payne of nowhere in particular, it will be much more difficult to find a suitable husband. I hope you will not look to me for help in the matter. It would be most inconvenient. We intend to launch Catherine this next year, and I shall need all my energies for that enterprise. Indeed, we hope for great things for her, don't we, my precious? I flatter myself that London will not often have seen such beauty as hers. There will be a great deal of expense, of course.'

Catherine Payne patted her blonde curls complacently. 'When Papa told us of your brother's death and that Herriards was consequently ours, we made such plans! Next year we are to take a house in London for the season, and I shall have a whole new wardrobe for my presentation! You cannot imagine how much I look forward to it—'

She jumped as her father's fist crashed on the table, and the storm finally broke.

'Hold your tongue! You don't know what you're talking about, miss! You none of you know what you're talking about!'

Catherine gazed at her father in hurt amazement. Then her eyes filled with tears and she turned to her mama. 'What's wrong?' she asked pathetically. 'What have I said? Why is Papa so cross? He promised we should go to London, didn't he? He promised!'

Mrs Payne said majestically, 'You are not to worry, Catherine. Your papa has guaranteed that you will be presented next year, and I shall see that he keeps his word, never fear.' She turned her attention to her husband. 'What is wrong, my love?'

Ignoring his wife, Henry Payne scowled at Katharine. 'Did it amuse you?' he asked heavily.

'What, Uncle?'

He got up and stood at the end of the table, glaring down at her. 'Don't pretend innocence with me, young lady! You allowed my poor wife to plan such changes here, you listened with a straight face while my poor little daughter talked of her dreams for her début, and all the time you knew that there wasn't the money to do half of it! How you must have been laughing!'

'What?' cried Mrs Payne. 'What are you saying, Henry?'

Henry Payne's outburst took Katharine's breath away for a moment. Then she said firmly, 'Sir, you are very mistaken. I knew of the situation, of course I did, but it was surely hardly my place to tell you of the terms of your inheritance. In fact, when I did make an attempt to say something at dinner last night, you forbade me to talk of it. But I assure you, I have never *laughed* at any of it. I don't believe I have felt like *laughing* since I heard that my brother had died and that I had…I had lost both him and my home.' Unable to continue, she got up and walked away to the windows. The gardens and terraces were bathed in the soft light of the dying sun. Herriards had never looked more beautiful. She told herself that she would survive this nightmare, she must. But she must get away from these people as soon as she could.

'Mr Payne, you will tell us, if you please, what you mean by all this!' said Mrs Payne. 'I insist! What is this talk of money?'

'Yes! Please tell us, Papa! *Please!*' Catherine's blue eyes once again filled with tears. 'Doesn't this place belong to us after all?'

'Herriards and the lands that belong to it are mine. The income from them is mine. But the lawyers here now tell me that the real wealth belonged to another branch of the family altogether. The Framptons. This girl's great-grandmother was an heiress, and her money, Frampton money, lies outside the entail. They say it has nothing to do with Herriards. It is all in a trust for your cousin here.'

'For Kate!' Aunt Ellen stared at Katharine in astonishment. 'What could she possibly want with it? No, I don't believe it—the lawyers must have made a mistake! You must question them further, Henry.'

'I'm afraid there's no mistake. My grandfather was free to leave the Frampton-Payne fortune where he wished,' said Katharine stonily, turning round again to face them.

Shock kept Aunt Ellen silent for almost a minute. Then she said blankly, 'So what are we to live on?'

Walter, who had been sitting very still throughout these exchanges, gave his father a significant glance as he got up and joined Katharine at the window. 'We must seem to you to be very mercenary,' he said. 'My father's words have obviously distressed you. But we have all had a great shock. Can you forgive us? I should imagine Herriards provides more than enough to live on, surely?'

'But not in style!' said his mother. 'Not the way we intended.'

Casting a glance at Katharine's set expression, Walter frowned at his mother and said, 'I am sure the situation is not as hopeless as it seems, Mama. We shall have to see what can be done. Meanwhile, I think my cousin has had enough of this conversation. She is looking very pale. Would you care to show me something of the garden, Kate?' He put Katharine's arm through his and led her firmly from the room, ignoring the rest of his family. Katharine, too weary to object, went with him without protest.

Chapter Three

The next day Katharine was furious to find when she went round to the stables that her Uncle Henry had already taken the phaeton out. She was forced to change her plans and, instead of driving to Basingstoke to consult her guardians, she decided to walk to Herriard Stoke to visit Tilly. The time would not be wasted. It would be useful to talk matters over with a friend before tackling Sir James and the General.

Tilly was delighted to see her, and ushered her through to the garden without ceremony. The cottage had been kept in good order during her absence and the little garden at the back was full of scent and colour. The two ladies sat under an apple tree and made themselves comfortable.

'Now, Katharine, you can tell me what is troubling you.'

She gave Tilly an account of the previous evening's discussion and ended by saying, 'One thing is certain. I could never live with my uncle and his family. I must see my guardians. I must get away.'

Tilly had never been one to beat about the bush. 'You haven't anywhere to go,' she said.

'Couldn't I stay here with you?'

Tilly smiled. 'There's nothing I would like better, but there really isn't room, my dear. Besides, your guardians would never hear of it.'

'I shall see them tomorrow! They must agree, they must! I refuse to stay with the Paynes!'

Katharine got up and walked around the garden. Miss Tillyard watched her with a worried frown. She said, 'If I were you I should wait a little before approaching General Armitage and Sir James. They will be more prepared to listen if you can speak calmly to them, show them that you are not being unreasonable. They must be persuaded that you have given living with your uncle a chance.'

'Tilly, what I fear most is that they would *never* be prepared to listen objectively. They are tired old men, and they have no notion of what they would do with me if I *didn't* stay with my uncle! What on earth my grandfather was thinking of to saddle me with such guardians I do not know!'

Though she privately agreed, Tilly did not say so. Instead she said persuasively, 'It is very early days yet. You haven't seen the Payne family at its best. People sometimes behave uncharacteristically when they have suffered a great disappointment. If Mr Payne had assumed that your grandfather's fortune, as well as Herriards, would be at his disposal, it would come as a great shock to them all to discover that this was not the case.'

'They have Herriards!' cried Katharine in tones of anguish. 'Why do they need any more?'

'Not everyone thinks of Herriards as you do. And *you* must stop thinking so much of it, my love. It is no longer your business. You must put it out of your mind and concentrate instead on what you are going to do with your own life. What can't be cured—'

'Must be endured. I know. And this is beyond curing.' There was a pause, then in a determinedly cheerful tone Katharine said, 'You're right, as usual, Tilly dear. It would be better to wait. I'll try to be patient. It's true that I can't do anything without my guardians' consent—my allowance is ridiculously small.'

'You should have had it increased when your grandfather died.'

'I know, I know! But while Tom was there, I had his authority to draw on funds from the estate, and I used them. I never thought—' Katharine stopped and swallowed. After a pause she went on, 'I was lazy, I suppose. I should have looked into it a long time ago.' She paused. 'Those old men still think of me as a child. And, worse still, a female child! It would be so much better if I had a man I could trust to represent me, someone they would respect...'

'What about your brother's friend, the one who wrote to you?'

'Lord Calthorpe?'

'Yes. He offered his help and it sounded as if he meant it. Why don't you write to him again? I should think he is exactly the sort of person the General and Sir James would listen to.'

'I think I will,' Katharine said slowly. 'You're right. Lord Calthorpe sounded like a man one could trust. I wonder if he is still in England? Tilly, you're a genius!

I'll write to Lord Calthorpe tonight! And this time I shall ask him to come and see me.'

Katharine was reminded of Tilly's words when she came downstairs the next morning. Uncle Henry seemed to have recovered from his displeasure of the previous day, and greeted her with a benign smile. He led her personally into the breakfast room, where her aunt was sitting. Neither Walter nor Catherine had yet appeared.

'My dear Kate,' her aunt said as she sat down, 'my dear Kate, what must you be thinking of us? I'm afraid we have not behaved as we ought. You will forgive us, won't you?'

'Of course,' Katharine murmured uncomfortably.

Her uncle cleared his throat and added, 'I hope you will overlook what I may have said last night, my dear. I'd had a hard day, d'y' see?' He gave her a look. 'You didn't take me seriously, I hope?' Katharine shook her head wordlessly, and he laughed and went on, 'Of course you didn't! I told Walter so. Kate's too sensible a girl, I told him, to be upset by a few hasty words. He was quite concerned about you.'

'The dear boy,' said Mrs Payne fondly. 'It has been very hard for us this past month, Kate. My health is not good, and when I am tired I, too, sometimes make mistakes. I dare say you thought me a little harsh and unfeeling when I arrived. It was all so confusing… But believe me, your rooms are yours for as long as you want them. I would not dream of turning you out of them.'

'You are very kind, ma'am,' said Katharine. 'But I intend to consult my guardians about my future. Miss

Tillyard and I have considered setting up house together.'

'You want to live with a *governess!*' exclaimed her uncle.

'As I said when you first arrived, Uncle, Miss Tillyard is a friend.'

'Oh, she may well be a very good sort of creature, but she is not exactly suitable company for a young lady of fortune! I don't imagine for one moment that your trustees would agree to such a plan.'

Aunt Ellen cried, 'No, indeed! It is an absurd idea!'

'I do not think so, ma'am,' said Katharine.

'Child, you do not realise what it would mean. Social ostracism! No, no, you would do much better to live with us, your family. It is only right!'

'Thank you, but I will see my guardians first, ma'am,' said Katharine firmly.

'Oh, don't be so obstinate, girl!' snapped Aunt Ellen, forgetting herself.

Giving his wife a warning look, Uncle Henry said gently, 'My love, discussing business with older gentlemen is no occupation for a young lady. I think you should leave it to me to deal with them.'

'No!' exclaimed Katharine. She made herself speak more calmly. 'Thank you, Uncle, but your intervention is not necessary. My guardians are elderly, but I have known them all my life.' Then, taking some liberty with the facts, she went on, 'In any case, I already have someone to act for me if it should be required.'

'Oh? Who is that?'

'A...a very good friend of Tom's. Lord Calthorpe. I have already written to him.' She did not say that the letter had not yet been despatched. It was at present in the hall, waiting to be taken to the receiving office in Basingstoke.

Her uncle eyed her thoughtfully. He said, 'Well, it all seems very odd. Your guardians received me very kindly yesterday.'

'Indeed, they seemed inclined to regard your uncle's plans with favour,' added Aunt Ellen with a satisfied smile.

Katharine felt a surge of anger but asked evenly, 'What plans are those, sir?'

'As your aunt said—that you should remain in our care for the foreseeable future. After that…well, we shall see, we shall see.'

Katharine rose. 'Your thought for me does you credit, Uncle Henry, but it is somewhat premature. I should prefer to settle my future for myself, directly with Sir James and General Armitage. By the way, exactly when did you see them?'

'Yesterday, my dear. I thought it only right to make myself known to them. And I took Walter along with me. We had a very pleasant half-hour with both Sir James and the General.'

'Since it was such a large party, I am surprised that you did not think to invite me to go with you, sir. Any discussions with my guardians surely concern me more directly than they do your son.'

'There you go again, Kate! When will you realise that it really isn't proper for a young lady to be so independent? You are no longer alone in the world. Your aunt and I are here to look after your interests.'

'Do you not rather mean ''my fortune'', Uncle Henry? Forgive me, but it seems to me that your concern for my safety is so much greater since you discovered the truth about the Herriard estate.'

Henry Payne smiled blandly. 'You're right, of course. But what is wrong in that? You are a considerable heiress, Kate. Would you rather you were left to the mercy of a selfish and self-seeking world? I think not.'

Aunt Ellen took one of Katharine's hands in hers. 'Our only concern, Kate, is to protect your interests. Poor child, you have no one else to look after you.'

'Indeed, ma'am, you underestimate me,' Katharine said, removing her hand. 'I have looked after myself, and this estate, for years. I need no protectors. And I wish most of all to make my own decisions about my future.'

Uncle Henry shook his head. 'Sir James said that you were wilful, that you had had your own way for far too long, and I can now see that he is right. But I fancy he will soon bring you round to our way of thinking. By all means see him, if you wish. It will make little difference.'

Katharine felt a shiver of apprehension. She said desperately, 'Sir James's notions are somewhat old-fashioned. But he has always been fond of me. I cannot believe he would force me to do anything which would make me unhappy. I must see him today. And I'll talk to General Armitage, too. Excuse me.'

Katharine ordered the phaeton and set off for Basingstoke as soon as she had changed her dress. Delay had already cost her the initiative. She would not wait another minute before talking to her guardians herself. She would not let them ignore her. To remain with the

Paynes was impossible, and she must make them see it.

In Basingstoke she had difficulty at first in seeing Sir James—his manservant said that his master was distinctly unwell, and unwilling to receive visitors. But Katharine knew her guardian of old. When faced with a problem of any kind, Sir James took refuge in illness. She insisted on being seen.

'I don't know why you have to disturb me, Katharine. You always were a headstrong child. What is it?' said Sir James testily.

Katharine explained her plan to leave Herriards and live somewhere else with Miss Tillyard as a companion.

'Why on earth do you want to do such a foolish thing?'

'I…I do not think that my uncle and I will deal very happily together,' said Katharine uncomfortably.

'What nonsense! Mr Payne seems an excellent fellow! And that son of his is as agreeable a young man as I've met in a long time!'

'Please believe me, sir! My uncle and I will never agree. Indeed, I refuse to stay at Herriards with them!'

'Refuse? Refuse? What do you mean, miss? Of course you won't refuse!'

'But I—'

'Don't say another word, Katharine! The trouble with you is that you've been allowed to go your own way for too long! I always thought you had too much say in the running of Herriards. That ain't work for a female. And now it has gone to your head.'

Katharine was incensed at the injustice of this remark. 'Taking charge of Herriards was not by my choice, sir. When my grandfather was ill and Tom was away there was no one else to do it!' she said hotly. Sir James glared at her, and she forced herself to speak more reasonably. 'But you are quite right. I am bound to feel injured when my uncle takes over the estate I thought would be…would be Tom's. So surely it would be wiser to let me go elsewhere?'

'Oh, no! You are not going to cozen me like that, girl! It's time you learned a bit of humility. Dammit, a chit of a girl like you ought to be *happy* to leave the running of Herriards to someone else. You should be thinking of dresses and dances, not trying to tell grown men what to do.'

'But I don't want to think of nothing more than dresses and dances!'

'It's time you did. And about marriage. If your grandfather had taught you to think more about that instead of running estates and the like, we wouldn't be in the fix we are now! However, your uncle has some very sensible ideas on that subject, too…but we'll speak of that another time.'

'What ideas has my uncle been suggesting? What right has he to suggest anything about my future? Please let me leave Herriards, Sir James. I—'

'No, not another word, Katharine. My mind is made up. The General and I may be two old bachelors, but what your uncle said made sense to us. He and his wife have children of their own—they understand young people, and from all accounts they are already very fond of you. We believe that they can give you exactly the sort of attention a young girl needs.'

When Katharine made a gesture of protest Sir James

went on firmly, 'You must put away this resentment and give them a chance.'

In despair Katharine said, 'Will you at least increase my allowance, Sir James?'

Sir James leaned back in his chair, put one hand to his brow and rang the bell on the table at his side with the other. 'No I shan't! Now, no more, please! My head is aching, and I'm sure one of my attacks is imminent. I should never have agreed to see you. I knew I should pay for the exertion.' He waved a vague hand at his ward. 'Come back another time, Katharine, when you are in a more reasonable frame of mind. Meanwhile, be grateful for your uncle's kindness. Ah, Roundell, see Miss Payne out, if you please. And then return immediately to attend to me. I must lie down. I don't feel at all the thing, not at all!'

Katharine left Sir James's house feeling angry and distinctly worried. Her uncle seemed to have worked his spell on one of her guardians at least. But, she told herself, General Armitage would have been harder to convince. She set off to see her second guardian full of determination to put her case to him as convincingly as she could. However, when she arrived at the General's house she suffered an even greater disappointment. He had left that morning for Bath and would be away for several weeks. Her heart sank. Henry Payne must have known about this, she thought bitterly, but he had said nothing to her. Once again her delay in coming to Basingstoke had cost her dear.

As Katharine returned to Herriards she was dismayed, but not yet defeated. It might take longer than she had planned, but she was determined to get her guardians' permission sooner or later. Sir James had always been something of a hypochondriac, and he was not fond of any disturbance. But she would ask to see him again as soon as she thought expedient. He couldn't refuse forever. And Bath was not the other side of the moon. She would write to the General straight away. Sooner or later she would escape from Herriards!

But even after summer had faded into autumn, and autumn was beginning to decline into the first signs of winter, Katharine had still not found a way of leaving.

October 1815

One dismal day in late October Katharine stood in her sitting room and frowned as she looked down at the garden below her window. It showed the signs of neglect which were beginning to be seen all round Herriards. She shut her eyes and gave the glass a thump with her fist. She must not give way to despair, she must not. But how long could she stay strong? Never before had she felt so helpless, so alone. There was still no prospect of escape, and now, to add to her worries, the plan hinted at by Sir James and her uncle was becoming all too clear. She was to marry Walter, thus at one stroke solving the problem of her future, and at the same time returning the Frampton fortune to the coffers of the Herriards estate. The prospect horrified her. Though she was certain that she would never, not even for one moment, consider such a match, everyone else in the house seemed to take it for granted.

Katharine was under constant pressure to spend time with Walter, to respond to his overtures, his offers of help and sympathy. In the early days, it was true, she had accepted his company, though it hadn't taken her long to realise that Walter's charm was all on the surface. Underneath he was essentially a cold man, seeking his own advantage in everything he did. But once she realised what the Paynes were planning, she had avoided Walter wherever possible. It wasn't easy. He was inordinately vain, and seemed to find it quite impossible to believe that Katharine was not attracted to him. For a time he had continued to exert his charm, teasing her for her shyness, suggesting that she was playing games with him. But recently he had begun to realise that she was serious in her refusals, and, though it hadn't put him off, his attitude had changed. He was becoming more persistent, while at the same time taking less trouble to disguise his true character. Katharine had found that the best way to avoid him was to keep to her rooms, and, apart from meals, she now spent very little time with the rest of the family. It all added to her sense of isolation.

There was a knock at the door, and it opened before she could say anything. Walter came into the room. She looked at him coldly. As usual he was immaculately dressed in clothes that were the acme of suitability. Today he was the country gentleman. His linen was, as always, spotless, his boots shone brilliantly, his buckskins were without stain or crease, his coat fitted like a glove. The guinea-gold hair was brushed with contrived carelessness over one brow, and his smile gleamed whitely as he sauntered in.

Katharine winced as a sudden vision of her brother Tom, coming into this very room a year ago, flashed across her mind. The contrast was painful. Tom had been out for a ride, his fair hair blown by the wind into a tousle of curls round a laughing, bronzed face. His buff breeches were spattered with mud, and his old green riding coat sat comfortably rather than elegantly across his broad shoulders. She had been annoyed with him, she remembered, had protested at his coming into the house in such a mess. With his usual insouciance he had only laughed the more, and in the end she had laughed too… They had seemed to spend most of their time together laughing…

Dear God, why wasn't Tom here to help her now? But Tom was dead, he had died at Waterloo, leaving her on her own to deal with the consequences—including the unwelcome attentions of her cousin Walter.

Katharine pulled herself together and said coolly, 'How many times do I have to tell you, Walter? Your father returned these rooms to me for my own private use. This is *my* room. And you are not welcome in it. Please leave! Now!'

'Demme, if you're not the most unfriendly girl I ever met, Kate,' he said with unimpaired good humour. 'As prickly as a bramble bush. How else can I talk to you if I don't come up here? You're never seen downstairs except at mealtimes. Come on, Kate! Be nice to your cousin. I'm starved for the sight of you.'

Katharine stiffened as he came further into the room, but she didn't move. Any sign of weakness would encourage him. She said stonily, 'I've told you. I like my own company.'

'That ain't very friendly, Kate.'

Katharine didn't answer, but turned back to the window. Walter came up behind her and put his arm round her waist. 'What's wrong with me, sweetheart?'

Katharine twisted out of his grasp and pushed him away. 'Stop fondling me, Walter. I don't like it, any more than I like you. I am not your sweetheart, and I wish you to go!'

Walter frowned and said, 'I wish I knew what the devil goes on in that mind of yours, Kate. Why are you always so hard on me? It's not as if there's anyone else—is there? If so, I don't know where you can have met him.' He studied her for a moment then shook his head. 'No, I'll swear that you haven't met anyone else...but there's something...' He moved closer and she stiffened.

'I've warned you, Walter. Stay away from me!'

Her cousin smiled. 'You look so fierce—like a little wild creature. The temptation to master you is almost irresistible. But there's no need to fight me, Kate. I'm on your side. I'd be your friend if you'd only let me be.'

'A real friend would help me to get away from this place and your wretched family!'

'I'll take you from here the minute you say the word, sweetheart! All you have to do is to marry me.'

'That is not a solution I would contemplate for one second. Now please get out of my room and leave me in peace!'

Walter regarded her thoughtfully. 'You have a great deal of spirit, Kate—I admire that. But you'll give in sooner or later, my dear. Apart from that old woman in the village, you have no friends that I can see. And, for all your fortune, you can't get your hands on very much cash. How will you ever escape? I shouldn't place your hopes on your guardians, if I were you. They aren't going to take you away from us. They'd have to find somewhere else for you to go, and Sir James isn't going to give himself that much trouble. Besides, they are delighted with my father—and with me. They think we are excellent fellows and quite right, too! We've worked hard to persuade them. No, Kate, face up to it. You'll have to give in in the end. Why not sooner rather than later? I'm sure I could make you happy.'

'You'll never have the chance! I'm as much of a fighter as Tom in my own weak, helpless, female way! I won't be beaten by such contemptible creatures as you and your father.'

'You poor deluded thing!' said Walter laughing softly. 'But I can wait. I'm looking forward to the fight. You won't be the first I've tamed.'

'Are you going, or shall I call one of the servants?'

Walter laughed again, his blue eyes alive with merriment. 'I'm going, my sweet. But I'll just take something on account…' Without warning he pulled Katharine towards him and bent her back against his arm. His fingers pulled her hair cruelly until she was forced to look up at him. He kissed her hard, then pushed her away, so that she stumbled against the window. All pretence of good humour quite gone, he said coldly, 'You'll have to learn something about me, Kate, my dear. I don't like being called a contemptible creature by a dab of a female. It's apt to make me rough. Don't do it again.' With that he turned and went out of the room. Katharine was left shaken and trembling by the window.

She stayed there staring out for some time. Walter's

attack had shocked her. Nothing remotely like it had ever happened to her before. Till now the men in her life might have been careless, had often forgotten that she belonged to the weaker sex—indeed, Katharine herself had frequently denied it!—but no one had ever before humiliated her in such a manner. In some ways she was very innocent for her age. At sixteen she had been forced to abandon a normal life in Society in order to look after her grandfather, who had become increasingly reclusive. In her few dealings with the outside world she had deliberately suppressed any femininity, preferring to treat the men she met in a businesslike manner. But now Walter's attack had made her aware of her vulnerability as a woman. And, for all her courage, Katharine began to feel the stirrings of fear.

For the first time she looked at her future realistically. Her uncle had made clear his desire—no, his *intention*—that his son should marry her. She could not forget the ruthless speed with which Henry Payne had acted immediately after his arrival. No sooner had he discovered that the Payne fortune was in Katharine's hands than he had persuaded her guardians to say she must stay at Herriards in his care. Even at that early stage he had taken Walter with him to visit them, Walter with his charm and his manly appearance, who was bound to make a favourable impression on them. At the moment Henry and his son were still hoping that Katharine's isolation from any other company, her loneliness, would make her vulnerable to Walter's powers of attraction. But when that failed she was fairly certain that other, less scrupulous, ways of per-

suasion would be found. And where could she turn
then?

Her distress grew. Fear mingled with feelings of
rage and frustration—not only with the living but,
worse than that, with the dead, too. She had loved her
brother and her grandfather, had grieved, and was still
grieving, for them, but between them they had left her
alone in the world, with no one to help her to fight
Henry Payne, or to cope with his son. Clouds of resentment were beginning to obscure her memories of
the two people she had loved best in the world. A
groan of despair escaped her. She *must* get out of the
house! She would go to Tilly. They *must* find some
way to save her from catastrophe.

It was a cold, grey day and the wind was tossing
the branches overhead. As she marched along the path
to Herriard Stoke, the weather seemed in keeping with
Katharine's mood. Her sense of injustice was growing
by the minute. She was only twenty-one, but she felt
that the cares of the world were bowing her down. Her
guardians were useless! Why on earth hadn't her
grandfather done as she had asked and replaced them
with younger men—his lawyer, perhaps, or his man
of business? General Armitage and Sir James Farrow
might well be the men of repute and honour he had
called them, but they were of little help in her present
predicament. Katharine kicked a branch which lay in
her path and gave an exclamation of angry frustration.
Tired old gentlemen, however honourable, were not
the ones to deal with a scheming, conniving villain
such as Henry Payne. Nor with his *worm* of a son!

Where in Heaven's name was she to find the help she needed?

As she came through the gate which led into the churchyard a sudden gust of wind caught her cloak and blew it up into the air. It was too much! Muttering, desperately trying to hold her hat in one hand, and anchor her cloak with the other, she ran full tilt into what felt like a wall. She staggered and sat down.

'I'm sorry! Ma'am, are you hurt? No, don't move, let me see if you are hurt first.' A tall figure squatted beside her and started to feel her legs. This was too much!

'Don't *touch* me, sir!' Katharine exclaimed fiercely. 'And don't try to help me get up, either! You've done enough damage already.'

To her annoyance the stranger ignored her words and, taking hold of her arm, helped her to rise. 'Let me escort you to your home, ma'am. I shan't be happy till I know you are not hurt.'

As soon as Katharine was on her feet she shook his hand off her arm and looked up angrily into his face. It was a good face, not exactly handsome, but definitely attractive. Just now it showed nothing but concern, but there was discipline and firmness in the jaw and mouth, and lines of laughter round the steady hazel eyes.

Katharine saw none of this. She said furiously, 'I told you! I'm perfectly able to manage, thank you! Will you kindly get out of my way?' Without looking at him again she started to walk away, brushing some leaves and mud from her cloak as she went. But Fate was not on Katharine's side. Her hat, without a hand to hold it, was attacked by another sudden gust of wind and was borne aloft, sailing away across the churchyard.

With a speed and dexterity which secretly impressed her, the unknown gentleman leapt after it and trapped it after a short chase. He returned and presented it to her with a bow. There was a distinct twinkle in his eye as he said, 'Forgive me for interfering yet again, ma'am. May I assist you to put it on?'

Katharine tied the strings of her cloak with a vicious tug, then more or less snatched the hat from the gentleman's hand. She was almost in tears. The fall had winded her more than she would admit even to herself. And now this…this *man* was laughing at her! 'I…I…' Her fingers were trembling as she fumbled with her hat.

'Allow me.' He took it from her, placed it carefully on her head and tied the strings under her chin. His touch was deft and quite impersonal. 'And now I shall accompany you to wherever it is you're going. Come!' He put his hand under her arm. She was appalled to find herself feeling helplessly feminine, experiencing an almost irresistible desire to lean on this stranger's arm and let him take control. If only she could just once place her burdens on such a man's shoulders… She stiffened. How could she be so weak? In her present situation she could not afford such idiocy. Strength came from independence.

She thrust him away from her again and said pugnaciously, 'Thank you for rescuing my hat. But I neither need nor want any more of your help. Goodbye, sir.' She marched along the path and turned into the street without a backward glance. But at Tilly's gate she turned and looked back. He was standing at the corner, presumably waiting to make sure she arrived safely at her destination. What a *busybody* he was! When he saw her looking he gave a slight bow, but Katharine ignored him and went in through Tilly's door.

Chapter Four

There was a small fire in Tilly's tiny grate. Katharine went over and warmed her hands, while her governess hung up her hat and cloak.

'What on earth have you been doing, Katharine? Your clothes are covered in mud!'

'I...I fell. In the churchyard. The wind caught me just as I came round the corner.'

'Did you trip?'

'No. I...I...er...bumped into someone and lost my balance. But I shall be fine in a moment. I'm a little cold, that's all.'

'You shall have a warm drink in an instant. Mrs Banks from the inn brought some of her raspberry cordial this morning. Sit there while I get it.' Tilly hurried to put a kettle on the hob and fetch the cordial and some beakers. Then she sat down in the chair on the other side of the fire and said, 'But what are you thinking of coming out on a day like this, my dear? I am delighted to see you, of course, but it's hardly a fit day for walking.'

'I had to get out, Tilly. It...it suddenly all seemed

too much.' To Katharine's shame her voice trembled and she was hard put not to cry.

'Oh, my dear child! Is it Walter, or his father?'

Katharine gazed at Tilly's concerned face and tried to pull herself together. 'It's hard to say. I don't know which of them is worse. I feel so…trapped. Oh, Tilly, I never thought…never thought I should long as I do to leave Herriards. I once loved it so.' Her voice broke.

Tilly sighed and said, 'I assume that you haven't heard from General Armitage?'

'No. He promised to come and see me when he returned from Bath but there has been no word. I assume he's still there.'

'But he's been away for three months now!'

'The trouble is, Tilly, that he doesn't see any need for urgency. Oh, what a fool I was! If I had known three months ago what a cunning man my uncle is, I would have made sure that the General heard what I had to say first.'

'You mustn't be too hard on yourself, Katharine. Tom's death was still too close. You weren't thinking very clearly.'

'Well, whatever the reason, it gave my uncle his chance. He impressed those two old men the way he impresses everyone outside the house. And now Sir James doesn't think it important to see me again, and the General thinks I'm unhappy simply because I haven't yet resigned myself to the new regime at Herriards.'

'I suppose that's natural…'

'Oh, yes! And so patronising! You'd think I was twelve, not twenty-one! Instead of coming to see what was wrong, he recommended me to be a good girl and do my best to learn to live with the changes.'

'That would be good advice, Katharine, in other circumstances. But as it is… My dear, why don't you try again? Write to him once more! More strongly this time.'

'What is the use? My cousin has pulled the wool over that old man's eyes, in the same way that he has deceived Sir James. Neither of my guardians will listen to me. I'm not to be taken seriously.'

'Sir James is ill. You can't blame him for not questioning your cousin's motives.'

'I don't blame *him!* I blame my grandfather for not replacing them both with younger men! I blame my brother for leaving me alone like this with no one to turn to…' Katharine got up and walked about the tiny room, twisting her hands. 'Day after day I watch that…that greedy villain milking Herriards till there will soon be nothing left. The fences go without repair, roofs are leaking, fields are left unplanted… And yet Henry Payne has only to smile, to flatter, to clap people on the back and tell a few stories, and everyone in the county thinks he is a great fellow! I tell you, Tilly, I am heartsick to see it all.'

'There, there, my love. There, there!' Tilly put her arms round Katharine and led her back to her chair. Then she sat her down and poured out some cordial. 'Drink that, and listen to me. General Armitage was right in one respect. You *must* stop feeling personally responsible for Herriards! I know it is hard, but, indeed, there is nothing you can do, Katharine! If you go on in this way you will be ill! I am rather surprised that you can't see this for yourself—since you grew up you have always been such a sensible girl. But I suspect it is more than this, isn't it? Tell me!'

Katharine straightened up and tried to speak calmly. 'Uncle Henry is determined to push me into marriage to his son. He has my guardians' approval. And now Walter is… Walter is pushing his claims as well. He gets bolder by the day. I have absolutely no intention of giving way, but if you only knew what a strain it is! They are both so devious. I am so afraid that I shall have a brainstorm one day and wake up to find myself married to Walter after all. I have nightmares about it…' Katharine got up again as if she couldn't bear to be still. 'Worst of all—' She stopped, then went on, 'Worst of all, Grandpapa and Tom—' She broke off, then went on doggedly. 'I used to find consolation in remembering the happy times we had together, but now I can only feel resentment! Why have they left me to face all this alone? Oh, Tilly, I feel so wicked! So ungrateful! What am I to do?'

Tilly's face showed real anxiety. 'You must get away, my dear!'

'I can't! I haven't anything worth mentioning to live on! And, until I am twenty-five, I can't have my allowance increased without the consent of my guardians. That's another four years away.'

'It is a pity you never found anyone you could marry before now. To be so alone in the world is not pleasant.'

Katharine shook her head. 'I suppose before Grandfather was ill I might have met someone, when Tom and I used to visit the neighbours. But, compared with Tom, they all seemed so uninteresting! And my grandfather never allowed Tom to invite his friends to stay—he didn't approve of most of them.'

'Old Mr Payne,' said Tilly carefully, 'was the best of employers and a wonderful man. But he had a tendency to seek his own comfort rather than the best interests of others, especially when he was older.'

'You mean he didn't *wish* me to meet anyone I liked? Oh, no, Tilly! I am sure if I had found someone he would have been delighted. Oh, you're wrong! He loved me—I'm sure he wanted me to be happy. Later, of course, when he was ill… Well, it was different then. I didn't even want to leave him on his own. And in any case I never seemed to have the time for gadding about—with Tom away I was always too busy. So I lost touch with what friends we had…so many of them have died or moved away. And now…there's no one but you.'

Katharine came back to the fire and sat down. She took a sip of her cordial, then hugged the beaker close to her as if seeking comfort from its warmth. Tilly gazed at her in concern. Katherine's fingers were bone thin, and her face was pale and worn. It was difficult to believe that just four months ago she had been a lively young girl, full of energy and enterprise, running Herriards estate, looking forward to her brother's return, to the time when Tom should come home and take over. Now she looked years older, the spring had quite gone out of her step, and that wonderful smile, which had been so appealing in both the young Paynes, seemed to have vanished forever. The shock and distress of Tom's death and its consequences could have accounted for it during the first few months. But she should now be recovering, shedding the melancholy, which had enveloped her then. This growing resentment towards people she had adored was seriously worrying. Tilly cast about in her mind for something—anything—that might be done.

'Why don't you write to Lord Calthorpe again?' she said at last.

This suggestion roused Katharine, but not quite in the way Miss Tillyard had intended. 'Yes!' she said bitterly. 'There's another miserable specimen! So eager to write the moment Tom died. Such a charming letter, too! Saddened and grieved by Tom's death… di…da…di…da…such close friends, heard such a lot about me…would like to come to see me…entirely at my service… You yourself said what a charming letter it was. Someone to trust, we both thought. And what happened after that? Nothing! Now that I really need someone, charming Lord Calthorpe isn't available. And he must be back from France again by now! '

'You did say in your first letter that you needed time—'

'I did need time! But I wrote again later…'

'I remember. It was soon after Mr Payne and his family had arrived.'

'Yes. Even as early as that I thought that I needed someone. Someone who had known Tom, who might even help me to talk to my wretched guardians. So I wrote again. Uselessly. There wasn't a whisper from our noble friend.'

'Perhaps your letter went astray? You weren't sure of his address.'

The burst of energy had faded. 'It might have,' Katharine said listlessly. 'But I doubt it. I sent it to the War Office address in London which Tom gave me to use. No, it's far more likely that Lord Calthorpe found life in London too amusing to bother. After all, his great friend died in June—a full month or more before. That's a *very* long time for a busy man to remember a great friend, don't you agree? Why should he feel obliged to leave his friends and come all this way to see a stranger? He probably assumed that my cousins were all the protection I needed.'

'I don't like to hear you speaking like this, Katharine. You are not usually so bitter. Besides, it's possible your brother never mentioned Mr Henry Payne and his family. Lord Calthorpe is probably unaware of the real situation.'

'I don't suppose he would care if he did! Don't let's talk of him any more, Tilly. He is just one more disappointment in a world that seems to be full of them. But if I ever meet him...' Katharine looked moodily at her drink, then finished it off. 'I must go back—it will soon be dark. I'm sorry to have been such a misery. I promise to be more cheerful next time. Goodbye, dearest friend!' Katharine bent over and kissed the little governess's cheek. Tilly held the girl's slender form to her for a moment, then let her go to walk her out to the gate.

'Think about writing to Lord Calthorpe again,' she said. 'And this time let me take the letter to the Receiving Office.'

Katharine stared at her. 'What are you suggesting?'

When Tilly stared back at her without saying a word, Katharine asked incredulously, 'You're surely not saying that Uncle Henry somehow stopped the letter?'

'I'm not suggesting anything. Except that you write again—and let me take it to the Receiving Office. Goodbye, my dear. Something will turn up, you'll see.'

As Tilly went back into her cottage she muttered to herself, 'Pray God it does! And soon!'

Meanwhile Katharine's stranger had walked back through the churchyard and into the church. Here he went into the Payne Chapel to the left of the chancel and stood gazing up at a new white marble plaque on the wall.

Sacred to the memory of
Thomas George Frampton Payne
1791–1815
Killed in action at the glorious battle of Waterloo
Only son of the late George Frampton Payne and
his wife Harriet
and beloved grandson of the late Thomas Framp-
ton Payne
of Herriards House
He won the affection of his fellow-officers
and the respect of his commanders
for his courage in action and his loyalty to his
friends
throughout campaigns fought in Portugal, Spain,
France and Belgium
Deeply mourned by his loving sister Katharine
who has lost the best of brothers and a very dear
companion.

Adam Calthorpe stood for some minutes before this silent tribute to Tom, laughing, devil-may-care Tom.

They had more than once saved each other on the field. And he had so often kept Tom out of trouble *off* the field. It seemed wrong that he should not have been there when Fate at last caught up with Tom Payne…

If she was married to you she'd be safe. Tom's words echoed in Adam's mind as he studied the simple tablet. He had not expected to be so moved at this memorial. So much had happened in the last months that memories of his life in the Army before Waterloo had been pushed to the back of his mind. But now he stood in the chapel, remembering so many campaigns, remembering the warmth of his friend's vivid personality, the ever-present laughter, the golden hair forever flopping over one eye, the reckless courage, the ready repentance when his impish sense of humour had taken him too far… And then the night of the Duchess of Richmond's ball, the night before the last great battle. Tom had been ablaze with excitement for most of the evening. But shortly before their ways had separated he had been, just for a few moments, uncharacteristically serious, worried about his sister's future… *If she was married to you she'd be safe.*

Adam stirred restlessly. That was the last time he had seen Tom. Ivo had given him the news two days later. The battle was almost over, the French in retreat when a shell from one of the last French guns to fire had killed Tom outright.

'I shall never forget the last I saw of him, Adam. You remember that look of his? The rest of us were fairly worn—it had been a long, hard fight. But Tom was charging up and down, urging his men on as if he was fresh out of barracks. He was laughing! If ever a man died doing what he loved most, that man was Tom Payne.'

'You're right,' Adam had said sombrely. 'He was a born soldier. And could have been a great one. I'm sorry he's gone—I'll miss him.' After a moment's silence he went on, 'That sister of his is in trouble. Tom's death will bring problems, as well as grief. I'll write to her immediately.'

And he had. And he had written again. He had written four times in all. But apart from a polite acknowledgement of his original letter, putting him off from visiting her in the immediate future, he had not heard a word from Miss Payne.

It had taken longer than he had thought it would to get back to England. So many of the Duke's staff had been killed or injured at Waterloo that Adam had been required to accompany his Commander-in-Chief to Paris. He had eventually managed to get away in September, and only then by pleading that his newly acquired estates in England urgently needed his attention. Since his return he had spent all his time on his estate near Bath, working with his lawyers and agents to sort out the tangle caused by his uncle's unexpected death and his own long absence abroad.

But he had not forgotten his responsibility towards Katharine Payne, and when there had been no reply to his fourth letter he had voiced his anxieties to his mother.

'It's clear, Adam! You must go to Hampshire at once. The poor girl might be in *danger!*'

'Ma'am, don't let your imagination run away with you! Katharine Payne is living in her old home, surrounded by her cousins. How could she possibly be in danger? Old General Armitage seems happy enough about her.'

'General Armitage? What has he to say to anything?'

'He's one of Miss Payne's guardians.'

'Really? How did you know that?'

'Tom once mentioned him. So when I was in Bath on business recently I looked the old fellow up—he's taking the waters there. Since I was already acquainted with him, I thought it would do no harm to have a word about Miss Payne. His memory may not be what it was, but I would respect his opinion on most matters.'

'What did he say?'

'He is quite sure that Katharine Payne is being well-looked after, though she's naturally a bit down at the moment. She was always a touch strong-willed and he thinks that having to give up control of Herriards has upset her, as well. But he has no fears for her. He's met Henry Payne and likes him. He thought him a very sound chap, a sensible, kindly fellow, and well-respected in the neighbourhood, too. The son Walter made a very good impression on the old man, too. Though…' He paused.

'Well? What is it?'

'Tom didn't like Walter Payne. But there wasn't anything specific. There's nothing to suggest that these cousins, apparently perfectly respectable people, would keep Katharine Payne locked up incommunicado! Isn't it far more likely that she is happy enough not to need help from outside?'

'I still don't like it, Adam! Unless the girl is shockingly ill-mannered she ought to write to reassure you, at least!'

'Well, that's what worries me, too. Tom was careless, but he knew how to behave. I confess that I should like to see for myself what is going on at Herriards. I don't at all mind paying them a visit, now that most of Calthorpe's problems have been sorted out. The difficulty is—'

'That you don't like the idea of forcing yourself on a girl who would apparently rather not meet you? My dear boy, you're being far too scrupulous! I don't know why she should be so reluctant. You're a handsome enough fellow. Most girls would be delighted to make your acquaintance. You're very eligible!'

Adam grinned. 'You wouldn't be biassed in my favour, would you, Ma?'

'Not at all!' Mrs Calthorpe reached up and kissed her son. 'I was never so happy as when you returned from the wars safe and sound, Adam. But you cannot call me a doting parent. I just wish that you would find a wife! I have an absurd wish to be a grandmother! It's time you married!'

'I assure you, Mama, I fully intend to!' He grew serious. 'It's strange. The night before Waterloo Tom suggested that I should marry his sister.'

'Just out of the blue? Gracious me! What a very odd suggestion! You've never even met her, have you?'

'No. But Tom was worried about her. I had told him that I would look for a wife, you see, and he saw it as a solution to his problem.'

'I should hope you can do better than to take an unknown girl to wife merely to solve someone else's problem, Adam!' said his mother somewhat tartly. 'Why did her brother have to ask among his friends to find her a husband? She must be an absolute anti-dote!'

'I don't think she can be. Tom was a handsome fellow—blond, blue eyes, regular features—and he always said that his sister was very like him. She's an heiress as well. I don't think finding her a husband would be difficult.' He considered for a moment. 'He was quite pressing. Poor Tom!'

Some business matter intervened, and their conversation had to be abandoned. But the next day his mother broached the subject again. 'I think I may have solved your problem, Adam.'

'Which particular problem is that, ma'am?' asked her son with a harassed look. Life in charge of a large country estate was not all enjoyment and ease.

'The Payne place is in Hampshire, is it not? Not far from Basingstoke? Well, I have some good friends near there who would be delighted if we paid them a visit. We could stay with the Quentins and still be in Dorking for Christmas.'

'Dorking?'

'I should like to spend Christmas in Bridge House, Adam. It's our old home. Calthorpe is beautiful, but it won't be a real home until it has a mistress. Your father brought me to Bridge House when I was a bride, and I've always loved it. Christmas there was always so…so cosy! Will you not spend Christmas with me there?'

'Of course I will! Are…are the Redshaws still our neighbours?'

'Oh, yes—and grander than ever! Ever since Julia

married Viscount Balmenny, John Redshaw has been extending the Court to match Balmenny Castle. You never saw so many turrets! But Julia hardly ever comes to visit her parents—she spends most of her time in London—or Ireland.'

Putting Julia Redshaw firmly out of his mind, Adam said, 'Spending Christmas at Bridge House is an excellent idea! And to visit the Quentins on the way is an even better one. If we were staying within reach of Herriards, it wouldn't be out of order for me to pay a visit. Miss Payne could hardly regard that as an imposition.'

'I shall write tonight. The Quentins will be so pleased—they have been urging me to visit them for a year or more.'

Everything had gone very easily after that. The day after Adam and his mother had arrived at the Quentins', the two ladies settled happily in Mrs Quentin's boudoir for a day of gossip about old times. But with a touch of embarrassment Mr Quentin excused himself to Adam. It was most unfortunate, but he was not free to entertain him that day. Adam assured him quite sincerely that he was perfectly happy to find his own amusement, and lost no time in riding over to Herriard Stoke. He left his groom in charge of the horses at the local inn, and walked to the church. Just a couple of miles away was Herriards, where Tom and his sister had grown up. And here was the last of Tom, this simple tablet on a church wall... *If she was married to you she'd be safe.*

It had been an absurd idea, born of Tom's sudden fear of leaving his sister alone in the world. But though

Adam had not made any commitment to marry the girl, he had promised to make sure she was looked after. His mother was right. Writing four letters and consulting General Armitage was not enough. He would call at Herriards in a day or two, and ask to see Miss Payne. He would ask his mother to come with him. That should avoid any awkwardness. Then, if the girl was happy and not in need of his help, he would consider his obligation to Tom fulfilled. That was what he would do.

Now it was time to collect his horse and get back to the Quentins. This had been just a lightning reconnaissance of the ground. Herriards was a good ten miles from the Quentins' place, and a proper visit would take the better part of a day. He made his way back to the inn to collect his horse and his groom. Before leaving he would have a pint of ale and a chat with Jem Banks, the landlord.

Banks was civil enough but rather taciturn. He couldn't say anything of the Paynes—since the old man had died the village hadn't seen that much of them. Miss Katharine's governess, though—Miss Tillyard—lived in the village.

'I think I saw her today,' Adam said. 'Does she live in the cottage next to the big white house?'

'The big white house… Oh, you mean the one belonging to Mr Cruikshank, the surgeon? Aye, that's the one. Miss Tillyard lives in the cottage next door to Mr Cruikshank.'

At dinner that evening he asked the Quentins about the Payne family.

'The Paynes?' Mrs Quentin said. 'Ah, yes, it was

very sad. That poor girl. We tried to visit, you know, after Tom Payne was killed, but Katharine didn't wish to see anyone, and I'm afraid we haven't bothered since. We don't hear a great deal about them now, Lord Calthorpe. Herriards is on the other side of Basingstoke, and we tend to mix with the folk on this side. We knew the old gentleman, of course—everyone in the county knew him. But since Mr Henry Payne has been in occupation we have seldom seen him. He seems an amiable enough man.'

'Young devils, the Paynes were, when they were children,' said Mr Quentin. 'They used to get up to all sorts of tricks! And Katharine was as bad as her brother. How they used to make us laugh! But since Tom went away…no, I don't think any of us has seen her. You were in action with Tom Payne, weren't you, Calthorpe? A pity he died. Great fellow. Would have been an asset to the county. Don't know about the new man or how he's managing. Entails are the very devil. I know Tom loved the Army, but…' He paused, unwilling perhaps to criticise. 'I hear you have just sold out yourself—do you miss Army life?'

For a while the talk was of the great battle which had been fought earlier in the year, the prospects for peace, the problems of owning land. Then Mrs Quentin said, 'Your mother tells me that you were in Herriard Stoke today. Did you not manage to gather some information about Katharine while you were there?'

'I only spoke to two people—the landlord at the inn, and a Miss Tillyard. In fact, I'm afraid I knocked Miss Tillyard over!'

The company demanded to know more, and Adam recounted the accident in the churchyard.

'But, Adam, I hope you saw that she was all right!'

'I tried to, Mama. I made sure that she wasn't seriously hurt, and then watched till she arrived safely at her cottage. Miss Tillyard wouldn't have thanked me if I had tried to do more. Indeed, she practically bit my head off when I rescued her hat.'

Amid laughter, Mrs Calthorpe said, 'This gets more and more bizarre! What happened to her hat?'

Again Adam explained.

'How ungrateful! She sounds rather a shrew, Lord Calthorpe.'

'A veritable tartar, ma'am!'

'If she had to keep the young Paynes in order, I'm not surprised!'

'She seemed a touch young to have done that…I wouldn't have said she was more than thirty. All the same, I hope I am not called upon to come to her rescue a second time! Once is quite enough!'

Chapter Five

But Adam had cause to remember his words two days later when he and his mother were approaching Herriards House. As they went Adam cast a critical eye over the condition of the drive. His recent experience at Calthorpe had shown him that the place had formerly been well managed, but had now been neglected for months. The drive itself was covered in places with dead weeds and grass, and the ground under a splendid avenue of elms on either side was obscured with a tangle of brambles and brushwood. Paths which had once been pleasant walks under the trees were overgrown. He shook his head. Henry Payne might well be the best of fellows, but he was not looking after his inheritance.

Something caught his eye—a flash of white on one of the paths. The woman he had encountered in the churchyard two days before was walking in some haste towards the drive. As he watched, a man who had obviously been following her came into sight and put a restraining hand on her arm. She shook it off impatiently whereupon the man pulled her round to face him, and snatched her into his arms. It looked as if the situation could become serious and Adam ordered the coachman to pull up. But even as he leapt out and started towards the couple the woman suddenly swung her arm in a wide arc and gave her companion a cracking punch on the nose.

'Leave me alone, Walter Payne! D'you hear me?'

Adam stopped where he was—this lady needed no rescue at the moment. Indeed, the man was in a worse way than she was. Blood was pouring from his nose and dripping down the front of his coat. He was making an effort to staunch it with a lawn handkerchief, but it still seeped through.

'Good God, what did you do that for?' said Walter Payne thickly. 'I wasn't meaning any harm! Look at this!' He gestured at the mess on his coat.

'It's your own fault!'

'My own fault? I was only trying to have a word with you, for God's sake! You've ruined my coat! I'll see you later about this.'

He went off in a rage, and the woman sank down on to the tree trunk nearby and put her face in her hands. Adam decided it was time to intervene. 'Are you all right, ma'am?' he asked gently.

She jumped up, startled. 'Oh! Oh, it's you again,' she said. 'What do you want now?'

'I asked if you were all right.'

'Why, yes, of course! I *enjoy* being mauled about by creatures like Walter Payne!' she said harshly. 'What do you think?'

'I think you have an impressive right hook, ma'am. Did he deserve such punishment?'

'Perhaps not,' she said. 'I didn't stop to debate it.

Perhaps I overreacted. But I was frightened… I dare say you thought it wasn't exactly ladylike…' Her voice wobbled and she put a hand to her brow. 'Oh Heavens, how I dislike men!'

Adam moved to her side. 'I'm sorry,' he said. 'Forgive me. But may I give you a piece of advice for the future? It is dangerous to hit a man when he is aroused. Another time you might not be so lucky.'

She regarded him with dislike. 'I've said before, sir. I neither want nor need your help, and least of all do I want your advice!'

Adam kept his calm. 'Very well,' he said equably. 'Consider it unsaid. Now, what can I do to make amends? Can I escort you somewhere?'

He had to admire her spirit. Pale and dishevelled though she was, she was not about to give an inch. 'No, thank you!' she said. 'I'll be all right now. He won't come back.'

'Adam? What is wrong?' Mrs Calthorpe had not seen what had happened, but was now leaning out of the window of the carriage.

'Stay inside the carriage, Mama!' he called. 'It's cold out here.' Then he turned to the 'governess'. 'You are still pale,' he said urgently. 'I really can't leave it like this. Can we not at least give you a lift to the house—?' Then, remembering too late that she had been dismissed, he corrected himself. 'Or to the village, if you prefer.' When she seemed to hesitate he added, 'You needn't be afraid, Miss Tillyard. My mother is with me, you would not be in any danger. I'm Calthorpe, by the way. Adam Calthorpe.'

She looked at him expressionlessly. After a mo-

mentary pause she said, 'Are you, indeed? Adam Calthorpe. Well, well! Er…who told you my name?'

'Someone in the village said you lived in the cottage
next to the doctor. I watched you go in there.' He
added, 'I wanted to make sure you were safe.'

'Really?' she murmured, almost to herself. 'Well,
better late than never, I suppose.' He was not sure he
had heard correctly, but then she continued, 'Thank
you, Lord Calthorpe, but I…I think I would rather
walk.' She looked at him once more, and gave him a
small smile. 'Goodbye, Lord Calthorpe. I wonder if
we shall meet a third time?'

Adam bowed and watched her walk away down the
path. What a strange woman she was! She was obviously a gentlewoman, and when she was not being
rude, her voice was most attractive. On the other hand,
she was also a first-class shrew, uncivil, ungrateful…he would even say ill bred. And then, her last
words had been spoken in a curiously semi-serious,
semi-mocking way. Adam was both intrigued and re-
pelled. What sort of governess was she?

'Adam, are you coming? In a moment I shall *die* of
cold and curiosity! Who was that girl? Why didn't you
offer her a lift to the house?'

Adam rejoined the carriage. 'I *think* it was a Miss
Tillyard, ma'am. And, if I am right, the last place she
would wish to be taken to would be Herriards—for
more reasons than one!'

When his mother demanded to know more he answered her as best he could, but Miss Tillyard remained an enigma to them both.

They drove up before the house in a few minutes.
Herriards was a beautiful old mansion, built just over

a hundred years before in the time of Queen Anne. It was not a large building, but handsomely proportioned with well-laid gardens surrounding it. Like the rest of the estate, it showed signs of recent neglect.

They were shown into the hall by a flustered housekeeper. 'If your lordship will wait here, I'll tell the master. Lord Calthorpe, was it?'

'And Mrs Calthorpe. Yes.'

'To see Miss Payne?'

'That is correct.'

A few minutes later a gentleman with a beaming smile on his face came through, holding out his hand. 'Come in, come in! I don't know why they kept you out here, Calthorpe! I am delighted to make your acquaintance. And Mrs Calthorpe, too. How delightful!' He shook their hands enthusiastically, but frowned when the housekeeper asked uncertainly,

'Er…shall I fetch Miss Katharine, sir?'

'That's not necessary,' said her master. 'You can fetch some more cups instead. Off with you!' He turned to Mrs Calthorpe. 'Come along, come along! It's warmer in the parlour.' He led them into a well-furnished room warmed by a large fire. Here they found the lady of the house sitting on the sofa next to the prettiest girl Adam had seen in a long time. Guinea-gold curls surrounded a delightfully pointed little face, long eyelashes lifted to reveal gentian-blue eyes before they fluttered modestly down again, the delicate rose in her cheeks echoed the deeper rose of a mouth shaped for kissing. Looking at this vision, Adam began to think that Tom's sister had a great deal to recommend her.

'Ellen, my love, may I present Mrs Calthorpe and

her son Lord Calthorpe?' The lady exchanged a look with her husband, then inclined her head graciously. She did not smile. In fact, she looked distinctly put out.

'And this is our Catherine. Miss Catherine Payne.' The diminutive Venus got up and gave a graceful curtsy, together with a smile which revealed pearl-like teeth. Adam was delighted. Katharine Payne was a prize indeed!

'Won't you sit down? Catherine, my dear, ring for some tea.' Mr Payne smiled benevolently at the company. 'My son Walter is somewhere about, Calthorpe. You might know him—he has spent some time 'in London.'

Adam smiled, but rather hoped Walter Payne would find it impossible to join them. He had no wish to be introduced to the fellow. Tea was brought in and the company talked desultorily. While Mr Payne chatted with Adam's mother, Adam spoke to Miss Payne. She listened to him with a charmingly modest air, just occasionally looking up at him through those long curling lashes. Tom's descriptions had led him to expect a rather more lively young lady, but Adam found little to criticise in this delightful creature. How fortunate it was that his mother had insisted on coming to Basingstoke! He gave his mother a smile and was surprised to see her frowning. What could possibly be wrong? But then just at that moment the door opened and a startled hush fell on the Payne family.

'Katharine! What are you doing here?' exclaimed Mrs Payne sharply after a brief pause. 'We never see you at this time of day! Is there something you want?'

As Adam rose to his feet, he was as startled as the

rest, for in the doorway stood a figure which was already familiar to him. The old cloak and stout shoes had been replaced with a simple round dress and slippers, the untidy hair was neatly, though not extravagantly dressed, but the young woman now closing the door was undeniably 'Miss Tillyard'. There was a slight pause while she turned and looked slowly round, her eyes resting on Adam.

'I heard you had company, ma'am. Asking to see Miss Payne. So I thought I would join you,' she said with a cool smile.

'Yes, yes, of course! In fact, I was…er…I was about to send for you, Katharine, my dear,' said Mrs Payne. 'Mrs Calthorpe, may I present Miss Katharine Payne?'

Adam's mother looked surprised. 'Miss Katharine Payne?' she said. She cast a glance at the girl sitting on the sofa. 'How…unusual. Two members of the same family with exactly the same name!' Looking round at the expressions of dismay on the faces of the Payne family, she added innocently, 'Does it not sometimes give rise to confusion?'

Mr Payne glanced sharply at her, but responded with a laugh, 'None, I assure you, ma'am,' he said. 'My daughter spells her name with ''C'', and is known as Catherine, whereas our dearest cousin Katharine is usually known as Kate.' He hesitated, then said to Adam, 'This is Tom's sister.'

Adam possessed considerable address—indeed, no one could have survived long on the Duke of Wellington's staff without it—but he was having a struggle to disguise his sharp disappointment. Tom's sister was not the enchantress on the sofa, but the shrew, the virago! The fact that she was not a governess did not altogether surprise him—somehow, the girl had not sounded like a governess—but that she was Tom's sister…! What had she said when they had parted in the drive? *I wonder if we shall meet a third time?* She had been laughing at him! Adam felt disappointment giving way to annoyance. Why the devil hadn't she told him who she was when he had given her his own name? What could possibly have been the reason? Pure malice? A desire to put him out of countenance when he learned the truth? It was almost as if she wished to take some sort of revenge—but for what? Confound it! The more he learned of this girl, the less he understood her!

With regret he looked once more at the girl on the sofa. Fate had truly played him a nasty trick. She had appeared to be everything he had hoped for. Pretty, compliant, dainty… She had fitted his own picture of Katharine Payne perfectly, and he had been well on the way to taking Tom's request quite seriously. But this was not Tom's sister!

He looked at the girl now advancing into the room. The contrast between the two Miss Paynes could not have been greater. How the devil could this tall, thin— no, *skinny*—dowdily dressed girl be the delightful creature Tom had described? Dull brown hair was a poor substitute for Tom's golden curls, and as for her eyes—not clear blue like those of her brother, and of the other Catherine—but a…a sort of mud colour! And he knew from personal experience that, far from being the fun-loving, tolerant girl he had been led to expect, she was a belligerent shrew!

However, his innate good manners did not desert

him. When he saw that no one else appeared to be anxious to offer Katharine Payne a seat, he gestured to his own, which was next to that of his mother. 'Miss Payne?'

She gave him a look, moved to the chair and sat down. 'Thank you, Lord Calthorpe. How kind of you. And how kind of you to respond to my letter…at last.'

Adam frowned and was about to ask what she meant, when Henry Payne interrupted him. 'Are you staying long in the neighbourhood, Calthorpe?'

Courtesy demanded that Adam reply. He turned away from Katharine and said, 'I'm not sure. My mother wishes to spend Christmas at our home in Surrey, so probably not more than a week or two.'

'I shall be glad to have a degree of comfort at last, Mr Payne,' said Mrs Calthorpe with a smile of apology at Adam. 'Calthorpe has been sadly neglected for years, and I have been helping my son in his efforts to restore it ever since he got back to England in September. But it is not yet the sort of place where one would wish to spend Christmas.'

'September?' said Katharine. 'I thought you would have been back in England sooner than that, Lord Calthorpe.'

'After Waterloo I was in Paris for nearly three months on the Duke of Wellington's staff, Miss Payne.'

His mother continued, 'You can imagine how much he has had to do to catch up! The house is still not in order even yet.' Mrs Calthorpe gave Katharine a rueful smile. 'So it isn't altogether surprising that this is the first time my son has been able to visit you. Has he not explained that?'

'He has not yet had an opportunity, ma'am.'

'But—' began Adam. He was interrupted again, somewhat arbitrarily, by Mrs Payne.

'Are you staying locally, Mrs Calthorpe?' she suddenly asked. 'Not that we know many of our neighbours as yet.'

Her husband broke in. 'Oh, come, my dear! I am sure we know at least a dozen families! All of them delightful company. Are you staying with the Faulkners, perhaps?' he said, turning to Adam. 'The Faulkners are a charming family, Calthorpe. He is Master of the local hunt, y'know. A very good fellow. Do you hunt?'

Adam's suspicions were aroused. It occurred to him that the Paynes seemed very anxious to prevent him from talking to Katharine Payne. In fact, their attitude had been curiously obstructive from the start. He answered politely, 'When I can. And no, we are not staying with the Faulkners, but with the Quentins, who live on the other side of Basingstoke. Mrs Quentin is an old friend of my mother's.' Then, before either of them could interrupt again, he went on, 'I hope you will excuse me, sir, but I should very much like a word with Miss Payne. I knew her brother very well. If she could bear it, I should like to have a private talk with her.'

After an infinitesimal pause his host said, 'By all means, my dear fellow, by all means! Go ahead!'

Adam turned to Katharine. 'Might I suggest a short walk? It is still quite light.'

Katharine said quickly, 'I should like that very much, Lord Calthorpe.'

'My dear child, it is far too cold—'

'Please excuse me, Uncle Henry. I intend to talk to Lord Calthorpe.' Henry Payne was obviously not particularly pleased, but there was little he could do in the face of such a very direct statement.

Katharine fetched her wrap and put on some boots, and she and Adam walked a short way down the drive.

'There are many things I should like to ask you, Miss Payne,' said Adam. 'Why you failed to tell me who you were when we last met is one of them. But we don't have much time. It is cold, and will soon be dark.'

'I see no reason to explain anything to you, sir. And I agree that we mustn't waste time. Now that you are here I…I have a favour to ask of you. I suppose I'm asking for your help, after all!'

Adam thought with a twinge of amusement that she didn't have the appearance of someone who was asking a favour. Her air was aggressive rather than ingratiating. He said, 'That's the third time you have made a comment which I don't quite understand!'

'Really?'

'You have three times implied that I have been somehow negligent. What did you mean?'

'I should have thought that was obvious. My brother died in June. It is now November,' she said shortly.

'But—'

'I know, I know! I put you off coming at first. Perhaps that annoyed you. Is that why you never wrote again? I…I would have expected you to have more understanding, Lord Calthorpe!'

'You are wrong. I was not annoyed, and I did understand.'

'Then why did you not answer when I wrote again?'

'Again?'

'I wrote to ask you very particularly to come. I hoped you would!'

'I have never had a second letter from you.'

She gave a snort of disbelief. 'Oh, come! There's no need for this, I am not a simpleton. You must have!'

Adam looked at her for a moment. Then he said coolly, 'Miss Payne, you have no reason to trust me, I know. But I was a good friend of your brother's. Tell me why you appear to have such a low opinion of me.'

She stared at him. Then she said slowly, 'I know I had no right to expect anything. But Tom thought the world of you. And you wrote such a...such a comforting letter after his death. At the time I didn't want to talk to anyone. But then...afterwards, when I really needed someone, you failed me.'

Adam was angry. 'How?'

'I asked you for your help last August, and since then this visit is the first I have heard from you. You don't think that is ''negligent''—your word, I believe?'

'I assure you on my honour that I have never had a second letter from you.'

Katharine looked searchingly at him as if trying to read the truth from his face. Then she said reluctantly, 'I suppose it could have gone astray. I wasn't sure of your direction so I sent it to your headquarters in London.'

'It could have—but most mail sent there has reached me. But I'm puzzled—why do you say that you have never heard from me again? I have written four times!'

She stopped and stared at him. 'When?'

'At intervals spread over the months since Tom was killed.'

'*Four times!* I suppose you sent them here? To Herriards?'

'Of course. Where else?'

'How odd! How very odd!'

'Are you telling me that you've had none of my letters since the first one?'

'Not one.' They looked at one another in silence for a moment. Then Katharine said nervously, 'Could they have all been lost in the post…?' Her voice trailed off. There was an awkward silence. Then she said harshly, 'Tilly suggested I should write to you again and give her my letter to post. I refused to accept what she implied.'

Adam said gravely, 'Miss Payne, I'm afraid Miss Tillyard's suspicions were fully justified. Someone has been…intercepting your correspondence.' He glanced at Katharine Payne. She was whiter than ever. A new emotion joined the others he had felt towards this girl. He felt pity. He put his arm round her, half expecting the usual rejection. But instead she gave a sob and turned to hide her face against his coat. Almost without volition his other arm completed the circle of comfort, and, for a moment, they were held in a curious bond, which neither of them quite understood. Then she gave a muffled exclamation and threw his arm off.

'I've asked you before not to touch me!' she said belligerently.

He might have known she would react badly,

thought Adam. This was obviously a woman who didn't believe in the weakness of the weaker sex! After a pause he said calmly, 'You wanted my help, I believe. How can I oblige you?'

'I would like, if possible, to live elsewhere. My cousins are… I don't trust… What we have just found out…' Her voice wavered. She stopped, then began again more firmly, 'I do not find my cousins at all congenial.'

'I noticed that this afternoon,' Adam said gravely.

'You are laughing at me again! And I assure you it is no laughing matter.'

'No, truly, I am not. I am here to serve you. Tell me what it is you want.'

'Tom may have told you that I am not exactly poor, but perhaps he didn't make it clear that I have no control over any money until my twenty-fifth birthday. And that is still four years away.'

Adam looked at her in surprise. So she was only twenty-one! He would have said she was considerably older.

She went on, 'I need your help in persuading my guardians to increase my allowance from the estate my grandfather left me. If I had a little more, just enough to live modestly with my governess somewhere away from Herriards… And before you say anything, I have already written to General Armitage, to no effect. He approves of Henry Payne, you see, and thinks I am merely suffering from the vapours.'

'I saw the General in Bath before I came here. You're right. He thinks very highly of your cousin.'

'I suppose you do, too,' she said bitterly.

'Don't be absurd! Of course I don't! Not now. And as for Walter…'

'They are trying to force me to marry him. And my guardians are not averse to such an idea.'

He stopped and stared. 'You can't be serious! That would never do!'

'I'm relieved you agree,' she said with a touch of irony. 'To some, the idea of reuniting the Payne wealth with the Payne estate, regardless of feeling, might seem quite rational.'

'They can't *make* you marry anyone!'

'No, they can't. But the pressure is sometimes almost more than I can bear. Which is why…which is why I may have overreacted this afternoon. Walter is determined to marry me, and he never stops trying to…to persuade me. He is convinced that I will eventually give in. He knows that I have no one to help me, you see. Tilly has been the only person I could even talk to.'

'Ah! The real Miss Tillyard, I take it?'

'Tilly was my governess, and became a very good friend, especially after my grandfather died. Though she is powerless to help me, I don't know what I would have done without her to confide in.'

He thought for a moment then said, 'I know General Armitage. Who is your other guardian?'

'Sir James Farrow. He lives in Basingstoke, but he's ill. He doesn't receive visitors. Not me, at least. He, too, approves of Henry Payne.' Katharine Payne's voice cracked.

Adam suppressed his impulse to offer her a sympathetic arm. He was beginning to know Miss Katharine Payne and was pretty sure she wouldn't accept it. But he was concerned for her, all the same. Her eyes were huge in her pale face, every line of that thin body expressing tension. She had clearly been under an unbearable strain for months. He made up his mind. Even without his promise to Tom, he would have done all he could to rescue any woman from Henry Payne's tyranny. The man was clearly a villain. His boldness in suppressing their letters was astonishing, and his lack of scruple would be a continuing threat to Katharine. As for Walter…

After a moment's thought, he said, 'I wonder how ill Sir James really is? And if the Quentins know him?' He took Katharine's hand in his and held it reassuringly. 'I'll talk to them tonight and see Sir James as soon as I can. Try not to worry. We shall find something to do.'

For a moment Katharine Payne gripped his fingers so tightly that it was almost painful. She looked directly up at him, eyes wide open in appeal. They were beautiful eyes, he thought in surprise. Not mud-coloured at all, but the golden brown of sherry wine. Then she let go of his hand and said quietly,

'Thank you! You…you have no idea how much this means.'

It was as well that he had not expected effusive thanks or desperate pleas for speed. Not from this lady. Katharine Payne may be near the edge, but, as long as she remained in control of herself, she would regard desperate appeals or tears of gratitude as signs of weakness. Such determination to be strong was admirable, but not attractive in a woman, Adam thought.

'From what you have told me, your ''escape'', as you call it, will mean a lot to your cousin, as well.

Too much, perhaps. May I suggest that you keep our plans to yourself until they are complete?' He looked at her ironically. 'We don't want him worried before it is necessary. How often do you visit your governess?'

'Once or twice a week.'

'Can you call on her tomorrow afternoon? Is she discreet?'

'Absolutely.'

'Then I will leave news of any progress with her. We might even meet there.'

On their way back to the Quentins Adam and his mother discussed what they had seen and heard.

'Thank heavens we came, Adam! They are a *dreadful* family! Poor Katharine Payne!'

'Surely the daughter is charming? I rather liked her. In fact—'

His mother looked at him pityingly. 'My dear boy, I would have thought maturity would have given you more sense! Catherine Payne—how confusing those names are!—Catherine Payne, by whom I mean the blonde miss who sat by her mother, is a spoiled little minx. Another Julia Redshaw, if ever I saw one.'

Adam shook his head at his mother and smiled. 'Do you still condemn Julia for my unhappiness ten years ago? You mustn't be too hard on her, ma'am. I forgave her a long time ago. After all, she merely faced reality before I did. At the time I had nothing to offer her. Much as she loved me—'

'Loved you! No more than she loved all the other young men who buzzed around her like bees round a honey pot!'

'You are mistaken, Mama. I *know* that Julia loved me—she just didn't love me enough. But why are we discussing something that was over long ago?'

'Because Henry Payne's daughter is another such girl. However, you are quite right. We shall forget Julia Redshaw. What are you proposing to do about Katharine? Tom's Katharine.'

'I have promised to help. I shall certainly write to-night to General Armitage—he ought to be informed of our visit and what we have discovered. I'm sure he'll agree that Kate should leave Herriards.'

'But that will take weeks! The girl needs more urgent help than that.'

'I agree. I'll see Sir James Farrow, her other guardian, while we are here. He lives in Basingstoke. The Quentins probably know him.'

'And supposing you do convince these guardians? What then? Where will the girl go?'

'She proposes to set up house with her old governess.'

His mother turned round in her seat to stare at him. 'Are you out of your mind, Adam? You mustn't allow that!'

'Mama, Katharine Payne is a very determined young woman. I don't think anyone could stop her doing exactly what she had decided.'

'Nonsense! Of course you could! What is more, those guardians would never consent to her scheme— and I would agree with them! The girl is far too young to cut herself off from society in that way. She should be enjoying herself, going to balls, to parties, wearing pretty dresses, meeting eligible young men...'

'And how am I to arrange that?'

'Offer her a home yourself.'

Adam stared at her in astonishment. 'With the utmost respect, Mama, I would say that it is you who are out of your mind! How could I offer Katharine Payne a home—unless I married her? And now that I have met her, that is something I am not prepared to do, whatever Tom said. She's not the sort of woman I would ever wish to marry.'

'I expressed myself badly. I meant you could offer her a home with *me*. I should love Miss Payne to come to live with me at Bridge House.'

'The idea is absurd! I'm sorry for the girl, of course, but I'm not sure I like her very much.'

'Why not?'

'She is everything I find unattractive in a woman. Aggressive, strong-minded, ungraceful, ill mannered…'

Mrs Calthorpe shook her head. 'Oh, Adam, you are still so blind, for all your experience! I suppose you liked the other Miss Payne better?'

'Of course I did! Any man would.'

'I'm surprised. I suppose I must just hope that you'll learn before it's too late.'

'What on earth are you talking about?'

'Quality.' He looked blank and she went on, 'Nothing. It's just my nonsense. Now, how soon will Tom's Katharine be ready to join me at Bridge House? Could she be ready to travel with us when we leave here?'

'Wait, wait! I haven't said—'

'But I have! If you won't do it for Miss Payne, then do it for me. I should truly like her company. Oh, Adam, it could be so amusing! Katharine could spend the rest of the winter getting back her…her *joie de vivre,* and in the spring we would take a house in London for the season. I should love to do the season again, Adam!'

'I really don't think—'

Mrs Calthorpe gave a small sigh. 'You really are the most obstinate person of my acquaintance.'

'If you think that, then wait till you have more to do with Katharine Payne. She is far worse than I am.'

'She's had to fight to survive, Adam! No wonder she is determined. Look, if you won't do it for me, perhaps you should do it for Tom? How is his sister ever to be safe if she never meets anyone we can trust to look after her? You may as well give in—my mind is quite made up. Katharine shall stay with me, and I shall sponsor her presentation in Society next year. And you could join us.'

'Oh, no! I couldn't possibly spare the—'

'Of course you could spare the time! Calthorpe will be in better order by then, and you will need some amusement after all your labours. You mustn't let yourself grow *dull,* Adam! Next spring is the time for you to mix in Society yourself. How else will you find a wife?'

'I don't think…'

'Though why you don't wish to marry Miss Payne is beyond me. She is the only sister of your friend, well bred, an heiress, pretty—'

'Pretty!'

'Perhaps not. Pretty isn't the word.'

'Of course it isn't!'

'I should have said beautiful. At least, she will be, once she is herself again.'

Adam regarded his mother with exasperation.

'Mama, I wonder sometimes whether you know what you're saying. How can you call Miss Payne beautiful?' His mother would have answered, but Adam went on, 'And if she were the queen of beauty herself I *still* wouldn't marry her!'

'Why not?'

'I've told you. She's a strong-minded shrew! She has a tongue as sharp as a sabre. I'd die the death of a thousand cuts before we had been married a year!' Remembering Walter Payne's bleeding nose, he added, 'And she is not afraid to use physical violence, either.'

Mrs Calthorpe burst out laughing. 'You poor defenceless lambkin! Has she attacked you?'

'Not yet,' said Adam. 'But she probably would. And it's all very well for you to laugh, but it isn't easy for a gentleman to deal with a lady who doesn't behave like one!'

'The girl is cracking under the strain of living with Henry Payne's family. Nothing she did at the moment would surprise me. But, Adam, she would soon change once she was free of those cousins of hers.'

Adam raised a sceptical eyebrow.

His mother went on, 'Well then, I shan't try to persuade you any more. But if you don't wish to marry her yourself, you ought to see to it that she meets suitable alternatives. And she won't do that cooped up with her governess in a cottage in the country.'

Her son was silent for a moment. There was some truth in what his mother said. Moreover, she seemed to have taken a liking to Katharine Payne—the girl would be company for her during the winter while he was busy at Calthorpe. He said at last, 'I must speak to Sir James. And then we shall see if it can be arranged.'

'Henry Payne won't let her go without a fight,' warned Mrs Calthorpe.

'If I have the support of her guardians, I can soon settle Henry Payne. But what if Katharine doesn't wish to live with you, Mama?'

'I assure you, my son, after Henry Payne and his delightful family, she would be glad to live with anyone. As you know, I can be very persuasive when I choose. In any case, what normal girl would refuse the prospect of a season in London?'

Chapter Six

Armed with an introduction from the Quentins, Adam called on Sir James Farrow the next day. Sir James, dressed in a brocade dressing gown and velvet-tasselled cap, received him in a stiflingly warm study. Next to his chair was a revolving bookcase full of books and papers. A decanter of wine and a glass, a dish of nuts and biscuits, a bowl of fruit and a plate and silver knife were arranged on the small table on his other side.

'Come in, come in and shut the door, Calthorpe! I can't abide draughts, they're not good for me. Sit down where I can see you and tell me about Waterloo! They say it was pretty close. Is that right? What was your regiment? Help yourself to a glass of wine.'

Adam obediently helped himself and sat down on the other side of the fire. 'I was in the same regiment as Tom Payne.'

'The Fighting 52nd, eh? Colborne's lot. They did well, I hear.' He paused. 'Were you with Tom when he was killed?'

'No, I wasn't with the regiment at that point. I'd

been seconded to the Duke's staff and was doing liaison work on that last day with the Prussians at the other end of the battlefield.'

For a while Adam answered the old man's eager questions about Wellington and the changes of fortune at Waterloo. Then, after a while, he paused. Sir James sat up a little.

'Talked yourself dry, have you? Have another glass of wine!'

'Thank you, Sir James, I still have some. But I would really like to talk of Tom Payne. You knew the family well, I gather.'

'Ah, yes! His grandfather was a great friend of mine. The boy was called after him—Thomas Frampton Payne. Sad business, his death. Very sad! What did you want to say about him?'

'Tom had a sister.'

'Did he? I never knew that! Fancy old Tom Payne not telling me that! Wrong side of the blanket, was she?'

'I mean the grandson had a sister. Katharine.'

'Oh…oh! Well, I know that, my boy! You don't have to tell me that! Her guardian, ain't I?'

Adam patiently worked his way through a series of explanations to the point where he could raise the question of Katharine's future.

'Want to marry her, do you? I thought she was to marry that cousin of hers. What was the fellow's name, now…? Walter! That's it! Sensible thing to do. As Henry Payne said, gets the money back where it belongs. You can't run an estate like that on nothing. Eh? What does a female know about it? Pretty little thing, Katharine, but when all's said and done, she's a female, ain't she?'

Adam reflected that Katharine's Uncle Henry had done his job well. He had used exactly the sort of argument which would appeal to the old man, and as a result Sir James was obviously inclined to look favourably on a match between his ward and Henry's son. It took all the guile and negotiating skills Adam had acquired during ten years in the Army to persuade the old man to agree at least to hear Katharine's views on the matter.

'You'll bring her along yourself, will you? Can't stand dealing with females on m'own. Never could. Why I never married. Come the day after tomorrow.'

'Thank you, sir.' It occurred to Adam that some reinforcement might be advisable. 'Er…Miss Payne would perhaps like some lady to accompany her?'

'Not that governess female! Can't abide her.'

'May I bring my mother, who is with me in Basingstoke? She is an old friend of Mrs Quentin's, you know.'

'Ah! The only sensible woman I ever knew, Quentin's wife. Very well. Bring your mother, my boy. Why not?'

Adam's plans nearly foundered at their birth. Katharine raised strong objections to the changes he was proposing to make to her future.

'I told you what I wanted!' she said. 'To live quietly with Tilly. Your mother is very kind, but I have no wish to live in a big city, to be presented to a crowd of strangers, to make conversation with people with whom I have nothing in common. I shan't know what

to wear, what to say, I don't know the latest dances…
I shall feel totally out of place. The idea is absurd! I
won't even consider it.'

Adam held on to his calm. 'You really are the most
unexpected female I have ever met! Most young
women would be delighted at the prospect of having
a season in London. Your own cousin Catherine, for
example, would give anything to be in your shoes.'

'Oh, yes, Catherine would—but she is a feather-
brain.'

'She is a very pretty one.'

Katharine looked at him, then uncannily echoed his
own thoughts. 'And would be a huge success. What a
pity I am not more like her—that's what you are no
doubt thinking! Well, with a little luck, you will be
able to indulge your admiration for her as much as
you wish next season. She fully intends to be in London then. So why do you need me there? I assure you
that I would much rather be in my own house in
Tilly's company.'

'Thank you,' Adam said ironically. 'You really
shouldn't flatter me so.'

Katharine had the grace to look ashamed. 'I didn't
mean it quite like that,' she said. 'It's just that…' She
hesitated, then burst out, 'I'm sure you mean well, but
I have managed my own life for so long. I resent being
told what I am to do!'

'I had noticed,' murmured Adam. 'But I quite
thought you had asked for my help?'

'I did! But I wanted you to arrange for me to live
with Tilly! Not to go gallivanting about the town! I
tell you, I won't do it!'

'Katharine Payne!' said Adam in a voice his junior

officers would have recognised. 'Do you or do you not wish to leave your uncle's house?'

'Well, of course I do! It's just—'

'Then for once in your life you will do as you are told!'

'But—'

'No buts! If you wish me to persuade Sir James to change his present plans for your future—which, if you remember, favour a marriage to Walter Payne— then you will remain silent and leave all negotiations to me. Understood?'

Katharine gazed at him mutinously. 'He's *my* guardian.'

'And you have so far been conspicuously unsuccessful in dealing with him. Look, it's not altogether your fault. Sir James doesn't like women, and he doesn't like exertion. Left to himself, he won't take kindly to what *he* sees as the rebellion of a spoilt female, nor will he make the slightest effort to find a more agreeable alternative for you. But if we can present him with a ready-made plan which fits in with his notions of what is proper, and moreover one which makes no demands on him, he will listen. It's your only hope, Katharine. Choose now—Herriards, or Bridge House and London.'

'It has to be Bridge House. But I don't like it!'

'You ungrateful brat! You don't deserve my mother's offer!'

When Adam vented his exasperation to Mrs Calthorpe she was unsympathetic. 'You must have handled the matter very clumsily, Adam. There isn't a girl alive who would not wish to visit London in the season at least once in her life.'

'So I told her. Her cousin Catherine—'

'You surely didn't mention her, did you?'

'Yes. Why not?'

'*Why not?* You have to ask me why not?' said his mother in exasperation.

'I merely said that her cousin would love to have such a chance,' said Adam defensively. 'I thought it might persuade our Miss Payne to change her mind. But that was when she announced that she would prefer Tilly's company to mine!'

His mother looked at him in amazement. 'Adam, you have managed to be the positive embodiment of tact for years, but Tom's poor sister seems to have a strangely adverse effect on you. Why on earth did you bring Catherine Payne into it? Your Katharine may not have been very polite, but I really cannot blame her for what she said! You deserved it. But believe me, your Katharine would without doubt like to go to London, though she would never admit it—not in her present state.'

'Please, Mama! She is not "my" Katharine!'

'Well, how am I to distinguish between the two girls? It is a ridiculous situation!'

'You could call her "Tom's Katharine", or at a pinch she could be "our" Katharine. Or better still we could call her Kate. But she is not my Katharine! Please!' His mother put her head on one side and regarded him quizzically.

'She really has upset you, hasn't she?'

'Not at all. But I know you. Now tell me what has persuaded you that Kate wants to come to London in spite of all her words to the contrary. I have to confess you have lost me.'

'Consider for a moment, my dear! In the space of a few months she has lost everything which made her feel secure—her grandfather, her brother, her home…even her fortune has proved to be not an asset, but a source of stress. Her guardians have ignored her, and for months she thought you had deserted her, too… She has had to learn to fight her own battles with little prospect of help from outside. Is it any wonder that she is exhausted? Your obvious admiration of her cousin Catherine must have been the last straw.'

Adam looked uncomfortable, as his mother went on, 'Kate is not conventionally pretty. The other Catherine's attractions are so much more obvious, and, what is more, that little minx has learned to make the most of them. Tom's sister was brought up by two male relatives and a governess. She has never been encouraged to spend much time on her appearance, and, if she thinks about them at all, she probably rates her looks rather low. It isn't surprising that she is nervous when faced with the prospect of submitting herself for inspection by Society. Perhaps you don't know how critical the *ton* can be.'

'Nervous? Kate Payne?'

'Yes,' said his mother firmly. 'Whatever you may think, Kate Payne's confidence is at the moment non-existent. I am convinced that all the things you disapprove of, Adam, her rudeness, her aggression, her desire for independence, they are all a form of defence. But you needn't worry. Once she has been in my care for a month or two you will be astounded at how she will change.'

'It can only be for the better,' muttered Adam.

His mother decided to ignore him. But, she thought ruefully, the next few months would prove quite interesting if Katharine Payne agreed to come and stay, and Adam persisted in this disapproval of her.

Adam was still not completely sure how Katharine would behave in the all-important interview with Sir James, so he arranged for them all to meet at Tilly's beforehand. Mrs Calthorpe had been given the task of persuading Katharine to look more favourably on the idea of being presented next season. She even pointed out that six or seven months were not a lifetime. If Katharine were of the same mind after experiencing life in London, she could still, supposing her guardians would consent, look for her house to share with Tilly.

'But pray do not mention that today, Kate! Today we all have to concentrate on getting Sir James to allow you to accept my invitation. If he has the slightest notion that you might revert to your original scheme, he might well refuse to listen to anything further.'

'I really don't see why he would object—Tilly is eminently respectable.'

'Kate, believe me, I know what I am talking about. It won't work! To be frank, I should be very surprised if any guardians worthy of the name would ever consent to such a scheme. In their eyes it would certainly mean virtual isolation from your proper position in society, and they would regard it as their duty to your grandfather to see that it doesn't happen. In fact, the very possibility might cause them to insist on your returning to your uncle.'

This gave Katharine pause. Then Tilly added her voice to the debate. The governess told her plainly that Lord Calthorpe was acting beyond the call of duty, and that Tom would have been astounded and very angry if she refused Mrs Calthorpe's invitation.

'I don't understand you, Katharine. For months you have thought of nothing but escape from Herriards, and now, when such a golden opportunity is presented, you hesitate, merely because it isn't quite the rescue you wanted. Not the retreat we planned, but an adventure into a new world—a world that should have been yours years ago. Yes, it needs courage, but you have never wanted for courage in the past. I shall think you a coward, if you do not do as Lord Calthorpe suggests. Learn to enjoy life as you were meant to, my dear!'

When they reached Sir James's house, Adam presented his suggestion for Katharine's future, claiming that he was fulfilling the promise made to Tom at their last meeting.

'Tom said that, did he? Asked you to look after his sister? He should have been here to look after her himself, the young scamp! But you may be right, Calthorpe, you may be right. You've shown sense in your career, you probably know what you're doing otherwise,' Sir James said at last. He turned to Mrs Calthorpe. 'What do you think, ma'am? You know the world as I do not. What do you say?'

'You can hardly expect me to give you a completely unbiassed view, Sir James. I would regard it as a great kindness on your part if you would grant me Katharine's company. But, since you ask…' She hesitated.

'Well? What is it?'

'Katharine has spent all her life at Herriards. I mean no offence, but have you considered how the world might regard it, if you agreed too readily to Mr Payne's plan for her to marry his son?'

Sir James sat up a little. 'How is that, ma'am?' he asked, a trifle coldly.

Mrs Calthorpe was undisturbed. She went on calmly, 'The temptation to bring a fortune back into the Herriards estate must be strong, especially to Mr Payne, and his wish for his son to marry into the Payne fortune might seem very reasonable. Though it is odd that such a thought had not occurred to Katharine's grandfather. Was it because he did not approve of his cousins? One cannot tell. But how will the world regard it? Living retired as you do, it may not have occurred to you that young ladies of Katharine's birth and wealth are generally expected to be presented to Society before marriage. Sir James, Katharine really ought not to be married off before she has seen anything of the world.'

'Ha! I never thought of that! You're quite right, ma'am, quite right! But we can't do it!'

'Why not, Sir James?'

'You see a sick man before you, Mrs Calthorpe,' said Sir James, sinking back into his chair. 'And I dare swear old Armitage's state is not much better, for all his cures in Bath. How could either of us junket about arranging chaperons and dressmakers and milliners, and I don't know what else besides?' He took a sip of wine, and settled himself more comfortably. 'It can't be done!'

Katharine began eagerly, 'In that case—' but Mrs Calthorpe's voice drowned hers.

'If that is the only difficulty,' she said cheerfully, 'then it is easily overcome! There's nothing I should like better than to introduce Kate to Society. And we women, you know, positively enjoy visiting mantua makers and buying gloves, shawls and all the rest. There is no problem there, I assure you.' She paused. 'Er…Kate will need to have her allowance considerably increased…'

'Strange,' said Sir James shaking his head. 'There's no accounting for female taste. Still, if you mean what you say, ma'am, that you're prepared to stand the racket of it all, you needn't worry about the cost. Send the bills to my man of business. He'll deal with them. And I dare say your son here will take an interest in her welfare, too, eh? Well, well, well!' He smiled benignly at his ward. 'I hope you're grateful for all the trouble I'm taking over you, miss!'

Katharine opened her mouth. 'But you've not heard my—'

'She is indeed, Sir James. Quite speechless with gratitude,' said Mrs Calthorpe firmly.

'All I wanted—' Katharine began again.

'Was to have your permission to travel with us when we leave for Dorking in a day or two's time. She is such a dutiful child,' said Mrs Calthorpe with an admonitory look at Katharine and a sweet smile for Sir James.

Since the 'dutiful child' was beginning to look prepared to argue, Adam decided it was time to take their leave. Pleased to have solved the problem of Katharine with so little trouble, Sir James readily agreed that she should leave Herriards when the Calthorpes set off for Dorking in a few days' time. This was all subject to General Armitage's agreement, of course, but there was no doubt that he would give it.

There was only one small flaw, as far as Adam could see. Sir James seemed to think that Adam had a deeper personal interest in his ward. And though there was nothing he could put his finger on, Mrs Calthorpe appeared to have fostered this belief. For some unaccountable reason she seemed to find Katharine far more attractive than her son did. Adam decided that he must be on his guard against whatever plans his mother was brewing. She had a knack of getting her own way before anyone noticed what she was up to. But in this she would be defeated—Katharine Payne possessed none of the qualities he was looking for in a wife. Not even her fortune was enough to tempt him!

Katharine did not seem to have noticed any of this—she was too preoccupied to question anything. But just before the carriage reached Tilly's cottage the Calthorpes realised that she was still fighting.

'I shouldn't have agreed so easily,' she said, turning to Mrs Calthorpe with a worried frown. 'What will Tilly do? How can I leave her to fend for herself?'

'It seems to me very likely that once Miss Tillyard knows that you are safe and well she will be perfectly happy in her little cottage. Dorking is not a hundred miles away, you know. But ask her yourself. If she is anxious to keep a closer eye on you, I am very willing to offer her a room in Bridge House while you are with us.'

Katharine sighed and sank back. 'You are so kind,'

she said in a slightly depressed tone. 'How will I ever repay you?'

'I'll find a way,' said Mrs Calthorpe, with a twinkle. 'Give me time.'

They all agreed that Katharine's departure had to be sprung on Henry Payne without warning. If he knew of her plans in advance, he would certainly set up some reason to delay her. Surprise was their best strategy. So it was arranged that Katharine would pack a small bag for herself, and that Adam and his mother would simply pick her up on their way from Basingstoke to Dorking. A carrier would be sent later in the day to collect the remainder of Katharine's possessions under the supervision of Miss Tillyard, and she would see that it was sent on.

On being asked what she herself wanted to do, she had kissed Katharine affectionately and said, 'I would prefer to stay where I am for the moment, Katharine, dear. Let us see what comes of your London excursion. Perhaps I shall change my mind after that. Meanwhile I shall be quite happy here. There's so much to do.'

The day for departure came about a week later. Adam arrived at Herriards in the morning and asked to see Mr Payne. At first Henry was all affability, but when he learned that Adam was there to take Katharine away with him, he denied at first that Katharine was in, then he said she was ill.

'And even if she were not indisposed, Lord Calthorpe, I could not in honesty consent to a mad scheme like this. What? Allow you, on the spur of the moment like this, to…to whisk my little cousin away from the only home she has ever known? To remove her from the company of those who regard themselves as her guardians and friends? No, no! I know my duty better than that. Katharine is a considerable heiress, an innocent in the ways of society. She needs protection from those who might seek to exploit her.'

'Am I to suppose you count me among such people?' asked Adam. His voice was quiet, but something in it caused Henry Payne to take a step back and hastily disclaim any such suggestion.

'No, no! You misunderstood me, Lord Calthorpe. I am sure you seek to act from the best of motives— your friendship for her brother, for example. But whatever sort of friend you were to Tom Payne, it is not at all necessary for you to concern yourself with his sister, sir! She is not, as you might have thought, alone in the world. I am, after all, her guardian.'

'You surprise me,' said Adam politely. 'I understood that Sir James Farrow and General Armitage were responsible for Miss Payne?'

Henry Payne gave him a malevolent look, then pulled himself together and gave Adam a smile of forgiveness. 'I should have said that they regard me as one,' he said. 'Her real guardians are elderly—they know they can trust me to look after her as if she was my own daughter, and have been happy to delegate their responsibilities to me. Lord Calthorpe, I'm afraid that on behalf of Katharine's guardians, I must decline your very kind invitation. I cannot allow her to go with you.'

Adam had had the forethought to arm himself with

a letter from Sir James. He now handed it over in silence.

'What is this?' Henry Payne read it through twice. When he looked up the expression on his face was ugly, his mask of benevolence quite gone. 'What are you trying to do, Calthorpe?' he muttered. 'The money, that's behind this, isn't it? Payne money—*my* money, if I had my rights! You're going to carry the heiress off and marry her yourself, is that it?'

'You would naturally think so,' drawled Adam, allowing the distaste he felt for the man to show through. 'However, that is not my purpose. I am merely escorting the ladies to Dorking. My mother, who is in the carriage outside, has simply invited Miss Payne to pay her a prolonged visit—an invitation which your cousin has accepted. It is very possible that my mother will do as the Payne trustees wish, and bring Miss Payne out next year.'

Henry Payne snarled his opinion of this idea. Adam raised his brows.

'Really? I am disappointed in you, Payne. One might have thought that you and Mrs Payne, as Katharine's self-styled ''guardians'', would be delighted to see her introduced to Society at such little cost of time and trouble to yourselves. Fortunately there is no need for debate—it is already settled. Discussing it further would be a waste of time. Now, where is Miss Payne? She assured me she would be ready… Ah! Here she is.'

'My cousin doesn't need to be introduced to Society or to anyone else!' Henry Payne said between his teeth. 'She's going to marry Walter. She's going to marry him any day now! I won't let you take her, do you hear?'

'You must know that is not true, Uncle Henry,' said Katharine as she came into the hall. She was carrying a small valise and was dressed for travelling. She looked pale, but steadfast. 'I think Lord Calthorpe has explained the situation. We must not keep his mother—and his horses—waiting any longer.' Adam watched in some admiration as she said, without the slightest trace of irony in her voice, 'I must thank you for giving me a home for the last few months. And please convey my best wishes for their future to the rest of your family. I'm afraid I haven't been able to speak to them—they are still in their rooms. A carrier will call for the rest of my things later today.' She looked at Adam, who took her valise, gave the briefest of bows to Henry Payne and escorted her to his carriage.

Henry Payne came to the door. 'You haven't heard the last of this!' he shouted, his face contorted with rage. 'Abduction, that's what it is!'

The groom was standing at the door of the carriage. Mrs Calthorpe was at its window, waiting to welcome her. But Katharine stopped and turned. 'The only abduction I have ever feared,' she said, the tremble in her voice revealing the depth of her feeling, 'was that threatened by you and your son. Goodbye, sir!'

She entered the carriage, followed by Adam. The groom closed the door and got up behind. The coachman gave his orders, the horses moved slowly off, and Katharine's journey to a new life had begun.

Chapter Seven

It was a distance of forty miles or so to Dorking, and now in winter the hours of daylight were limited. Adam had taken the precaution of reserving rooms for them at the Bush in Farnham, which was about halfway, and it was as well, for darkness was already falling as the carriage drove up the main street of the pleasant little town. Katharine had hoped to see the castle, which was the ancient seat of the Bishops of Winchester, but she saw little more than a tantalising glimpse up a broad street to the left just before they reached the inn.

A hearty welcome awaited them at the Bush. They were quickly taken to their rooms and maidservants scurried round to make them warm and comfortable. Both ladies were glad of a few minutes' rest after the somewhat fraught circumstances of their departure from Herriards, followed by a journey of twenty miles on a cold winter's day. But then they tidied themselves up and came downstairs for the evening meal. Winter was not a time when many people travelled, and though Farnham was on the main road to Winchester,

the inn was not full. However, there was a great deal
of noise and bustle about the place—a celebration of
sorts appeared to be going on in the main taproom—
and Adam and his ladies were glad to be served in a
private parlour.

The food was good and plentiful, but Katharine
found she had little appetite. She felt drained, both
emotionally and physically. Reaction had set in after
months of tension. Adam saw how it was with her—
he had observed the same symptoms in his junior officers after a particularly vicious bout of fighting. He
gave her a glass of wine and told her to drink it all.

'And, if you will take my advice, you will go to
bed as soon as you have finished it,' he said. 'Tomorrow will be a different story. You'll see.'

Katharine was too worn out to object. She made her
excuses and went slowly upstairs, leaving Adam and
his mother to finish their meal together.

But once alone in her room she felt restless, unable
to relax. Though she was exhausted, the thought of
undressing and settling into bed simply did not appeal.
She dismissed the maid and sat by the window. She
was missing Tom more than ever. Nothing could bring
back those days of sunshine and laughter at Herriards
when they had both been children. But today, when
she had left behind everything they had shared, the old
life had never seemed so dear.

Impatiently she stood up. This was no way to go
about it! Katharine Payne was no watering pot, no
weakling to mourn what she couldn't any longer have!
She must start on a new life, with new friends and
new interests. Herriards was no longer a haven of
happy dreams. It was a place of fear, of nightmare,

even. She should be thanking her lucky stars that she had escaped at last. And perhaps thanking Adam Calthorpe, too.

The thought of Adam Calthorpe gave her pause. Something of an enigma, his lordship. Did he never lose his temper? Though she had been impossibly rude to him, he had maintained his calm. Though Henry Payne had insulted him, Lord Calthorpe had remained a gentleman. He must be a fighter—he wouldn't otherwise have had such a long and successful career in the Army. But she had seen no evidence of it, apart from a certain officer-like arrogance which set her teeth on edge. But he was otherwise so impartial, so patient, so…cool! How unlike his mother he was! She was all impulse and warmth, and Katharine already liked Mrs Calthorpe a great deal. But not the son! What a contrast he was to Tom—laughing, mischievous, reckless Tom! Her heart sank as she realised that she was back with thoughts of Tom again…

This would not do! She was never going to be able to rest. She looked desperately out of the window. The moon was full, silvering the streets and houses opposite. The castle would look magical in this light… Katharine made up her mind. She snatched up her cloak and, without questioning whether she was being wise, slipped down the stairs and out through the side door. The street that led to the castle was only a step or two away. She would see if a little lunar magic would calm her, make it possible for her to sleep.

The castle was just as she had imagined—spectacular in the moonlight, the essence of fairy tales, the embodiment of dreams. Katharine stood at the bottom of the street in rapt contemplation. But she was given a rude awakening. A pair of arms grabbed her around the waist and brandy-soaked fumes breathed over her.

'Well, well! What've we here, then, eh? Lookin' f'r company, sweetheart?'

The voice was that of a gentleman, but the gentleman in question was more than half drunk. He must have been part of the crowd in the tap room.

'You are making a mistake—'

'No need to b' coy, girl! What else would you be doing loose on the town like this? C'm here!' He pulled her closer. Katharine managed to wrest herself free of his embrace, and, deciding that discretion was the better part of valour, started to run back towards the inn. Unfortunately, the young buck had a companion, equally well to the wind. He caught her as she turned and half-carried her back to his friend, laughing at her efforts to escape. Katharine was in a panic. She forgot discretion and hit out wildly, fists bunched the way Tom had taught her. She caught one of them full in the face. Shock and pain made him angry, and, instead of letting her go, he stopped laughing and retaliated. Katharine could do nothing to stop them. One hit her straight away, then held her while the other prepared to take his revenge. Katharine strained desperately against the cruel arms holding her. She closed her eyes… Then she heard a voice she hardly recognised saying furiously, 'Leave her alone, you scum!' and she was suddenly free as the fellow holding her fell back, and measured his length on the cobbles.

A powerful arm skimmed past her ear and Katharine heard the crunch as a fist met its target. Her second attacker went staggering back, holding his jaw. If she had been less frightened she would have felt sorry for the man. She looked round. Lord Calthorpe was standing behind her, legs apart, rubbing his knuckles threateningly. The moonlight had turned his face into a mask of steel.

'Are you all right?'

She nodded, whereupon he looked round, ready to turn his attention on her attackers again. They had, wisely perhaps, vanished.

'Do you need help to get back to the inn?'

Katharine shook her head, still unable to speak. They went back to the inn and up to her room in silence.

Then she said in a subdued voice, 'Goodnight, sir.'

'Oh, no, Miss Katharine Payne! You don't get off as lightly as that!' Lord Calthorpe pushed Katharine into the room and shut the door.

'What…what are you doing?' she asked nervously.

'You needn't be afraid I have designs on your virtue!' he said in a scathing voice. 'I merely want privacy to ask you what the *devil* you thought you were doing? Were you actually *looking* for adventure? Is that why you left us early?'

Katharine fired up. 'Of course not! How dare you suggest such a th—'

'That's as well. You would have found more than you bargained for, believe me! *And* you chose to disregard the excellent piece of advice I've already given you!'

'Which bit was that?' asked Katharine mutinously.

'Not to hit a man when he's attacking you. Scream for help, run away, but don't respond in kind! You're bound to lose.'

She pulled the rags of her dignity together and answered him with spirit. 'I…I assure you, sir, I was far from looking for any kind of adventure. I…I merely went for a walk! I wanted to see the cas—'

'A *walk!*' Words seemed to fail Lord Calthorpe, but not, thought Katharine miserably, for long. He proceeded to express with fluency and feeling his contempt for her intelligence, for her complete lack of any sense of self-preservation, and finally for her want of any consideration for his mother, not to mention himself.

'You are meant to be in our care, Miss Payne, but how can we protect such a want-wit? How on earth is my mother to cope with such stupidity?'

Katharine was angry and ashamed. She hated to admit it, but the man was right. She had been stupid. She wondered briefly whether he would disown her and send her back to Hampshire, and said forlornly, 'You need say no more, Lord Calthorpe. I was foolish. I see that now. I suppose I am not used to towns— though that is no excuse. I…I am ashamed. And grateful to you for rescuing me.'

Lord Calthorpe looked at her closely. 'This doesn't sound like you! Are you sure you are all right? Let me see!' He took her chin in his hand and turned it to the light of the candle. 'There's a nasty bruise there. Why didn't you say you were hurt? My God, I should have hit those brutes harder!'

'I don't think you could have,' Katharine said, trying to smile. She winced as the bruise on her cheek made itself felt.

'Sit down, here by the light!' His voice was peremptory, but his hands were gentle. She allowed him to examine her face. 'Just the one bruise on your cheek. What about the rest of you?'

'They didn't have time to do any real harm. You appeared almost as soon as they did. There's nothing amiss, other than the bruise here.'

'Thank God for that! You've been luckier than you deserve.'

'I know,' she said, trying not to sound resentful at his tone.

He gave her a look. 'You have courage, Kate Payne, I'll give you that, but you're reckless, like your brother. I can see we're going to have to teach you some sense. But enough said. That cheek must hurt like the devil. I'll get something for it.'

He disappeared, but returned as discreetly as he had gone, with a small bottle. 'Arnica,' he said. 'It will deal with the worst of it. And I've brought some drops. My mother uses them occasionally when she can't sleep.'

'I don't think—'

'Don't argue, Miss Payne! Just do as I tell you. I'll bathe that bruise, and then wait while you take the drops. There'll be time to undress after I've gone.'

'Well, that's a relief,' Katharine said rebelliously. 'I was afraid you were going to deal with everything.'

He smiled. 'I see that your spirits are improving. Shall I send a maid to help you? Or shall I undo the necessary hooks before I go?'

'I'll have the maid, if you don't mind,' said Katharine hastily.

'Good! Then drink this…' He poured one or two of the drops into a glass of water and handed it to her. She hesitated, but he looked at her calmly until she downed them. 'And now I'll find a maid. Goodnight, Miss Payne.'

The maid came, not without a slightly puzzled air, but Katharine was too tired to notice. In spite of her bruised cheek she smiled as she fell asleep. She had been mistaken. When roused, Adam Calthorpe was not at all cool... And that punch had been as good as she had ever witnessed—even Tom couldn't have done better.

The next morning Mrs Calthorpe exclaimed at Katharine's cheek, which was now purple. 'You may well have a black eye!' she cried. 'My dear girl, how did you do it?'

Scarlet mixed with the purple in Katharine's face. She hesitated.

Adam came to her rescue. 'Perhaps Miss Payne knocked her head against the post,' he said. 'I very nearly did myself—the beams in our rooms are very low. Did you do it last night?' Katharine nodded. 'Then though it looks ugly—it does, though you must forgive my saying so—it is a good sign that it has discoloured so quickly. A day or two and it will have disappeared completely. No black eye. How did you sleep, Mama?'

'Oh, there was so much to-ing and fro-ing that I took my drops before I got into bed. You know I always sleep very soundly after I have those. You needn't look like that, Adam! I hardly ever take them now. Indeed, I'm not even sure where I put them last night. They weren't on my bedside table this morning.'

'Perhaps you put them on the washstand?'

'Perhaps. But, Adam, you were not very sympathetic with Kate. She is not one of your soldiers, you know, but just a frail girl. Look at her—a breath of wind would blow her away. Are you fit to travel on, my dear? We could easily wait a day here. We might even visit the castle.'

'I think Miss Payne has seen enough of Farnham for the moment, ma'am. She would probably like to get to Dorking. I certainly should.'

And Katharine was, for the first time in their acquaintance, in complete agreement with Adam.

They arrived at Bridge House just as the sun was bathing it in a late afternoon glow. Katharine found it altogether delightful. It was built of brick, in a soft rose colour, and was surrounded by a park, which sloped down to the river. At this season few of the trees had any leaves, but Katharine could see that they had been planted by an artist. A small channel had been diverted from the river to create a lake, and as the carriage drove along its edge towards the house, Katharine was entranced to see moorhens and coots, ducks and swans, all busy about their affairs on the reed-fringed water. Nearer the house shrubs and flowerbeds enclosed a terraced lawn, dotted with specimen trees. There was little of grandeur or formality in the disposition of the house and grounds, but much that paid tribute to the owners' thought and taste.

'You like it, Kate?' said Mrs Calthorpe with a pleased expression.

'It is beautiful! Oh, I can well sympathise with your wish to spend Christmas here at Bridge House! Indeed,

I cannot imagine how you could spend as long as you have away from it!'

'I confess I am glad to be back. I have great hopes for Calthorpe, Adam's house near Bath, once it is occupied and given the attention it deserves, but my brother-in-law never spent a penny more than he had to on the place, and as a result it is somewhat bleak. Adam has already worked miracles in the grounds. And when he has a wife they will work together inside the house. That is what Adam's father and I did here, and I think it turned out well.'

Adam was not listening. His attention had been caught by a herd of deer which had appeared to the left of the house.

'That damned agent of yours, Mama!' he said. 'He can't be supervising the men properly—those deer ought not to be able to get so near the house. The ditches must have filled up. What the devil does Frenton think we pay him for?'

Katharine leant comfortably back again against the cushions and eyed him covertly. Even though his words were strong, he still spoke judicially, without undue heat. Perhaps last night had been uncharacteristic after all, and this was his usual mode—calm, even-tempered, unruffled. Together with his air of confident authority it was rather irritating... What sort of husband would he make? Of course, he was immensely eligible; even she, ignorant as she was of the world, could see that. Rich, titled, well bred, a Hero of Waterloo... And far from being the bewhiskered older man she had pictured when she received his letter, he was really quite handsome. He could undoubtedly take his pick of the young ladies who would appear next season, looking for a husband. Lord Calthorpe might be a touch too sure of himself for her taste, but there were probably any number of girls who would be impressed by his habit of command. And his manners were unquestionably impeccable. Apart from his outburst last night he had always been unfailingly courteous in her experience. Yes, he would be a protective and considerate husband. But fun to be with? Exciting? Romantic? Passionate? She thought not. Unlike Tom, Adam Calthorpe would never rush headlong into an adventure of any sort, and she could not imagine that he would ever lose his head over a woman.

What sort of wife would he look for? Certainly not one who expected fun, excitement or passionate romance. The future Lady Calthorpe would probably be blonde with blue eyes, and be chosen for her suitability and propriety; the sort who would defer to her husband, even in the management of her house and children. She would have impeccable manners, too. She would never employ rough tricks taught her by her brother, scorn tears as a form of weakness, refuse to surrender one jot of her right to form her own opinions, resent interference with her decisions... She would never fall headlong—and unsuitably—in love, either. Katharine sat up with a jerk. Where on earth had that thought come from? How in Heaven's name had she come to connect herself with falling headlong in love? A fine thing that would be—especially with a cool fish like Adam Calthorpe.

'What startled you, Kate?'

'Startled? Er...I wasn't startled, ma'am. The...the deer look so pretty I sat up to see them better.'

Mrs Calthorpe raised an eyebrow, but made no comment.

Adam said, 'Admire them while you can. They'll be back where they belong tomorrow.'

Katharine found it very easy to settle in at Bridge House. The release from stress seemed to give her boundless energy, and she was soon well acquainted with the house and grounds. She spent quite a little time with Mrs Calthorpe, delighting in that lady's gift for scatty conversation, which always seemed to end up making sense. They grew close, and before long Mrs Calthorpe was treating Katharine more like a daughter than a guest, calling her Kate, inspecting her wardrobe, declaring it unfit and taking her to buy new and prettier dresses. Little was seen of Mrs Calthorpe's son. He seemed to be very busy putting the affairs of Bridge House in order. But he did find time to send for Katharine's phaeton and horses, including the powerful stallion which had been Tom's.

'He's a splendid brute,' said Adam. 'But I'm not sure what we are going to do with him.'

'Why, ride him, of course!' Katharine said in amazement. 'I always exercised him when Tom left him behind at Herriards.'

'You won't do so here, however,' said Adam firmly. 'The horse is simply not suitable for a lady.'

'Oh?' said Katharine with a dangerous lift to her chin. 'Then perhaps you do not think me a lady, sir? For I assure you, Sholto is entirely suitable for me, and I intend to ride him. As I have for the last four years.'

Adam looked unconvinced. 'Tom never had a great

deal of sense, but I cannot imagine he would allow his sister to risk her life on a brute like that.'

Kate laughed. 'The only reason Tom kept Sholto for himself when we went out together was that he knew I could beat him on any other horse. You needn't worry about me. Sholto won't get the better of me—I know his tricks.'

'All the same, you will please me by not taking him out while you are here. I'll get one of the grooms to exercise him when I can't do it myself.'

Mrs Calthorpe sighed. She was beginning to know her young guest quite well, and directing her what to do or not do was not the best way to manage her. She had not changed her mind about Katharine Payne. She still thought that the girl would make her son just the sort of wife he needed, though whether he would ever come to recognise that fact she was not so sure. He was still hopelessly prejudiced about the girl, and it was true that Katharine did not show herself to advantage in his company. Adam's calm assumption of authority seemed to rouse the worst in her.

But Mrs Calthorpe was a woman who saw below the surface. Katharine Payne had spirit and character, and underneath the cool facade was a loving, passionate heart. The man who captured that heart would be fortunate indeed. However, the girl still had a lot to learn. Her life till now had been far from ideal as a preparation for success in polite Society. Dancing and deportment, dress and social customs could be taught relatively easily in the months before next April. But persuading Katharine to adopt the attitude of a debutante would be far more difficult. The girl had been neglected, left to run her own life for far too long.

Forced by circumstances into managing her grandfather and the Herriards estate, she was now more accustomed to giving orders, rather than taking them. Adam was equally used to giving orders and expecting them to be obeyed. It was inevitable that the two should frequently clash—and they did!

But to Mrs Calthorpe's relief, Kate seemed in this instance, at least, to have no desire to argue. She merely gave Adam a straight look, and then turned to Mrs Calthorpe to ask about engaging a dancing master.

Life was comparatively peaceful in the weeks leading up to Christmas. Adam took the opportunity of going into London to see one or two of his old friends from Army days, and the two ladies spent their time supervising preparations for the feast, and decorating Bridge House.

'I cannot say how delighted I am that you are here, Kate,' Mrs Calthorpe said as they were busy winding garlands of green round the banisters in the hall. 'I seem to have spent so many Christmasses on my own, and now I am to have both you and Adam with me.'

'I am very happy to be here, ma'am,' said Katharine. 'And especially grateful that you rescued me from a Christmas spent at Herriards. Even if my aunt and uncle had been the pleasantest people imaginable I would still have felt unhappy there. There are so many associations with Tom.'

'You were very close.'

'Very,' said Katharine in the detached manner she adopted when talking of Tom. 'My mother was always an invalid, and after she died my father travelled a great deal. So Tom and I were left at Herriards with my grandfather and each other for company. I was several years younger than Tom and a girl. I suppose many brothers would have ignored me, but not Tom. He treated me very much as a younger brother, and we did everything together.' She paused in her work. 'We loved each other, but we quarrelled a lot. I suppose we were quite competitive in a way. Tom always wanted to win, and so did I. Grandfather used to laugh at us.'

'Did you never have an older person to look after you? Someone to teach you the ways of the world?'

'I had Miss Tillyard. And after my father died and Tom went to Eton, Grandfather engaged a chaperon for me. But she didn't last a month. Grandfather was irritated by what he called her finicking ways. He was always reluctant to have strangers in the house, especially after he became ill.'

'You never went into society?'

'There never seemed to be time. I was usually needed at home. And even when he was in good health my grandfather never cared for making calls.' Katharine gave her hostess a challenging look. 'I didn't mind. I never had much to say to the young people we knew. And I never met anyone whose company I liked better than Tom's.'

Mrs Calthorpe nodded and appeared to concentrate on arranging a particularly difficult piece of greenery. But she was angry. Kate had had so little support from the men in her life. Old Mr Payne had ignored his granddaughter's needs and thought only of his own comfort and convenience. He hadn't bothered to change Kate's guardians, though he must have known himself that they were too old for the task. Nor had he taken the trouble to provide Kate with a proper chaperon, a gentlewoman who would prepare her for Society. Miss Tillyard was no doubt an excellent governess and had been a good friend, but she was not a suitable person for such a task as that.

And though Tom Payne had been her son's friend, Mrs Calthorpe was of the opinion that he had been as selfish as his grandfather. He should have been running the estate during his grandfather's illness, not burdening his sister with it. And much more than that—knowing what would happen if he was killed, he should never have risked his life in that last campaign.

Well, thought Mrs Calthorpe, she had spent some weary years since Adam had left home and her husband had died. She had often wondered what she should do with her life. And now, thanks to Adam's promise to Tom Payne, she had found something which was proving to be both enjoyable and rewarding. She could offer Katharine Payne some of the care and attention which she had so far lacked. The child would probably not welcome it at first—she had no idea what had been missing. But it would not be Mrs Calthorpe's fault if her protégée were not one of next season's outstanding successes! And there was always the hope that somewhere along the way her son would learn to value the girl as highly as his mother did.

Three days before Christmas Adam arrived back from London with an armful of interesting parcels. He brought with him as well an invitation from their neighbours to an evening party on Christmas Eve.

'I met Sir John in Bond Street, and he was most pressing, Mama. I hope I did right to accept the invitation?'

'Oh! How kind of him,' said Mrs Calthorpe somewhat flatly. When she saw her son's surprise at her tone, she visibly pulled herself together and spoke with more enthusiasm. 'My dear boy, of course you were right! You could hardly refuse. And I am glad for Kate's sake that we have somewhere to visit. She has hardly been out of the house since she arrived, except for a few shopping expeditions to Guildford. And her daily rides, of course, but one can hardly count those. Kate, my dear, you must wear one of your new dresses. The Redshaws like a touch of formality—especially since their daughter married into the aristocracy. Who else is to be there, do you know, Adam? Is…is Julia with her parents at the moment?'

'I believe so. Together with her husband. There will probably be quite a large party.'

Katharine looked nervous. She said, 'I…I cannot imagine your friends really want my company, ma'am. You and your son will have so much to discuss with them and I shall only be in the way. Pray make my excuses to Lady Redshaw.'

'What nonsense is this? Of course you must come,' Adam said briskly. 'I told Sir John you were staying with us—he will expect to see you.'

'Then he will have to wait!' said Kate defiantly. 'I am not yet ready to face strangers! I did warn you before I ever came that I do not like company!'

'Oh, Kate, my dear, pray do not disappoint me!' Mrs Calthorpe gave Adam a warning glance and went over to take Kate's hand. 'I was so looking forward to seeing you in your new dress—the one with the bronze velvet ribbons. And this would be the best possible occasion to practise the little tricks of manners and deportment we have been discussing, you know. Your first practice. You need not concern yourself about the Redshaws. They are really not important, except in their own eyes. They are never seen in London.' Then, as Katharine still looked hesitant, she said, 'Is it Adam? Has he frightened you off?'

Katharine's response was instant. 'Frightened me off? Of course not! What an idea! It was just…it was just… Well, then, if you think you would like me to come, then I shall,' she said somewhat desperately.

'Good! That's settled, then. I suppose there's hardly time to have some of this made up,' said Adam, fetching the parcels and putting them down in front of his mother. 'Besides, it sounds as if Miss Payne already has something to wear.'

'Adam! What have you brought us?' cried his mother, starting to unwrap the first one. She gave a cry of delight as she held up a length of silvery grey silk. 'It must be French!'

'I asked Ivo to bring over a selection of silks for you both from Paris. I hope you like them.'

'They are beautiful!' She held up a swathe of pale golden taffeta. 'Look, Kate! This would be perfect for you!'

'For me?' said Katharine. She looked at Adam in surprise. 'You asked your friend to bring some for me?'

'Don't look so amazed, Miss Payne. Tom must often have done the same.'

'No, never,' said Katharine, touching the delicate

material hesitantly. 'I don't think it ever occurred to him.' She looked up. 'Did you really mean this for me, Lord Calthorpe?'

'Of course!'

Mrs Calthorpe laughed at Katharine's stunned expression. 'I'm afraid you'll have to revise your opinion of my son, Kate! He has some good about him, after all!'

Katharine blushed. 'You make me sound so ungrateful, ma'am. Indeed, Lord Calthorpe is always very…kind. But this is quite unexpected.' She fingered the material. Then she came over to Adam and held out her hand. 'I don't think I have ever had a present that pleased me more. I'm not sure what to say…'

Adam took her hand in his, looked at her gravely, then lifted her hand and kissed it. 'Don't say anything—but have it made up, and wear the dress for our first outing in London.' He turned to his mother. 'I think Ivo put some lace for you in one of the other parcels, Mama.'

'Adam! You are very good. Let me see!'

The evening that followed was one of complete harmony. Katharine saw a new side to Adam as he entertained them with news of his friends in London and Paris. Tom's sense of fun had been strong but robustly simple, making no great demands on one's intelligence. But Adam Calthorpe's humour was a revelation to her. He had a dry, keen wit, and a strong sense of the absurd, and Katharine found herself stimulated and amused. His account of the Duke's reactions to the excessive formality of the newly reinstated French court had her laughing for the first time in months. This was Adam Calthorpe at his most charming, and

Katharine went to bed that night more in charity with her arrogant rescuer than she would have thought possible.

Adam had also been surprised. Katharine Payne had for once dropped the slightly belligerent air she adopted in his presence, and there had been signs of a different, more appealing personality. Laughter transformed her, and for the first time in their acquaintance he had seen something of Tom's natural, unaffected charm in her. Though she was still far from his ideal, he was more prepared to believe that she might have some success in London, after all.

Sadly, this happy state of affairs did not last even for twenty-four hours.

Chapter Eight

Katharine felt more cheerful than she had for months as she came out of the house for her ride the next morning. The sun was dazzling on the frost-covered lawns and she paused at the top of the steps to look at the view. It was incredibly beautiful, but cold! She took a couple of steps, then paused again. There was ice on the steps—the ground would be hard. Was she wise to take Sholto out? While Adam had been away she had ridden her brother's stallion every day, and, though she hated to admit it, once or twice recently it had taken all her skill to keep him under control. The downland in this part of the world was more demanding than the flat, soft acres of Hampshire, and though her riding ability was not in doubt, her strength had been more than once severely tested. Perhaps today she should leave it to the stable lads to exercise him?

Halfway to the stables she found Adam Calthorpe waiting for her. He was dressed for riding, but there was no sign of groom or horses.

'Good morning!' she called. 'Are you riding with me this morning? Where are the horses?'

'The horses are back in their stables. I've already been out with them. I have something to discuss with you.'

Katharine stiffened. This was not last night's charmer speaking. This was Lord Calthorpe, the officer in charge. 'What is it?' she asked coolly.

'Why have you been ignoring my wish that you should not ride your brother's horse? I understand that you have been taking him out quite regularly.'

'And why should I not?' asked Katharine, bristling. 'Sholto is now mine and whether I ride him or not is my concern, not yours!'

'Wrong, Miss Payne! While you are a guest in my mother's house, I regard you as very much my concern. We did not rescue you from your uncle's clutches only to have you break your neck on a horse which is manifestly unsuitable for a woman to ride— and certainly not in conditions like these. I cannot permit it.'

Katharine said angrily, 'Permit? What do you mean by *permit?* I shall ride the horse whenever I choose!'

Adam was unaffected by this defiance. He said calmly but firmly, 'I'm afraid you can't. There are several other horses in the stables which you may ride with my good will. But I have given instructions that Sholto is to be exercised by me, or one of the grooms—no one else.'

'How *dare* you!'

'Come, let us not be melodramatic!' said Adam with a touch of impatience. 'If you were not so headstrong, you would admit that I am right. I had him out myself this morning, and I simply cannot believe that you haven't had trouble with him. Once or twice it was all I could do myself to control the brute.'

When Katharine remained silent he went on, 'Can you honestly say that you have never had doubts when riding Sholto? Or are you too pig-headed to admit it?'

'No, I... I—' Katharine stopped short as she tried to keep a rein on her temper. She was too honest to deny what Adam Calthorpe had said, but detested having matters taken out of her hands in such an arbitrary fashion, and most unwilling to give in without a fight. 'I am not pig-headed!' she said.

'No? It looks remarkably like it to me. Does my mother know that you've been riding Sholto?'

'No.'

'Do you think she would approve?'

'No, I know she wouldn't. She has said he is too much for me. But she is wrong! And you had no right—'

He interrupted her. 'Miss Payne, could you not simply agree to my request—'

'Request? Is that what it is? It sounds rather more like an order to me.'

Adam took a breath and prayed for patience. 'I will try to put it differently,' he said. Then, speaking with exaggerated care, he went on, 'My dear Miss Payne, I know that my mother would be extremely anxious if she knew that you were still riding Sholto. It would relieve my mind enormously if you would promise not to ride him again. You need not worry about the horse. I shall make sure he is properly exercised.'

Katharine, feeling that she had been somehow out-manoeuvred, scowled and said ungraciously, 'Since you put it like that, and for your mother's sake—very well!'

'Good!' said Adam, starting back to the stables.

'But only till the weather is milder.'

Adam, who had been congratulating himself on his victory, turned round in surprised anger to give Katharine Payne the benefit of his tongue, but she had curtsied and gone before he could find the right words. He stood there impotently for a moment, then, unwilling to pursue her, he continued on his way to the stables. But he wondered as he went what had possessed him to take in Tom Payne's sister. She was a menace, a positive menace, with all of Tom's lack of subordination and none of his charm! And he, who had always prided himself on keeping cool in the most difficult or provocative circumstances imaginable, who had been famous throughout the Army for his patience and tact, had very nearly descended to her level! He could not remember when he had last felt so angry.

When they next met Mrs Calthorpe noticed at once that Adam was most unusually curt with Katharine, and that Katharine had again adopted a belligerent air towards her son. Mrs Calthorpe was very disappointed. She had been much encouraged by the improvement in relations the previous evening, and this change in the atmosphere did not augur well for the visit to the Redshaws, which was to take place the next day. Mrs Calthorpe had her own reasons for hoping for harmony on that occasion, so, when later in the day Adam excused himself and went out, she decided to do something about it. The two ladies were sitting in Mrs Calthorpe's little parlour—a favourite place on cold winter days, and a perfect setting for confidences.

'Kate, my dear, what is wrong? You and Adam are clearly at daggers' drawn again. And I had such hopes for you both last night. What has happened?'

Katharine had had time to think things over. Perhaps she had been a touch stubborn—though 'pig-headed' was a term she thought more suited to Adam, rather than herself! His ban on riding Sholto was really quite reasonable, but the arbitrary manner in which he had presented it had roused a devil of opposition in her. She said as much to Mrs Calthorpe.

'I must confess that I am highly relieved at your decision not to ride Sholto, though I am sorry if Adam's manner offended you—he doesn't always remember that he is no longer in the Army. I can understand *your* resentment, Kate. But why is *he* in such a mood? I haven't seen him as put out as this for years. He is normally the most even-tempered of creatures.'

'That is easily explained, ma'am. I dared to disagree with him!'

'It must have been more than that. He isn't usually so touchy. I have to say that I am disappointed in you both. I was so hoping we should all three present a united front to the Redshaws.'

'The Redshaws? Why?' asked Katharine, astonished.

Mrs Calthorpe paused. 'I think I shall tell you. But it is in confidence, mind.'

'I can be very discreet, ma'am.'

'Well, years ago, before he joined the Army, Adam once fell headlong in love.'

'*Your son!* Headlong in love? I can't believe it!'

'I suppose it does seem unlikely now. But at twenty he was the most idealistic, romantic creature you could imagine. He fell in love with Julia Redshaw, and, after leading him on for months, she rejected him.'

'This was your neighbour's daughter—the present Lady Balmenny?' Mrs Calthorpe nodded. 'I see. How did he take it?' asked Katharine, still struggling with the thought of Adam Calthorpe as a lovelorn young man.

'Badly. He went away and joined the Army. We saw nothing of him for years.'

'But he has surely recovered now.'

'Oh, yes. At least…he is a very different person now. I doubt that he would ever be as foolish as he was then.'

'Then, forgive me, but why are you so concerned?'

'Because though Adam is no longer passionately in love with Julia Redshaw, he still has a fondness for her. And she…'

'Yes?'

'I never shared Adam's admiration of Julia. She was, and still is, I believe, a heartless minx. There, I've said it. I dare say you're shocked. It isn't at all the sort of thing one ought to say about our neighbour's daughter.'

'I still don't quite understand why you are so worried, ma'am.'

'Think, Kate! Julia Redshaw was determined to marry into a fortune, and she did—she married an elderly aristocrat, whose assets are his wealth and position, rather than any personal charms. Now the wealth and position are no longer a novelty and Julia is bored with her husband. She has a reputation for flirting with any personable young man who comes near her. How will she behave when Adam comes back into her life? She was quite attracted to him when he was a tongue-tied student, fresh from Oxford, but now? A handsome, distinguished, self-assured man? I can't see Julia resisting that challenge!'

'Oh, come!' said Katharine, smiling. 'I may have reservations about your son's attitude to me, ma'am, but I am absolutely certain that, whatever a lady's charms, he would never allow himself to be tempted in the way you fear.'

'You haven't seen Julia Redshaw!' said Mrs Calthorpe.

There was a short pause. Then Katharine said, 'But if that is the case, how could I help?'

'You could help quite a lot. But there is one major difficulty.'

'What is that?'

'I think you are, at the moment, more likely to avoid Adam's company than to seek it, isn't that so?'

'Quite!'

'Could I possibly persuade you to change your attitude—even if it is just for tomorrow evening? Could you stay as close to him as you can?'

'Why on earth…?'

Mrs Calthorpe took a breath and said rapidly, 'I want to discourage Julia from trying to attract Adam again. I'd like her to believe that Adam is interested in you—that's why you are staying with us.'

Katharine was shocked into rudeness. 'That's absurd!' she cried. 'Oh, forgive me, ma'am, but I couldn't do it! I couldn't pretend anything like that!'

'You wouldn't have to pretend very much,' said

Mrs Calthorpe with a pleading look. 'All you need do is to stay by Adam, and manage to give him an occasional smile or friendly look. That is all the pretence I ask. You must admit that all he gets at the moment is a series of basilisk stares, which is not what is wanted! You may leave the rest to me.'

Katharine looked at Mrs Calthorpe with suspicion. 'And what does the rest consist of, ma'am?'

'Oh, hints, and glances. They will be enough,' said Mrs Calthorpe airily. Then she grew serious. 'Katharine, help me in this! I know Julia Redshaw. She is beautiful, clever and unscrupulous. Adam thinks she is everything he has always admired in a woman, and she will be careful to foster the illusion, to enmesh him again merely for her own amusement. Like you, I am quite certain that my son would never allow himself to be embroiled in anything scandalous, but he could be made deeply unhappy again. I don't want to run that risk. And, apart from forgetting your present quarrel with Adam—just for one evening—your behaviour really needn't be very different.'

'What—to pretend that I am…I am…interested in your son? That sounds like a big difference to me!'

'Kate, dear, you have a natural reserve about you. It is obvious to everyone that you are not someone who would ever wear her heart on her sleeve. Apart from disguising your present antagonism toward Adam you could behave quite normally. Let the world suspect that there is more feeling than there is. I am sure you could do that!'

'Well, if that is all, I suppose I could try,' said Katharine reluctantly. She gave Mrs Calthorpe a sudden grin. 'But I cannot answer for Lord Calthorpe's co-operation. He is not very fond of me at the moment, I think!'

'I will deal with Adam. Thank you, my dear.'

But by the time Katharine began to dress for the party the next evening she was bitterly regretting her promise to Mrs Calthorpe. Though she would never have admitted to anyone just how nervous she was about it, the visit to the Redshaws promised to have all the elements of a nightmare. She had never mixed a great deal in company, and to date her appearances in public could be counted on the fingers of one hand—every one of them with Tom there to support her. He had even taught her a few rudimentary dance steps, but there had been little time to practise them, and she had always felt stiff and awkward when dancing with anyone else. The thought of facing all these strangers without Tom terrified her.

And, worse still, Adam's mother had given her a task for which she felt hopelessly inadequate. How could she possibly hold Adam's attention in competition with a woman who, from all accounts, was both beautiful and sophisticated? Katharine stared at herself in the mirror and saw plain Katharine Payne, brown-haired, brown-eyed, compared so often unfavourably with her handsome brother. 'You've twice the character and only half the looks, Kate!' her grandfather had once said with regret. 'Why couldn't it have been the other way round?'

And even her short-lived chaperon had regarded her in despair. 'Katharine, you should take more pains with your appearance. You cannot afford to neglect it if you wish to be a success.' Then she had sighed, 'It's such a pity! Matters would be so much easier if you only had your brother's blue eyes and blond curls...' Such comments and others like them had never worried her—the way she looked had never been very important to her. But tonight... She frowned at the dress she had thought so pretty—a simple slip of white with bronze ribbons as its only decoration. Dull, that's what she was. Very dull.

Mrs Calthorpe's heart sank when she saw Katharine coming downstairs to join them. Far from looking affectionate, Kate scowled as she greeted Adam at the bottom of the stairs, and Adam's response was hardly any more pleasant.

'That dress suits you perfectly, Kate, my dear!' said Mrs Calthorpe warmly, suspecting that Katharine's expression was the result of nerves, not ill-feeling.

'Thank you. I'm sure you mean well.' Katharine's tone was curt, and Mrs Calthorpe saw Adam look sharply at her and start to frown at what he regarded as rudeness to his mother.

'Help Kate with her cloak, Adam,' Mrs Calthorpe said hastily.

She could not have suggested anything more suited to her plans. For, as Adam arranged the cloak, his hands rested on Katharine's shoulders for a moment, and he was astonished to find that she was shivering. He was touched. The girl might look perfectly self-possessed, but she was in a panic! He watched as she tried to tie the ribbons with fingers that trembled.

'Let me do that,' he said gently. Their hands met—hers were icy. He forgot his earlier anger and wanted only to reassure her. 'Do you remember the first time

I helped you to tie some ribbons?' he asked conversationally as he pulled the ribbons into a bow. 'It was the first time we met. You were quite ready to bite my head off, and I thought you a Gorgon. But then I discovered you were Tom's sister.' He put his hands back on her shoulders. 'You don't look like your brother, Kate, but last night when you were laughing I could see Tom in you.' He held her until she looked up at him. Katharine's eyes were huge. He noticed once again what a curious and beautiful colour they were— the amber-gold of the wines of Spain. Then he smiled ruefully. 'We really shouldn't fight. I promised your brother that I would make sure you were safe. Don't condemn me for taking that promise seriously.'

She dropped her eyes, cleared her throat and said slowly, 'I'll try not to. You were right about Sholto. And I know you mean well. I'm just not used to obeying orders.'

'Is that what they sound like? I'm sorry. Let's make a bargain. I will try to sound less peremptory, if you will make an effort to meet me halfway when I am doing my best to look after you. Agreed?' He put his finger under her chin and made her look at him again.

If Adam Calthorpe was always as nice as this when making his requests, thought Katharine, she might well agree without demur to anything he suggested. She smiled back at him and nodded.

'Good! That's settled,' said Mrs Calthorpe, who had been listening to this exchange with delight. As Katharine went out before them to the carriage Mrs Calthorpe said in a low voice, 'We shouldn't have insisted on her coming with us, Adam. It's too soon. The child is terrified of company, and she misses Tom.'

'I realise that now. But don't worry, Mama. I'll look after her.'

Well satisfied, Adam's mother preceded Adam to the carriage and they set off.

The ballroom of Redshaw Hall was at the back of the house, and Katharine looked curiously about her as they walked through the marble-columned hall and along what seemed like miles of tapestry-lined passage. The Hall was an imposing mansion, she thought, but not a comfortable home like Herriards or Bridge House.

They were met at the door of the ballroom by a major-domo who announced them in a resounding voice. The party was well under way with crowds of people milling round the room. But they had hardly gone a few steps when they were halted by an exquisitely diminutive figure.

'Adam!' called this vision. 'Adam Calthorpe, as I live and breathe! How *nice* to see you after all these years!'

'Lady Balmenny.' Adam bowed.

'What nonsense is this? I thought we were *friends*— you must call me Julia, as you did in the old days.'

Smiling, Adam said, 'You remember my mother, I think?'

'Oh, of *course*,' cried Lady Balmenny. 'How are you, Mrs Calthorpe? So *nice* you could come… Adam, we must have a long chat. I cannot *wait* to ask you about the Duke. Is he as bad as they say?'

'Julia, I don't think you know Miss Payne,' said Mrs Calthorpe firmly. 'May I introduce her?'

Julia stared at Katharine. 'How d'y' do, Miss Payne.

I heard Mrs Calthorpe had a friend staying with her. You must meet my parents. Do come with me.' She led the way through the crowded room across to an alcove to where a small group of people were sitting. Julia presented them to Sir John and Lady Redshaw, but then wasted no time in dragging Adam off to dance with her.

The Redshaws showed no surprise at their daughter's extraordinary behaviour, but greeted Mrs Calthorpe very kindly and expressed their pleasure in meeting Katharine.

'Is this your first visit to Surrey, Miss Payne?' asked Lady Redshaw.

'Yes, and I find it very attractive, even in winter.'

'Are you planning to stay long?'

'I'm…I'm not sure…'

'What Kate means is that she will be presented next season, and then…' Mrs Calthorpe allowed her eyes to rest on her son for a moment. 'We shall see….'

'Oh?' said Lady Redshaw, regarding Katharine with increased interest.

'I cannot say more as yet,' Mrs Calthorpe went on with a significant smile. 'Kate's guardians wish her to have her season first. But when that is over…'

Katharine blushed and looked reproachfully at Mrs Calthorpe, who gave her a fond smile and went on, 'The dear child would rather die than admit it, but she is at the stage when she feels lost without Adam,' she said. 'And he feels just the same. Look, he and Julia are coming back already. What did I say?'

Katharine began to feel annoyed. This was going too far! An occasional smile at Adam was all very well, but to be portrayed as a pair of lovelorn fools was too much! She was within a hair of denying it all when Adam and Julia returned.

'I now know *all* about you, Miss Payne,' cried Julia. 'Adam has been telling me of his friendship with your brother, and I am *deeply* impressed. It is *so* like Adam to take on the responsibility of looking after you. He is sometimes *too* good! But *do* say you will let me help him!'

'Good heavens, Julia! How do you think you can help?' said Mrs Calthorpe.

'Well, to take a share in teaching Miss Payne the ways of Society. Adam tells me that she has been brought up in the *depths* of Hampshire and knows *nothing* of the world. I should be *delighted* to guide her. *Do* let me help!' she said, turning to Katharine with a smile. Gentian-blue eyes surveyed Katharine's hair and dress. 'Adam couldn't *possibly* advise you on how to make the *best* of oneself, and what to *wear,* and so on, and I could. My friends tell me I have a gift with even the most *unpromising* material—' Julia put her hand to her mouth. 'Oh, do forgive me, Miss Payne! My wretched tongue! I didn't mean that the way it sounded. Oh, what must you think of me?'

'I think Adam has been spinning you stories, Lady Balmenny. I am by no means as helpless as he suggests,' said Katharine with a sparkle in her eye.

Adam looked slightly embarrassed, but protested, 'Believe me, Kate, I didn't suggest anything of the sort. I merely told Lady Balmenny that my mother had agreed to bring you out next season, and that you would spend the winter preparing for it. Your offer is generous, Julia, but it really isn't necessary. I am sure my mother will provide any help and advice Kate might need.'

Julia sighed and looked hurt. 'You think I've been tactless, and you are quite right. I shouldn't have said anything. But when I see something wrong, I can't *bear* not to put it right! I only meant to help, Adam.'

'I am sure you did and it does you credit,' Adam said with an indulgent smile. 'But it was hard enough to persuade Kate to accept even my mother's help. You have no idea what an independent creature she is.'

'Are you, Miss Payne? I do so *admire* you for it. But then you are *tall!* A tiny creature such as myself would merely look *ridiculous,* striding about, insisting on doing everything for myself.' Julia smiled bewitchingly at Adam. 'I have to rely on my menfolk.'

'And where *is* your husband, Julia?' asked Mrs Calthorpe briskly. 'I should love to meet him. Is he not here?'

'Julia, you and I will take Mrs Calthorpe to find Bernard,' said Lady Redshaw. 'He is probably over there by the buffet. Lord Calthorpe will look after Miss Payne, I am sure.' With a kindly smile at Katharine, Lady Redshaw gathered Julia and Adam's mother up and swept them off towards the other end of the room. Adam looked at Katharine.

'You're very quiet, Kate.'

'Am I? The conversation seemed to be flowing quite nicely without me.'

'It's amazing! Julia is still a most bewitching creature! I knew her years ago—in fact, at one time I was very fond of her. And now she has been married eight or nine years, but she doesn't seem to have changed a bit.'

'Really?' said Katharine, and, remembering Mrs Calthorpe's views on Julia Redshaw, she thought that was probably perfectly true.

'I hope you weren't offended by her words. I am sure she didn't mean to upset you—she is very good-hearted.'

'I did wonder what you had said to her…'

'Nothing you would have objected to! I told her of Tom. I said you missed him. And that is true, isn't it?'

'Yes,' sighed Katharine. 'I miss him a lot—especially on occasions like these. Mind you, we quarrelled nearly all the time. He was a most exasperating fellow…'

'He was, wasn't he?' Adam grinned. 'He was a first-class officer, but you'd be surprised at how often I felt like wringing Tom Payne's neck. But then he would look at you…'

'How well I know that look! His puppy-dog look. You would end up laughing with him, or feeling guilty for being so unreasonably annoyed!'

'And then you would finally risk your own reputation in order to save him…'

'Or make up all sorts of excuses to Grandfather for him and be punished yourself…!'

They looked at one another and burst out laughing. 'I am so glad someone else knew him as well as I did!' Katharine said impulsively.

Adam regarded her. Katharine Payne was a different creature altogether when she laughed. Her assertive, rather aggressive air disappeared, revealing a younger, warmer, and in some strange way more vulnerable woman. Which was the real Katharine Payne? It was irritating—even after nearly two months he was still as undecided about her as on that day in November when he had first seen her!

'Come!' he said suddenly. 'We shall dance.'

The laughter died, and she frowned. 'Thank you, but I don't wish to dance,' she said abruptly.

'Nonsense! That is why we're here. Come!' He took her arm.

'I said I don't wish to dance!' she whispered fiercely, and turned her back on him. At the other end of the room Julia Redshaw was staring at her. Katharine remembered her promise to Mrs Calthorpe, swallowed her temper and turned back. She gave Adam the most bewitching smile she could manage. It was not to be compared with Lady Balmenny's, of course, but it was the best she could do.

'You're sounding just a touch peremptory, Adam,' she said sweetly. 'I thought we agreed earlier that you would try not to give orders?'

'And you promised to meet me halfway,' he said.

'That's not—' Katharine stopped short. She had nearly forgotten again. Giving him a charmingly rueful look, she said, 'Oh, Adam, I see I shall have to confess the awful truth. I can't.'

'Can't what?'

'I have never learned how to dance properly! Tom taught me one or two steps, but that is all. It's one of the many things your mother was going to see to. We've already arranged for a dancing master to come after Christmas.' She came closer and put her hand on his sleeve. Adam looked surprised, but to her relief he didn't seem to object. With a look of appeal she went

on, 'But don't force me to make an exhibition of myself here and now—especially after telling your friend
that I didn't need her help. Please don't make me!'

Adam put his hand over hers. 'My dear girl, of
course I won't! I'm not a monster. We'll join the others at the buffet.'

'Oh…er…couldn't we sit somewhere else? I would
dearly love to hear some stories about Tom.'

'A much better idea! I'll get one of the servants to
bring some refreshments to that table over here. Come,
Kate!' He took her hand and led her over to the table
in a small alcove, and saw her seated. 'Stay there,' he
said with a charming smile. 'I'll be back in a moment.'

Really, thought Katharine, that was quite easy. Perhaps I have something to learn from Lady Balmenny
after all. But I'm not sure I could keep it up for long.
We tall women are too independent! And too honest!

Adam kept Katharine entertained with his tales of
life with Tom for a good half-hour, and then escorted
her over to his mother. They were introduced in their
turn to Lord Balmenny. After a few minutes' conversation, Julia once again took Adam off to introduce
him to some of her friends, and Katharine was left
with Julia's husband. Lady Redshaw and Mrs Calthorpe were deep in conversation a little distance
away.

'You a friend of Calthorpe's, Miss Payne?' asked
Viscount Balmenny, his eyes on the figures circling
the floor.

'My brother was, sir. I would say that I am rather
a friend of Lord Calthorpe's mother.'

'That's not what I hear,' said the Viscount, turning

to look at her. His eye closed in a wink. 'Still, if that's the story you want to spread, I shan't interfere. As long as m'wife knows the truth.'

'I'm not sure what you mean, Lord Balmenny,' faltered Katharine.

'Don't suppose y'do. Y'needn't concern y'self about it.' He turned back to the table and poured himself a glass of wine. 'I'll drink to your success and happiness, Miss Payne. Success and happiness.' He drank deep, then called to one of the waiters. 'You! Fellow! Give the lady a glass of champagne.'

'I don't think—'

'Yes, y'do, Miss Payne. How else can y'drink to *my* happiness?' He spoke in an ironic tone, but there was more than a touch of pain in his eyes. Katharine found that she liked Julia's husband.

'I'll do that with pleasure,' she said.

The evening came to an end before midnight. A number of the guests wanted to attend the midnight service at the church nearby. But later that night, when Julia was preparing for bed, Lady Redshaw came into her daughter's bedroom. She took the hairbrush from the maid and dismissed her. As she brushed Julia's hair she said casually, 'Did you know that Adam Calthorpe is as good as engaged to Miss Payne?'

Julia turned to look at her mother. 'I don't believe it!' she said sharply. 'Who told you? The girl herself?'

'No, Adam's mother.'

'I see.' Julia was silent for a moment. Then she shook her head. 'It doesn't matter. The girl is a nonentity, a dull, ungraceful beanstalk. She will never hold him.'

'Adam Calthorpe is not a boy any longer. I believe he is a man who will keep his word, whatever happens. But you should not concern yourself with him, Julia.' There was a warning note in Lady Redshaw's voice.

'What do you mean?'

'Bernard is no fool. And your exploits are starting to annoy him.'

Julia smiled scornfully. 'I can manage Bernard, Mama. And I fancy I can manage Adam Calthorpe, too.'

Lady Redshaw shook her head. 'I think you underestimate your husband. And I strongly doubt that you would find Adam Calthorpe as easy a conquest as you did ten years ago. I beg you not to try it, Julia.'

'Dearest Mama, you have just made it impossible for me to refuse the challenge! Do you seriously believe that Adam Calthorpe would resist me if I set out to capture him? You should have more faith in me!'

Chapter Nine

Katharine Payne had been given food for thought by the evening with the Redshaws. Till now her attitude towards the opposite sex had been regulated by her dealings with her grandfather, her brother, her guardians and those she had met in running Herriards. Her grandfather had demanded respect and obedience, and had spoiled her. Though she had loved her brother deeply, her relationship with him had been keenly competitive, each of them striving to outdo the other. Her guardians were elderly gentlemen, remote creatures whom she found a source of irritation, but had been forced to obey. And, up to the moment her uncle had arrived, her position at Herriards had been one of authority, in which she gave orders and expected them to be carried out.

Not one of these relationships had prepared her for social exchanges with eligible young men. Moreover, unlike most girls of her age, she had had very little instruction or experience in the manners and modes of polite society. As a result of all this, the most inexperienced débutante knew more about the arts of attraction than Katharine Payne.

Up to now this had never troubled her. She was not vain—the fact that Tom was so much better looking than she was had never disturbed her—and her personal appearance had never been a matter of importance in dealing with elderly gentlemen, her brother or her servants. But Katharine was no doormat, and she had not enjoyed being treated like one by Julia Redshaw. Her love of challenges and her lively spirit, which had almost disappeared in the dreadful months following Tom's death, had gradually been returning. And Julia Redshaw's obvious scorn was a spur which finally completed the process.

At the Redshaws, she had seen the liberties a beautiful, unscrupulous woman could take with an otherwise intelligent man. From the top of her burnished curls to the toes of her dainty slippers, Julia Redshaw's appearance and behaviour were designed to charm the gentlemen. And, to Katharine's amazement, Adam Calthorpe had been charmed, had seen only the surface beauty, not the lack of manners, the malice, the selfishness which lay beneath. It was a lesson worth remembering. Though she had no desire to be like Julia Redshaw, Katharine decided that she would profit from what she had observed.

Katharine's enterprise and energy now found a new outlet. The attention to detail, the determination to succeed, which had gone into making Herriards so successful, were now engaged in pursuit of a different goal. Katharine Payne, with Mrs Calthorpe's enthusiastic co-operation, would not become just another average débutante, one of many who appeared every

year on the London scene. She was determined to
make her mark. She might never be as beautiful as the
lovely Viscountess Balmenny, but her person would
be as exquisitely cared for, her dresses would be as
elegant and her dancing as graceful. And she would
put the lesson she had learned at the Redshaws to the
best possible use.

Life was very busy in the weeks following Christmas. Katharine paid a short visit to London in the
company of Adam and Mrs Calthorpe to set in motion
the arrangements for their stay during the season.
Adam spent his time finding a suitable house to lease,
while Mrs Calthorpe took Katharine round on a pre-
liminary tour of the dressmakers, milliners, and pur-
veyors of shoes, slippers, shawls, fans and all the rest
of the necessities for an aspirant to the highest society.
They were also visited at their hotel by a number of
ladies' maids, for Mrs Calthorpe was insistent that
Katharine should have the attentions of an expert
dresser. The wages demanded by these persons
seemed astronomical to countrified Katharine, but Mrs
Calthorpe assured her that they were perfectly normal.

'A good maid is very important, Kate. You have
great potential, but I should be less than honest if I
denied that your appearance badly needs the sort of
care and attention that an experienced maid can provide. We must engage someone straight away, and
then persuade her to spend the next couple of months
in the depths of Surrey—something not all of them
would be willing to agree to. You may have to pay
over the odds for the best, but I assure you she will
be worth every penny.'

In the end they were fortunate to find Miss Kendrick who had just left the service of Lady Abernethy, one of London's most fashionable women. Lady Abernethy was about to go to Vienna with her husband, and though she had begged her maid to accompany her, Miss Kendrick had regretfully declined the honour. She preferred, she said, to stay in England. The interview went very well, though Katharine thought one could be pardoned for thinking that she was the one being interviewed, not the prospective maid! Miss Kendrick graciously agreed to join them as soon as she was free.

Well satisfied with their endeavours, the ladies returned to Bridge House, where Katharine embarked on various courses of instruction. The dancing master took her through the basic steps of the dance, exclaiming all the while how badly she had previously been taught! 'No, no, no, Mees Payne! Not gallop, not like ze 'orse! Leap like ze bird, like ze feazher! Lightly! *Comme ça!*' And Katharine, remembering Tom's dancing, was forced to agree that it had indeed been 'like ze 'orse' and tried to do better.

Mrs Calthorpe spent a great deal of time with her. The friendship between Adam's mother and her young guest grew with every day that passed, and some of the time was spent in cosy gossip and reminiscence. But at least an hour a day was spent in serious discussion of the structure and habits of London's polite world. Katharine was soon familiar with the ramifications and politics of the great families who formed the major part of Society; she learned how she should address these august personages, and the different degrees of respect to be shown in her curtsies. More than that, Mrs Calthorpe had been a beauty in her day, and was well able to advise Katharine how to deal with compliments or, worse, impertinence.

'Not that I shall need such skills, ma'am,' Katharine said one day, rather dispiritedly. She had just come through a disastrous dancing lesson. Also, Adam had stayed behind in London, and Bridge House seemed surprisingly dull without him.

'What nonsense! It's time you woke up to the fact, Kate, that you are—or could be—an exceptionally striking female! You are not so commonplace, I hope, as to be wishing for blue eyes and golden curls?'

'I suppose not. But it is surely easier to be graceful if you are small. Leaping "like ze feazher" is quite difficult when you are as tall as I am.'

Mrs Calthorpe looked annoyed. 'I see I shall have to have a word with Monsieur Edouard. This isn't the right way to teach you. Kate, you have such a natural dignity! You walk like a queen! There is not the slightest necessity for you to leap about like a feather—if a feather *could* leap, which I doubt.'

'But the dance step—'

'Adam will be back tomorrow evening. You can discuss this with him.'

Katharine felt a lift of excitement, but she said sedately enough, 'Why Adam, ma'am? How can he help?'

'Kate! Surely you noticed? Or were you too annoyed with Julia Redshaw? Adam is a superb dancer! If he would be willing to take you in hand, you would have no problems at all. You would be dancing "like ze feazher" in no time. I shall speak to him. Indeed, you may well have two partners, for Adam is bringing a friend of his back with him. Lord Trenchard is on his way to the west country and will stay the night here. It is most annoying that that maid has not yet arrived! We could have impressed Adam with your elegant new appearance…and Lord Trenchard, of course.'

Katharine laughed at her. 'Your son will never be impressed with me, ma'am, whatever arts we employ! He remembers our first meeting too well. But perhaps I could have captured Lord Trenchard? What a pity it is not to be! Without my London maid I am still plain, unadorned Kate.'

'If the stories I've heard are true that is perhaps as well, my dear! Ivo Trenchard is the world's worst flirt.'

'Tom liked him.'

'Tom wasn't a bored society beauty looking for amusement.'

'Neither am I.'

Mrs Calthorpe laughed. 'That's true! Life is far too interesting for both of us.'

The weather had improved, so the next afternoon they took a walk down to the stables. The horses were in the paddock nearby, Sholto dominating the rest.

'I'm so glad you agreed not to ride that brute, Kate. He is far too big and powerful for you.'

'But you will admit he is a beautiful creature, ma'am. He has such spirit as well as strength. There isn't another to match him, not even in Adam's stable.' She sighed. 'But you are right, of course, and so is Adam. Sholto is a man's horse. He was bought for my brother, not me. I suppose I really wanted to ride him to keep a link with Tom, but I must admit he was often almost too much for me.' She turned to Mrs Calthorpe. 'How would it be if I gave Sholto to your son? He and Tom were very good friends, and Adam has done a great deal for me. Would he like it, do you think?'

'This is a new Katharine Payne!' exclaimed Mrs Calthorpe. 'I thought you disliked Adam!'

'Oh, I do!' Katharine said with emphasis. 'Quite a lot of the time…and especially when he starts telling me what to do. But I will admit it to you and to no one else—Adam is sometimes right!'

'Good heavens, Kate! Are you quite well?'

'I haven't felt so alive for months, ma'am! And I have you and your son to thank for that!'

'Nonsense! We have done very little. It was merely a matter of time.'

'I cannot imagine that I would feel like this if I were still at Herriards.'

'Perhaps not.' They walked in silence towards the house. 'I think Adam would be delighted with Sholto—if you are sure you wish to part with the horse.'

Katharine sighed. 'Yes, I am sure. I'll find another horse to suit me some time. But for the moment…' She pulled a face at Mrs Calthorpe. 'For the moment I must concentrate on other accomplishments. Like dancing.'

Mrs Calthorpe started to laugh. 'How was this morning's lesson? Is Monsieur Edouard still trying to teach you to "leap like ze feazher"?'

'No, this morning he gave up the steps of the dance, and demonstrated "ze grand curtsy". I was not exactly impressed. He looked like Madame du Barry wearing breeches. Then I had to try, and by the time we had finished he was in despair again.'

As they walked up the steps to the terrace outside the long windows of the saloon, Mrs Calthorpe was still laughing. Katharine stopped and said severely, 'It is no laughing matter! The poor man was practically in tears!' She put her hands to her head in a dramatic gesture, then threw them up in the air. '*Mademoiselle, mademoiselle*, why ees eet zat ze English womens is so stiff? You must move not like ze drilling soldier, but like ze waves of ze sea. *Comme ça!*' Katharine took a wide step, flung her arms out to the side, then swayed down to the ground in an impressive sweep. She looked up at Mrs Calthorpe and raised an eyebrow. '*Comme ça?*'

Mrs Calthorpe could hardly talk for laughter. 'Kate, that is absurd!' she gasped. 'Even the King couldn't expect such an obeisance! Get up, do!'

Katharine jumped up, her face sparkling with mischief. 'You don't like it? Did it not flow enough like "ze waves of ze sea"?'

'You ridiculous child! I ought to be annoyed with you for being so disrespectful to poor Monsieur Edouard—' A movement by one of the windows caught her eye. She stopped, then cried, 'Oh! Oh, Adam! What are you doing here? Kate, Kate, look! Adam has arrived!' She flew over to her son, who had stepped through the window door and was observing them both in amusement. Behind him was another, extremely handsome gentleman. He, too, was smiling as he regarded Katharine.

Adam kissed his mother, then greeted Katharine.

'Where are you thinking of making your début, Kate? At the theatre in Drury Lane?'

Katharine blushed. 'You weren't supposed to see that,' she said.

'No, indeed!' said Mrs Calthorpe. 'You weren't supposed to be here till this evening. This is a delightful surprise. Lord Trenchard, welcome. I am very pleased to see you again.'

Ivo Trenchard greeted Mrs Calthorpe with genuine warmth, then looked at Katharine.

'I don't believe you know Miss Payne, do you?' said Adam's mother. 'Kate, may I introduce Captain Lord Trenchard?'

'Miss Payne, I am delighted to know you at last,' said Ivo Trenchard, taking her hand and kissing it. 'Tom spoke so often about you. You are just as he described you.'

Adam raised an eyebrow. Ivo was at his tricks again. Kate might be looking a lot happier than she had in October, but she was still far from being the charmer her brother had described!

'Really, sir? Dare I ask how that was?' Kate asked with a look of mock apprehension.

'You would accuse me of flattering you, Miss Payne…'

Adam felt a spurt of irritation. He hoped Ivo was not about to start one of his flirtations with Kate! He would have to put a stop to it if it were so. Kate wasn't like the ladies of Spain and Brussels, she didn't know the rules.

'Do let's go in,' said Mrs Calthorpe. 'Now that the sun is lower it is getting cold again. We've been down to the stables, Adam.'

'Ah! Good! But you won't have seen the latest addition—she has just arrived. Could you bear to walk back again, Mama? I'd like you to see her. You too, Kate!'

Lord Trenchard clearly knew what was afoot, for he nodded to Adam and tactfully excused himself, explaining that he needed to see to some of his things. The two ladies followed Adam to the stable yard. In the centre of the yard, held firmly between two grooms, was a handsome bay mare.

'What a beauty!' cried Katharine, enraptured. 'Oh, Adam, where did you find such a lovely creature?'

'She may look well enough,' said Mrs Calthorpe doubtfully. 'But she seems a touch fiery to me.' She kept her distance as she examined the mare. The animal was restive and the grooms were having quite a job to hold her. 'I must say, Adam, that it's not a horse I should like to ride! In fact…in fact, she reminds me of Sholto. She's smaller, of course, but she looks just as wilful, just as full of energy and spirits.' She turned to her son. 'What are you going to do with her? I wouldn't have said that you needed another mount. And in any case, Katharine— No, let her tell you herself.'

'What is this, Kate?' Adam frowned. 'Have you been riding Sholto again?'

'I have not!' said Katharine.

'What? Even though the weather is milder?'

'Don't provoke the girl, Adam. Far from riding that great brute, she has been concentrating hard on her dancing.'

'Dancing? Is that what I saw?' He laughed when he saw Katharine bristling. 'Peace, Kate! We shall talk of the dancing later. Meanwhile, what were you going to tell me?'

'I...I have come to see that you were right. Sholto isn't really a suitable horse for me...' adding, with a touch of her old belligerence '...though that isn't to say that I can't manage him!'

Adam waited without comment. Katharine went on, 'So, if you wish it, I would like to give Sholto to you, Adam. I...I think Tom would approve.'

There was a short silence. Then Adam cleared his throat and said, 'That is breathtakingly generous of you, Kate. There is nothing I would like more as a remembrance of Tom. Thank you. I accept.' He took her hand and kissed it. 'But—' He smiled.

'Do hurry, Adam. I'm getting very cold!' said Mrs Calthorpe. 'I want to know what you are going to do with that mare now that Kate has given you Sholto.'

'I am going to do what I intended from the start—' Adam started to laugh again. 'I bought the mare for Kate! I thought she might enjoy riding her.'

'You bought the mare for me!' Katharine's eyes were shining. 'For me? Do you really mean it?'

'Of course.'

'But that horse is almost as dangerous as the stallion!' exclaimed Mrs Calthorpe. 'Just look at it! Kate will be killed! What were you thinking of, Adam?'

'There's no need to be anxious, Mama! That mare may be spirited, but she's not at all vicious. I've had her through her paces, and I assure you that, once she knows who is master, she is wonderfully responsive. Kate is too good a rider to be in danger.'

Adam was talking to his mother but his eyes were on Katharine, who had left them. She had taken something from one of the grooms and was now totally absorbed in the mare, feeding her a titbit, talking to her, stroking her, speaking to her all the while in a low voice.

He went on, 'Do you really think Kate Payne would be content with a steady, safe ride? You should know her better! She's like her brother in that respect—not content without a challenge. Sholto was too much of one, and I cannot tell you how relieved I am that she has seen it for herself. But she must have some adventure left in her life, something for her to enjoy.'

'I should have thought that learning the necessary social graces for entering London Society was enough of an adventure for anyone!'

'That's just it! The life ahead is bound to be difficult for her, but hardly enjoyable. We both know that Kate isn't likely to be one of the season's successes, in spite of her wealth—'

His mother raised an eyebrow. 'You're rather blunt. And a bit too pessimistic. She may surprise you.'

'Oh, come! I know you like Kate—'

'And you don't?'

Adam paused. 'I like her a lot better than I did. But she can still be irritatingly obstinate. And while I've no doubt you will do your best with her, she isn't likely to take the town by storm, is she? If only she had been more like Tom in looks...'

'Adam, I won't let you say another word! I am surprised at you. You may have had a huge success in your Army career, but it hasn't done much for your judgement of women!'

'Mama—!'

Katharine had finished her chat with her new acquisition and was coming back to them. Mrs Calthorpe said quietly and urgently, 'But whatever your opinion, help us, Adam. Help to make Kate as much of a success as we can. Do it for Tom's sake, if not for hers.'

'Of course, I will, though I still think…' He stopped. Katharine was too close. 'What is your opinion of the horse, Kate?'

'She's beautiful,' Katharine said. 'I shall call her Cintra. Tom once said what a beautiful place it was.'

'He was right. It's a good name for the mare.'

'Thank you, Adam. But it's cold and she ought to be indoors. Has she been fed and watered?'

Her tone was businesslike, almost cool, but Adam was not put off as he might have been earlier in their acquaintance. He had noticed before that, when Katharine Payne was most moved, her manner was most detached.

Ivo Trenchard had been almost as close to Tom as Adam himself had been. So that night, over an after-dinner glass of port, the talk naturally turned to Tom and from there to Tom's sister and Mrs Calthorpe's plans for her début. To Adam's amazement Ivo Trenchard, a true connoisseur of women, was inclined to agree with Mrs Calthorpe. He thought it quite possible that Katharine would be a success.

'But, Ivo!' Adam protested. 'You saw her this afternoon! She looks more like a…a governess than a débutante! In fact, that's what I thought she was when I first met her.'

'Well, I thought she looked remarkably like Tom—and he was a handsome enough fellow.'

'What the devil are you talking about? Tom was blond!'

'She hasn't the colouring, perhaps. But that smile…absolutely his. Very charming.' Ivo smiled as he remembered it. 'Completely captivating.'

'*Captivating?* How much port have you had?'

'Not enough,' said Ivo promptly, and helped himself to some more. 'Why are you so critical of the girl? I've seen you charmed by ladies a lot less pretty. There was one in Ciudad, I remember…'

'Yes, but she had other talents…'

'Well, what about Comtesse Whatshername's daughter? The one in Toulouse.'

'I hardly spoke to the girl! Her cousin was a charmer, though. A pity about the fiancé. Do you remember the night we…?'

From that point Katharine Payne was forgotten. The talk turned to past experiences, not all of them respectable.

Unfortunately Ivo had to continue his journey the very next day. He expressed his regret and took his leave of Mrs Calthorpe, with whom he was clearly a favourite. She pressed him to visit them when they would all be in London.

'I shan't be able to keep away, ma'am!' he said. 'I can't wait to witness Miss Payne's triumph!'

He told Katharine that he didn't need to wish her a successful début—that was assured. 'But I hope you will reserve at least one dance for me at the first ball we both attend.'

'I shall no doubt be grateful for at least one partner,

Lord Trenchard. But I have to confess that my dancing is not yet up to standard.'

'It will be, it will be! Get Adam to teach you—he was the best dancer on the Duke's staff. Twinkle-toes Calthorpe, we called him.' He laughed and dodged Adam's arm. 'Enjoy your new mare, Miss Payne. The next time I am in Surrey I shall hope to see her in action.'

Adam accompanied him to the carriage. 'Good luck on your mission, Ivo.'

'Thanks. I have no great hopes that my father will agree to see me, but I have to try. Meanwhile, don't you underestimate Tom's sister. She's worth some effort, Adam. Tom was right to be so proud of her. *Adios!*'

Adam walked thoughtfully back to the house. Was Katharine Payne as attractive as Ivo and his mother seemed to think? Had he been too strongly influenced by that first meeting in October? He had discovered later that she had been going through a very bad time for months—no woman would be at her best after such a prolonged strain. Perhaps he was prejudiced. He made up his mind to try to take a fresh look at her, to attempt to see her with his mother's eyes.

But when he found Katharine, her face and manner were most unlikely to improve anyone's opinion of her—rather the reverse. She was standing in the centre of the room face to face with a little man, who was gesticulating wildly, trying to make himself heard. Katharine herself was scowling fearsomely as she overrode him.

'You are unreasonable, sir! I can't remember everything at once! Waves and feathers don't know the difference between left and right, and no more do I when I am trying to imitate them. Which is, as we both know, a hopeless task! I wonder you continue to try!'

'What is this?' asked Adam.

'Milor' Calthorpe, ze case, it ees 'opeless! I 'ave taught many young ladies ze art of dancing, most of zem much younger, of course, but Mees Payne is impossible to teach. Impossible!'

'Indeed?'

But Monsieur Edouard was too angry to take heed of the warning tone in Adam's voice. He went on, 'She turns left when she should turn to ze right, and right when she should turn to ze left! And she argues! All ze time!'

Katharine's protests had ended when Adam had come in. She stood silent, head in the air, too proud to defend herself.

Adam said coldly, 'Monsieur Edouard, we seem to have made a mistake in engaging you. You have failed lamentably to appreciate Miss Payne's particular needs. You will be paid for the full course of lessons, but pray do not come again.' The dancing master started to expostulate but Adam said curtly, 'Thank you. That will do.'

When Monsieur Edouard had left the room Adam said softly, 'Come here, Kate.'

She looked at him mutely, but made no move. He smiled and said again, 'Come here!'

Still scowling, Katharine walked stiffly towards him.

'What has that fool done to you?'

'Don't blame him,' she said bitterly. 'I'm just not made for dancing.'

'I don't believe that for one moment. But I can believe that you're not quite made for teaching—not his sort of teaching, anyway.'

'Your mother was told he was the best dancing master in Dorking. Where shall we find anyone better?'

'I have no doubt we shall find someone when you are more…amenable to instruction. Meanwhile—'

'"Amenable to instruction"? What an unreasonable thing to say! I have tried as hard as I can to learn from that…that little popinjay!'

'Exactly. That is why you can't learn from him—you despise him. I suspect you despise the whole art of dancing as well. Am I right?'

'It all seems such a pointless exercise! I don't like jumping about all over the room, being pushed here and pulled there, with no rhyme or reason behind it! And all I've learned from Monsieur Edouard is how to fall over my own feet while this is going on!'

'Oh, my intractable Kate!' said Adam, laughing at this sad picture. 'Poor Monsieur Edouard. Teaching you must have given him nightmares!'

Katharine walked away from him and stood looking out of the window. 'Laugh away!' she said bitterly. 'But don't ask me to join in. I know that dancing is an important accomplishment, whatever my opinion of it. And I so hoped…I had such ambitions… Well, never mind.' She leaned her forehead wearily against the window.

Adam came over and stood close behind her. He said gently, 'Forget about the important accomplishment, Kate. Learn to enjoy it. Dancing isn't just noise and confusion, you know. It can give pleasure in so many ways.'

'How?'

'Well, there's the music—you like music, I know you do. I've heard you play. Then there is pattern, design, not confusion. Each dance has its own pattern, and surely there is satisfaction in seeing the pattern worked out to its proper end? And there are the steps. There are really very few of them—you could learn them in an hour, if you wanted to. But…'

He took her by the shoulders and turned her round to face him. 'But that's not where the difficulty lies, is it? You resist dancing because it means physical contact, and I think you've had very little experience of that. You're afraid of it.' He paused, but when she didn't speak he went on, 'There's no need to be.'

She kept her head down, refusing to meet his eyes, but slow colour covered her cheeks, as he slid his arms down to her elbows and pulled her closer.

'Do you think I mean you harm?' he asked.

She looked up, startled. 'Of course not!'

'Then why are your fists clenched?' He took one of her hands, uncurled the fingers and held it against his chest. 'Trust me, Kate. I want nothing but your good, believe me.'

'I do believe that. You've been very kind.'

'Then don't pull away. Let yourself lean against me. Relax.' He put his free arm round her, so that she was loosely held against him.

The scene in the churchyard at Herriard Stoke flashed into Katharine's mind. Even before she had known who he was, she had felt the same strange desire to let herself be guided by this man, to let his arms enfold her…but she mustn't…!

'You're tightening up again,' Adam said. 'Just when you were doing so well. What is it?'

'I…I have never…I have learned never to depend on anyone.'

'Now that I know more of your history I don't find it surprising. But that doesn't mean that you have to push people away.'

Held by his arm, her hand resting on his chest, Katharine considered this. 'You're saying I can't dance because I can't relax? But I can't think how to do that.'

'Don't try to think! Stay here like this, just for a moment.' The room was silent, shadowed except for a strip of pale sunshine through one of the long windows. Beneath her hand Katharine could feel Adam's heart beating steadily. Slowly the tension seeped away and, perhaps for the first time in her life, she felt at ease in close contact with someone else.

After a moment Adam said softly, 'You know, there's a new dance now called the waltz. It's danced all over Europe, and it's even beginning to be seen in England. The couples stand almost as close as this to each other. Shall I teach it to you?'

She stiffened again.

'Don't, Kate! There's no need. Put your left hand on my shoulder. Good! Keep your head up! Now follow my steps. Count in threes. Very slowly. Like this. One, two-three, one, two-three…'

He took her slowly round the room, his left hand still clasping her right, the other at her waist. His touch was light but firm and, after a stumble or two, she began to follow more easily. His pace gradually quickened, but she found that she could still follow, the hand at her waist always guiding, telling her which way to turn, when to slow down, when to move more quickly. The steady, rhythmical counting entered her bloodstream and she found herself swaying, dipping with the turns. It was like magic, like champagne, she was floating…

They came to a stop. Adam said, 'Kate…that was wonderful!' He put both arms round her, then bent his head and kissed her. The kiss may not have been passionate, but it was none the less real. To Katharine who, with the exception of Walter's onslaught, had never been kissed by any man other than her brother and grandfather, it was a revelation. That a kiss could be so warm, so comforting, and at the same time so spellbinding… She had difficulty in holding on to her reason, to stop herself from putting her arms round Adam's neck, from holding on forever to a moment of such enchantment…

Chapter Ten

The kiss came to an end and Adam briefly hugged her, putting his cheek next to hers. 'Dear Kate!' he said, his voice full of affection and warmth.

It was like a splash of cold water and it brought Katharine to her senses. 'Dear Kate!' No excitement, no desperately whispered 'Darling Kate', 'Sweetheart Kate', 'Kate, the love of my life'! Just an affectionate 'Dear Kate'—the sort of thing you called your mother, or your aunt, or your sister. That was how he regarded her, of course. A sister, as Tom had arranged. More than ever thankful that she had not succumbed to that mad moment of temptation, Katharine managed to smile as she released herself from his grasp.

'That…that was like no dance I have ever attempted,' she said shakily. 'The ending was…was… quite unique!'

Adam gave a shout of laughter. 'Oh, please, Kate! You needn't worry yourself. The waltz is daring enough, but a kiss normally plays no part in it! That was my own compliment to a wonderful dancer. Were you angry?'

'Not at all. Why should I be?'

'Good! Though I should really be scolding you, not paying compliments.'

'Why?' she asked in surprise.

'You are a fraud!'

'W...What?'

'Pretending you are unteachable, can't move, don't know the steps. Poor Monsieur Edouard—you really had him fooled!'

'What on earth are you talking about? I never pretended anything—I can't dance!'

Adam took her hand again and kissed it. 'You are as natural a dancer as I have met! The sense of rhythm, the instinct for movement... What do you mean by deceiving us all?'

Adam's touch had sent a frisson up her spine. Removing her hand, she pulled herself together and said calmly, 'I don't know what you are talking about, Adam! Th...that wasn't dancing! Not the sort I've come across, anyway.'

'The waltz is very different from the old dances, I agree. But that isn't what matters. Kate, the way you danced with me just now proves that you have the rhythm and grace to make you a first-class dancer! I cannot think why that fool of a dancing master couldn't see that!'

'I think you're underestimating the part *you* played in my performance just then,' she said. 'What was it Lord Trenchard called you? "Twinkle—"'

He put his hand over her mouth. 'Don't even think of saying it! And don't believe for one moment that anyone ever called me that. Ivo Trenchard's sense of humour got the better of him. He was making it up.

But don't lose sight of what I was trying to tell you, either. Edouard was the very worst sort of instructor for you. All you need to learn are a few special steps and four or five figures—there aren't many of them. And that is all. Any country dance is made up of a selection of these put together. I can teach you myself in the week I have left.'

'You're…you're going away?'

'If I am to have eight or nine weeks during the season in London, I must spend some time on Calthorpe beforehand. The place is still in need of a lot of attention. But don't look so worried—a week is more than enough to start you on the right track. The rest is merely practice. We'll arrange for some visits to Guildford or Reigate, where they have some Public Assembly Rooms. You can try your wings in relative obscurity there.'

Adam was as good as his word. He engaged a fiddler from one of the villages nearby and for an hour each afternoon he was a relentless taskmaster. Katharine learned to walk the patterns of the dances until she knew them by heart. He taught her to glide, to skip, to lift and fall to the music. When he found her dropping her head to watch her feet, he put a scarf round her eyes, and made her dance blindfold. The room resounded with cries of, 'Head up, Kate! Up, I say!' and 'You can't see your feet anyway, so don't look!' and 'Dammit, lift your head, girl! That's better! Beautiful!'

It wasn't all work. They rode every day, and Adam showed Kate the favourite places of his boyhood. She had never known such enjoyable companionship, not even with Tom. There was no sense of rivalry, no need to guard against any reckless tricks which would plunge them into danger. Adam was no coward, he rode right up to Sholto's capabilities, which were considerable, but she felt safer with him than she ever had with Tom. The kiss was never repeated and, though Katharine felt a curious ache in her heart whenever she thought of it, she was glad. Adam was growing fond of her, she could tell that from his manner, but it was clear that he regarded her as a sort of sister. Nothing more. And so, though it had taken something of a struggle, she had her feelings firmly under control again. But another kiss, however harmless, could easily undermine all her efforts.

At the end of the week Adam took his mother and Katharine to the Assembly Rooms in Guildford, where Katharine felt she acquitted herself reasonably well with a variety of partners. She found herself enjoying the occasion, and during the evening several young gentlemen reappeared to ask her to dance with them a second time. However, during the supper interval, Adam, who seemed to be slightly out of humour, disabused her of this conceit. He pointed out that her partners had not exactly been in a position to judge her, being so lacking in grace themselves, and added that she had looked down at her feet twice in the figure of eight, and missed two entries.

'I still think that I acquitted myself quite creditably,' said Katharine with a touch of her old belligerent tone.

'Quite creditably! Is that what you want? In that case, accept my congratulations. But it wouldn't be enough, for me!'

'Adam!' his mother protested. 'You are too hard! This is Kate's first venture into public. You mustn't put her off at the start. Remember how nervous she was when we first arrived. It isn't at all surprising that she forgot one or two details. She needs cherishing, not criticism. Why haven't you danced with her your-self?'

'He's ashamed to be seen with me, ma'am,' said Katharine with a malicious look at Adam. 'He has his reputation to think of.' She turned to Adam and asked innocently, 'What was that you were called? "Tw—"'

Adam pulled her to her feet. 'The supper interval is over, I believe, Miss Payne!' he said with a threatening smile. 'May I have the honour of this dance? Excuse us, Mama.'

He hauled her to the floor without waiting but, as he gazed at her laughing face while they waited to begin, his ill humour faded.

'You are a minx, Kate,' he said. 'And one day you will get your desserts. But for now we shall converse in the manner expected at a ball. What do you think of the orchestra?'

As they wound their way faultlessly up through the set and back again, Adam was surprised at Katharine's vivacity and charm. He found himself thinking that, if only she had had Tom's looks, she could have been a great success. But her colouring was against her. And, perhaps because of her height, she still had that irri-tating air of independence. Where were the dimples, the air of helpless femininity, the innocently coquettish glances which appealed to so many men, himself in-cluded? No, whatever Ivo and his mother thought, he himself could still not see how Katharine Payne could possibly be the success they predicted.

But, when the music stopped, he found himself strangely reluctant to release her. The time had passed so quickly, he felt they had not finished what they had been saying, though he was not sure what that was. It was very odd! He had spent many a duller half-hour, even among the cream of European society. And, as they walked back to join his mother, the memory of the first time they had danced together in the saloon at Bridge House flashed unbidden into his mind. She had felt so right in his arms, so responsive. And that kiss at the end... It had been extraordinarily sweet! He looked down at the girl walking so calmly beside him and decided to ask her to dance with him again later on. The waltz, perhaps...

In the event, he did not manage to engage Kate for the rest of the evening. She was never free. Katharine Payne seemed to be surprisingly popular with the young men of Guildford.

The next day two things happened. Adam left for Calthorpe, and they finally had news of Miss Kendrick's arrival. Katharine was glad of the second, for she had felt somewhat low ever since she had looked out of her bedroom window early in the morning and seen Adam setting off. Theirs had not been what you would call a friendly parting. Adam had been somewhat silent the night before, and, for someone who was leaving at the crack of dawn, remarkably reluctant to let the evening come to an end. When they got back to Bridge House he suggested that they should have a chat before retiring. He had one or two things to sort out with them, he said, before leaving the next day.

But the chat turned out to reveal Adam at what Katharine considered to be his worst. He issued orders, thinly disguised as advice, to both of them. In essence, Katharine was to take care when riding the mare, she was always to have a groom with her, and she was to avoid one or two places, which he named, where the going was not always safe.

'Would you prefer me to ride only in the paddock, sir?' Katharine asked with suspicious meekness. 'And perhaps it might be safer if the grooms used a leading rein on Cintra—though, even if *I* were to tolerate it, I doubt *she* would!'

'It's all very well to laugh, Kate, but—'

'I assure you I am not laughing!' said Katharine coldly. 'I think I know enough to ride sensibly, however.'

'That is arrant nonsense and you know it! You can be every bit as reckless as your brother when the mood takes you! And, as I think I said before, I didn't rescue you from your uncle merely to have you break your neck while in our care!'

Mrs Calthorpe decided to intervene. 'Adam, I think you may trust Kate. She knows how it would worry me if she took risks while you are away. Isn't that so, Kate, dear?'

Katharine scowled at Adam, but nodded and Mrs Calthorpe relaxed.

But then, when her son proceeded to give her suggestions for Katharine's further progress, Mrs Calthorpe herself became irritated. 'Really, Adam, you must think I am in my dotage! We shall go to as many

Assemblies as I think fit, and as Kate wishes! And of *course* I shall chaperon Kate to them all—why on earth should you think I wouldn't? Furthermore, you really have no need to ask me to keep a careful eye on her partners—any chaperon would do that quite as a matter of course. What *has* got into you?'

Adam, realising that his two companions, far from being grateful for his advice, were both bridling, sought to make amends. 'I'm sorry, Mama,' he said. 'I suppose I feel responsible for the success of our campaign. We have all worked so hard—I should hate to ruin it for want of a little foresight.'

Katharine stood up. 'Lord Calthorpe!' she said. 'Pray do not think me ungrateful for your help thus far. You have been...have been most...most...kind. But I am not a "campaign"! Nor am I one of the men in your command, to be told what to do and what not to do! Unlikely though it may seem to you, I think your mother and I will manage very well while you are away. May I suggest that you concentrate your mind on Calthorpe, and leave the success or otherwise of my début to such poor skills as your mother and I possess?'

Adam did not take this with his customary even temper. He bowed coldly and said with a most unusual bite in his voice, 'In that case, Miss Payne, I have no more to say. Except that my only wish has always been to see you launched into society as easily as possible. And that I hope to find you in a more amenable frame of mind when I see you next.'

They wished each other a frosty goodnight, and Katharine went to her bedchamber. But she could not sleep. She was suffering from such a turmoil of feel-

ings that sleep was impossible. She told herself that
Adam Calthorpe was a domineering, insensitive block,
and she was mad to feel as she did about him! But
after a while memories of the times when he had
shown a great deal of understanding began to haunt
her, and she decided that she had been monstrously
ungrateful. She was filled with remorse and wondered
whether to go downstairs and apologise. She even
reached the first landing, but then Mrs Calthorpe's
voice floated up to her.

'I have to say that I have some sympathy with
Kate,' she said. 'You can sound very arbitrary, Adam,
and she is not a girl who reacts well to orders.'

'I don't know why you always defend Madame Independence, ma'am! To my mind, Katharine Payne
should learn to accept perfectly well-meant advice
with more grace. The sooner the better! Her guardians
were quite right! She has had her own way for far too
long!'

'Adam! You are not usually so unjust! What *is* the
matter with you?'

Katharine didn't wait to hear any more. She went
back towards her room, fuming. Madame Independence, indeed! Who did Adam Calthorpe think he
was? What right had he to forbid her to ride any horse
she chose? But he *had* forbidden her. Sholto first, and
now Cintra! What a tyrant he was—telling her where
to go for her rides, how often to go to the Assemblies,
with whom to dance… If she gave in to him now she
would be condemned to be a spineless puppet, she,
Katharine Payne of Herriards, who had until recently
managed her life quite successfully with very little
help from anyone else. It was not to be thought of!

She entered the room, undressed and went to bed. Eventually she slept, but her last illogical thought was a wish, quite a desperate one, that Adam Calthorpe could see her more as a desirable woman, and less as one of his many responsibilities.

Miss Kendrick arrived two days later, and before the week was out had established herself as a force in the household. When asked what she wished to be called, Miss Kendrick said, 'Her ladyship always called me "Kendrick", miss.' After a pause she added, 'Below stairs I shall, of course, be known as "Miss Kendrick".'

She seldom smiled and a mere look from Miss Kendrick could strike fear into the hearts of the other maids. Even Wigborough, Mrs Calthorpe's long-established butler, addressed her with more deference than was his wont with the rest of the female servants, and she had a way of saying, 'Certainly, ma'am!' which frequently caused Mrs Calthorpe to re-examine her orders feverishly for unnoticed errors. But she was outstandingly good at her job. Fortunately for Katharine, it had been many years since Miss Kendrick had prepared a young lady for her début, and she rather liked the idea. She made no bones about the fact that she regarded Katharine a challenge, but nor did she expect to fail.

'Lady Abernethy was only moderately presentable when she first engaged me,' she said calmly. 'But, in the end, I believe she was one of London's most admired ladies of fashion.'

'Miss has excellent bone structure,' she said on another occasion, 'and her colouring is unusual enough to be interesting.'

'Interesting?' Katharine had exclaimed. 'Really?'

'We have quite a lot to work on, of course,' Miss Kendrick had added. 'Miss has neglected her appearance for too long. But I am optimistic about the result.' She was even inclined to look favourably on Katharine's height. 'Miss is tall, but that is by no means a disadvantage,' she pronounced. 'Present modes favour the tall figure.' She gave Katharine a severe look. 'As long as the lady in question carries herself well. Not one of my ladies has *ever* slouched.' Katharine didn't doubt it. Fear of Miss Kendrick would be more effective than a whole library of books carried on the head!

Throughout the weeks that followed Katharine's face, figure, deportment and dress were subjected to Miss Kendrick's iron discipline. Katharine had never thought much about what she wore, had never concerned herself about styles which flattered, or colours which complemented her own colouring. But now one disapproving look from her maid could send favourite dresses to languish at the back of the cupboard forever, and other gowns, in shades she had never thought of wearing, took their place. Fortunately they both agreed that simplicity was more Katharine's style than the feathers, frills, and ribbons depicted in the fashion magazines. But Katharine soon learned that Miss Kendrick's 'simplicity' owed a lot more to art than was apparent to the casual eye.

Mrs Calthorpe was delighted. She went around the house with the look of a cat that has found a whole bowl of cream, though in her letters to Adam she merely reported that Miss Kendrick was excellent at her task, and that Katharine was working hard at her dancing. She also took care to inform him that Katharine was well chaperoned whenever they went to the Assembly Rooms, and that it was just as well—Miss Payne was proving to be very popular. She added that she wouldn't be surprised if Katharine made an excellent match before the London season was halfway through. But though Mrs Calthorpe was a fond mother, her motive in giving her son these assurances was not to make him feel happier. It had not escaped her that Adam was becoming more personally interested than he realised in her protégée, that he had been not as pleased as one might have expected at Katharine's success with the young men of Guildford. Adam's mother saw no harm in giving him even more to think about.

Katharine's marriage prospects were being discussed a mere forty miles away, too. Henry Payne and his family were also preparing to go to London, though not in such splendour as they had planned. Herriards was a comfortable property, but without the income from the Frampton-Payne inheritance, it would not run to expensive luxuries.

'I hope you realise that we are all depending on you, Walter,' said his father one day in March. 'The only way to bring the Frampton fortune back to Herriards is for you to marry that confounded girl. You missed your chance once, and you mustn't miss it again. I don't know why she took against you—you're a personable enough fellow, and when you put yourself out the women usually seem to like you. But you'd better make sure you don't fail with her in London. Your cousin Kate is no beauty—she won't find it easy to attract the gentlemen on her own account. It'll be the money which will draw them. All you have to do is to persuade her that you're different from the rest, that you "love her for herself alone".'

'I'll try, Pa,' said Walter, pulling a face. 'But don't underestimate the task. She can be damned difficult.'

'Walter! You are not to let your dislike of the girl stand in your way! You surely don't need reminding that *we need her money!* Unless you know of another heiress you might persuade to marry you?'

'No, I don't. And I have to admit—there's a certain charm attached to the thought of getting that girl in my power. She wouldn't be so high and mighty for long.'

'You'll have to win her first.'

'Aye, there's the difficulty. What about the Calthorpe fellow?'

'He won't present a problem. From what I saw, he didn't like the girl much more than you did. I'd be willing to wager that it was his mother who pushed him into taking her away from here. She probably regrets it now. No, Calthorpe's swimming in lard himself, he doesn't need the Frampton money. He won't be interested in her. Look, Walter, you have to remember that you have one great advantage—you can offer your cousin Herriards. She was besotted about this place, God knows why. Tell her how much the people here miss her, remind her that in time she would be mistress here again. Play that tune, and she might well fall into your arms. But marry her you must. And soon.'

The two men sat in gloomy silence, contemplating the sheaf of bills and accounts on the table. After a while Walter said idly, 'I just wonder…'

'What?'

'Well, do we know what happens to that money if Kate Payne were never to marry?'

'She gets control of it when she is twenty-five. She can leave it wherever she likes then. For heaven's sake, don't waste time on speculation, boy! You can't afford to. If Kate marries someone else, or reaches the age of twenty-five without marrying, the money will be gone forever as far as we are concerned. You *have* to marry her, Walter.'

'And…if something happened to her before she is twenty-five?'

'I'm not sure, but I believe it reverts to the Herriards estate.'

'Does it really?' Walter got up and walked about the room. 'Well, well!'

'You're grasping at straws! As far as I know your cousin is in perfect health! She isn't going to fade away and die just to save you from having to marry her! Pull yourself together, Walter! Stop fantasising and concentrate on what is possible!'

Walter stopped pacing, and looked at his father enigmatically. Then he shrugged his shoulders and appeared to abandon whatever he had been thinking. He said, 'You're right, Pa. Kate has had time to get over her spleen at the loss of Herriards. And by now she must be over Tom's death, too. She'll probably be much more amenable. Don't worry. I'll get her.'

All was now ready for the Calthorpe household to move to London. The house just off Berkeley Square was ready to receive them, a few of the servants, together with numerous additional domestic comforts, were already installed there, and everything needed for the wardrobe of two fashionable ladies was finished and waiting to be packed. It only needed Adam's presence for the changeover to take place. Some business in Bath had caused him an unexpected delay, but he was now expected hourly. In the event, his arrival took them by surprise. Katharine had been out with Cintra and she returned to find Adam waiting for her at the stables. She quite forgot the cloud under which they had parted, and gave him a dazzling smile.

'You seem to make a habit of surprising us,' she said gaily as he helped her to dismount. 'Though I cannot say this time that you were earlier than expected. Have you seen your mother?'

'Not yet,' he replied, smiling at her in turn. 'I left the carriage to follow on, and rode the last bit of the way, in order to be here sooner. When I saw you and Cintra on the other side of the river I waited for you here. Shall we go in?'

They strolled up to the house. 'How are you and Mama? You at least are looking well.' She replied suitably and enquired after his journey and the progress of the work at Calthorpe.

It was all very companionable and easy, yet Katharine was a trifle put out. She had planned Adam's first sight of her, and it wasn't meant to take place in the stables after she had had a demanding ride. Her hair was all over the place, she was prepared to swear that her cheeks were red with her exertions, and her old riding habit was not nearly as flattering as any of her new gowns. It was a far cry from the newly elegant Miss Payne with which she had hoped to astonish him!

Adam, on the other hand, was feeling very pleased. Perhaps Ivo Trenchard had not been so far out, after all! Kate's smile was indeed captivating, and, in spite of her height and the absence of any dimples, she had a great deal of charm. He had been quite taken with her when he had first seen her just now—cheeks flushed, hair loose... The riding habit was old, of course, but it somehow suited her. Perhaps it was because he was used to seeing it on her. He had missed Kate at Calthorpe, had frequently thought of her riding with him on the Downs dressed in that same habit. He had recalled their conversations, her delight in the world about them, her determination to keep up with him, however hard the going... Adam found himself hoping quite passionately that she would not be disappointed in the new world she was about to enter. What if his mother and he had not between them prepared her well enough? He did not like to think of that smile growing dimmed, of Kate becoming once again the unhappy creature he had met last October... He mustn't let it happen!

They went into the house, where his mother greeted him with enthusiasm. Katharine excused herself and disappeared.

'And what do you think of Kate?'

'I told her—she is looking remarkably well, though not much changed. Is the new maid any good?'

Mrs Calthorpe began to laugh. 'My dear boy, never let Miss Kendrick hear you say so! And, in any case, what do you mean? Kate has been transformed!'

'Oh, really, that is going too far! The girl is happier,

certainly, and that adds a charm to her looks which was lacking before. But transformed? Surely not!'

His mother regarded him thoughtfully. 'You don't think so? Well, perhaps I am wrong. We shall see.'

Dinner was late that evening, after the last-minute preparations for their departure the next morning were complete. Adam was waiting at the bottom of the stairs when Kate came down, his mother having deliberately delayed her own descent to give him time to appreciate the new Kate Payne. At first he did not recognise her. For the moment before he came to his senses he found himself asking who this slender creature descending the stairs so gracefully could possibly be. Head held high, one hand holding the train of her golden silk dress, she had reached the bottom step before he had found his voice.

'Kate!' he exclaimed.

'Well, Adam? Do you like the dress? It was your Christmas present, you know.'

Stammering like the newest subaltern, Adam said, 'Y…yes, of course I do! It suits you very well.'

She gave him a cool sideways look. 'You sound doubtful?'

'No, no, I assure you! I was merely taken somewhat aback. You look so different.'

'I should hope so,' she said. 'But why do I still have the impression that you don't approve? Isn't it what you wanted?'

'It is! Of course it is! The dress is lovely. And…and your hair is very nice, too. I think.'

'I beg your pardon?' she said, beginning to sound annoyed.

'It's just that…it doesn't… It's all so elegant—it doesn't look like you at all! Oh, God, that's not what I meant to say—' Adam stopped in confusion.

Since Katharine was starting to look as if she would like to give Adam a most inelegant box on the ears, Mrs Calthorpe decided it was time she joined them. 'It is very strange,' she said, giving Katharine a wicked smile. 'Numerous acquaintances over the years have complimented me on my son's exquisitely polished manners. I believe the Duke himself has said as much. What has happened to them tonight, my dear?'

Adam pulled himself together and gave his mother a rueful smile. 'You are quite right, Mama. Forgive me, Kate! I was indeed overcome by your transformation! You look superb! I can see that I shall have a busy time keeping your suitors at bay.' He bowed formally to each of them in turn. 'Shall we go in to dinner, ladies?'

Mrs Calthorpe noticed with delight that, though Adam's eyes were frequently on Katharine, the girl did not allow this to put her off. Her company manners and conversation were exactly as Mrs Calthorpe had taught her, and if Adam's mother had ever entertained any doubt about Kate's suitability to be her son's wife it would have been dismissed that night.

Adam himself soon recovered all his famous aplomb, and the dinner table resounded with laughter and good humour. They talked of their plans for their stay in London. The dates for the various parties and outings which Mrs Calthorpe had planned were already fixed, of course, including one for the ball which Katharine's guardians had asked her to arrange. But they made plans for other occasions, and Mrs Calthorpe reeled off a list of people she wished Katharine to meet.

'That reminds me,' said Adam. 'I saw Ivo when I was in Somerset. He seemed quite eager to receive an invitation to your ball.'

'He is at the head of the list,' said Mrs Calthorpe. 'Dear Ivo! He is such a valuable guest at a party or ball. He loves dancing and is always extremely popular.'

'Until he makes off with the ambassador's wife, or some such lark,' said Adam caustically.

Later that night, after Katharine had gone to bed, Mrs Calthorpe tackled Adam about his behaviour.

'The dear child has worked so hard, Adam. I think she was a little disappointed that you did not immediately show more approval. And I have to say that you had me a little puzzled as well.'

'I'm not sure how to explain, Mama. There's no doubt that you and Miss Whatever-her-name-is have worked wonders. Between you—'

'And with Kate's help!' interposed his mother.

'And with Kate's help, you have produced a young lady of fashion who is bound to rouse a certain amount of admiration—'

His mother interrupted again. 'A great deal of admiration,' she said gently.

'Whatever you say. But…it isn't Kate. I found the girl I saw this afternoon down at the stables far more appealing than the elegant creature at the table tonight.'

Mrs Calthorpe paused. Then she said, 'Adam, what

was your aim in bringing Kate away from that uncle of hers?'

'I...I wanted to rescue her from a life of misery. I had promised Tom, and I could do no less.'

'Not to marry her yourself, I think?'

'Good heavens, no!'

'Well, then, what are you worried about? Kate doesn't have to appeal to you. If she is to find a suitable husband, she needs to be successfully launched into Society. The young lady at the table tonight will find that far easier than the girl you met this afternoon. You know what the polite world is like. Our job is to prepare her as fully as we can, to introduce her to the right people and then to try to make sure that she chooses a husband wisely. Your responsibility to Tom's sister will then be at an end.'

She looked sideways at her son. He was hunched over his glass of wine, looking anything but pleased at this description of the task ahead. She smiled. She didn't like it any more than he did, but then...she had an idea that Adam's responsibility for Katharine Payne would not come to an end with the London season!

Chapter Eleven

Their journey the following day was accomplished
without delay or incident, and soon, after three weeks
in London, Katharine felt as if she had lived there all
her life. She quickly adapted to London hours, rising
late and going to bed in the early hours, and in no
time at all she knew the latest *on dit,* which were the
most stylish shops, and where the most fashionable
coffee houses were to be found. And the capital soon
got used to the sight of Miss Payne dancing at Almack's, riding through the park, driving out to Kew,
or visiting Vauxhall, together with all the other activ-
ities which made up the life of the polite world during
the season.

Society agreed that Miss Payne was not quite in the
accepted mode. She was neither divinely fair, nor rav-
ishingly dark, her eyes were not celestial blue, but an
unusual brown and, though her figure was good, she
was taller than the ideal. She did not appear to set
herself out to charm, but behaved in an open, natural
manner. All of which made it quite astonishing that
she was on the way to becoming one of the season's

successes. Certainly the sight of her slender form weaving its way gracefully through London's ballrooms aroused a great deal of admiration. To evoke Miss Payne's dazzling smile was an object of importance with many an otherwise sensible young man. And numbers of eligible bachelors were impressed by the discovery that she sometimes preferred an interesting conversation to listening to extravagant compliments.

In short, by the time the Balmennys appeared in London, Katharine Payne was on the way to having the success her heart had desired. Adam was beginning to realise that he had been wrong and his mother and Ivo Trenchard right. And, as time passed, he got used to the new Kate Payne, and began to see her with the world's eyes. The shabby governess of Herriard Stoke churchyard was gone forever, replaced by an elegantly fashionable young lady with exquisite manners. Kate the virago was lost, buried inside a light-hearted, light-footed creature who danced and smiled her way into the hearts of Society. Adam was fascinated with the change, but was occasionally irritated by his own perversity in regretting the disappearance of the belligerent shrew and wishing he could see her just once more.

Mindful of his responsibility he kept a watchful eye on her, but took care not to appear to be too close. The world must regard Katharine as his mother's protégé, not as any kind of future bride for himself. In this respect he and his mother were at odds, he knew. But better acquaintance with Kate had not given him any reason to change his mind. He had grown to like her, but she possessed neither the sort of looks he admired, nor the qualities he was seeking. Life with Katharine Payne would never be easy—for one thing, she argued too much. And Adam was still looking for the kind of wife he had pictured back at the ball on the eve of Waterloo—gentle, calm and undemanding, someone for whom he would have a mild affection without the turmoil of passionate love. If she happened to be a blue-eyed blonde so much the better.

Another newcomer to the London scene would seem to be ideal. Kate's cousin, Miss Catherine Payne, enchantingly fair, with eyes the colour of summer skies, and a delicately submissive air, had already impressed him at Herriards, and she was now also in London for the season. And because of a curious set of circumstances he found himself quite frequently in her company.

Henry Payne and his family had arrived not long after the Calthorpes. Their paths did not cross at first, for they tended to move in different circles. But, ironically enough, it wasn't long before Society was divided into two camps, each claiming that the success of the season would be a Miss Payne. The smaller, more discerning, group declared that Miss Kate Payne was the cream of the débutantes. They refused to allow that her lack of more conventional beauty in any way detracted from her charms. The larger group, while granting that Miss Katharine Payne was very charming, swore that London had seldom seen as beautiful a creature as her cousin, Mr Henry Payne's daughter, the lovely Miss Catherine Payne. Rivalry between the factions increased, and society hostesses, eager to add interest to the endless round of balls and soirées, tried to make sure that both girls were present at their events as often as possible.

Katharine was thus forced to see far more of her cousins than she wished. To avoid them would encourage just the sort of gossip she disliked. Society already found it slightly odd that she was being sponsored in London by Mrs Calthorpe, rather than by Mr Henry Payne and his wife. If it was seen that she was reluctant even to talk to her cousins, society would soon start to speculate on the rift in the Payne family. Even less did Katharine want to encourage any thought of rivalry between herself and the family beauty, Catherine. So she hid her distrust of them, chatted to Catherine, danced with Walter, and listened with apparent attention to her uncle and aunt. And of course, Adam saw quite a lot of them too.

Walter was delighted. Matters could not have turned out better. After his failure to attract her in Hampshire, it was most unlikely that Kate Payne would have spent a second longer in his company than she had to. But now fate, and Society, had taken a hand, and it was up to him to take advantage of it. He took care to escort his sister to every occasion where Kate was likely to be present. Once there, he made sure he reserved at least one dance with his cousin before she could legitimately claim that her card was full. And during the dances he exerted himself as never before to remedy the damage done to his cause at Herriards.

At first Katharine froze him out whenever he became personal. But Walter was a fast learner and he soon knew how to hold her interest by giving her titbits of information about the people she had known at Herriards. He had always been an excellent improvisor and his accounts of how he had defied his father to defend the interests of the poor in the community were quite convincing. After a month or so, Walter began to feel that he was making some headway, that in a while Kate Payne would listen more favourably to his suit. And about time, too! Very few women had resisted him for this long before.

Into this intriguing situation came Lady Balmenny, beautiful, spoilt, trapped in a boring marriage and looking for amusement.

The day after she arrived, she appeared at the Marchmonts' ball halfway through the evening. It was one of the season's most prestigious events and the rooms were full. Julia wandered slowly through the throng, waving her fan languidly, apparently enjoying the scene. But she was searching all the while for one face among the crowd, and she finally saw it. Adam Calthorpe was dancing.

She turned to the person next to her, who happened to be an old friend. Hetta Jerrard was one of London's most notorious gossips. 'Who is that delightful girl?' Julia asked. 'The tall one dancing over there.'

'You mean the one with Lord Calthorpe, Julia?'

'I suppose I do. Yes.'

'That, my dear, is one of the latest stars. A Miss Katharine Payne. Charming, isn't she? Some say she is *the* star. But I myself prefer her cousin. She is infinitely prettier. You must meet her, Julia.'

Julia nearly dropped her fan. 'Wait! Katharine Payne! You said Katharine Payne? That girl dancing with Lord Calthorpe is *Katharine Payne!* I don't believe it! Is she staying with the Calthorpes?'

'Yes. Mrs Calthorpe is sponsoring her. We are led to believe that there isn't any other reason for Lord Calthorpe's interest in her. But one does wonder… they seem very close.'

Julia looked at the pair on the floor. They were laughing as they rejoined the set. 'That's nonsense,' she said sharply. 'It's easily explained—she's the sister of one of Lord Calthorpe's friends, who was killed at Waterloo. Adam made him some ridiculous promise about looking after the girl. That is all.'

'It can't quite be all, my dear. Katharine Payne is not alone in the world. She has some perfectly good cousins, who are also in London for the season. Why aren't *they* looking after her?' Lady Hetta sent a significant look in the direction of the dancers. 'Perhaps Lord Calthorpe's interest is more than just an obligation to a friend?'

'What nonsense you talk, Hetta! The girl isn't at all his style.'

'That's true,' said Lady Hetta with regret. 'He appears to be far more taken with her cousin.'

'What cousin?'

Hetta Jerrard started to smile. This was going better. Julia sounded quite annoyed. 'Another Miss Payne, Julia dear. Another Catherine Payne! And a real diamond. The two girls may be cousins, but they are not at all alike—one is tall and the other tiny. In fact…'

'Well?' said Julia impatiently.

'The other Miss Payne bears a remarkable resemblance to you—as you were years ago. You might almost be mother and daughter!'

Julia took a moment to recover, then snapped, 'You were never very good at arithmetic, Hetta. I dare say there's a bare seven or eight years between the chit and me. And what do you mean—as I was years ago? I look exactly the same now as I did before I married Balmenny. Everyone says so.'

'Well, they would, wouldn't they? But perhaps it would be better if you didn't meet the second Miss Payne, Julia. In fact, I would stay away from her altogether if you can. Comparisons can be very disconcerting, don't you think?'

'I don't know what you're talking about. Excuse me, I see that the set is ending. I must go and congratulate Katharine Payne on her début.'

Hetta Jerrard watched eagerly as her friend made her way through to Adam Calthorpe and his partner. She would eat her best hat if Julia's interest was in Miss Katharine Payne. Not when handsome, charming Lord Calthorpe was standing right next to the girl.

'Miss Payne!' called Julia. 'Miss Payne, don't go away! Remember me? You came to Redshaw Hall on Christmas Eve—' She turned and gave a start. 'Why, Adam! It's you! This is an unexpected pleasure. Still looking after Katharine, I see.' She smiled at him archly. 'When do you take time off for your *own* enjoyment, Adam?'

'Julia! When did you arrive in London?'

Julia fell into step with them as they walked towards the supper room. 'Last night. What a *journey* we had! The packet tossed us about till I thought we should *die!* And then the roads were *impossible!*'

'But here you are tonight, looking as beautiful as ever.'

'Oh, never say so! I am a *hag,* a positive hag!' said Lady Balmenny, looking deeply pleased.

Katharine was annoyed. She had not been taken in by Julia's apparent surprise at seeing Adam. The woman had probably come over with the express design of talking to him. And though Julia's barbed remark seemed to have passed him by, it had not been lost on her. Refusing to allow Julia to leave her out of the conversation, she said now, 'Have you come direct from Ireland, Lady Balmenny?'

'What? Oh, yes. Balmenny left everything so late that there wasn't time to stop for any length of time on the way. We spent but four days driving from Holyhead.' Her wonderful eyes turned back to Adam. 'I really wanted to be here much sooner,' she said wistfully.

Katharine persisted. 'Is Lord Balmenny here tonight?'

'I don't think so.' There was a slight snap in Julia's voice. 'He said he was going to rest this evening.' She threw out her hands and said, 'But you know me, Adam. I was *starved* for some company. Ireland is a *desert*. However, I have to say that I recognise very few people here tonight. I feel very alone.'

They had reached the supper room. 'In that case, why don't you join us for supper?' said Adam. Katharine gazed at him in disbelief. Even while they were walking the short distance from the ballroom, at least a dozen people had nodded to Julia! But the invitation had been made and it was impossible to get out of it. Katharine sighed. She had been looking forward to this supper with Adam. He seemed to spend so little time with her nowadays. And though she frequently reminded herself of his arrogant, domineering ways, of how often he had annoyed her, she had not yet found anyone else whose company she enjoyed more. Try as she might to stop herself, Adam's face was the one she first looked for, Adam's voice the one she wanted to hear…

And now, the rare prospect of a delightful supper party *à deux* with him had been ruined by this…this relic of the past! She was willing to wager that, if matters were left to Julia Redshaw, the *à deux* supper would consist of Lord Calthorpe and herself, and Katharine would be pushed to the fringe. But that was not going to happen. She could not get rid of Julia, but she could enlarge the party—perhaps not altogether to Lady Balmenny's taste. It wasn't to hers either, but in matters of war… Walter Payne was passing their table with his sister on his arm.

'Walter! Catherine! Do come and join us,' she called.

Walter could hardly believe his ears, but he didn't hesitate. 'This is very nice,' he said as he approached. 'Good evening, Kate. Calthorpe.' He nodded and regarded Julia.

'Lady Balmenny, may I present my cousins, Catherine and Walter Payne?'

Introductions over, Katharine ignored a glance of outrage from Adam and sat back. She wasn't particularly happy, but she found the situation intriguing. Adam, she knew, couldn't stand Walter, but he had a very soft spot for Walter's sister. And now, looking at Catherine and Lady Balmenny as they sat together, she could see why. Julia Redshaw had been the love of his life ten years earlier, and Catherine Payne must be almost the image of Julia at seventeen. Even now they were very alike, but Catherine's beauty still had the dew on it, a rose which was delicately unfurling. Julia was a strikingly beautiful woman, but her looks were just beginning to owe less to nature and more to art. The comparison was cruel.

Conversation flourished, in spite of the tensions round the table. Julia did her best to dominate Adam's attention, but was not altogether successful—largely because Adam's innate good manners wouldn't allow the rest of the party to be excluded. When Adam was talking to Catherine or Kate Payne, Julia turned her attention to Walter, who was, after all, a very handsome young man. He responded gallantly, for Lady Balmenny was an illustrious member of the highest circles, and he found her overtures most flattering. However, it annoyed Julia to note that the true focus of Walter's attention was always his cousin Katharine, and as soon as he could he turned to talk to her again. Catherine Payne contributed little, merely gazing shyly at Adam and blushing whenever he addressed her.

Katharine found this most irritating. How did the girl manage it? she asked herself. She sits there, saying nothing worth listening to and blushing to order, and Adam looks at her with a warmth in his eyes which I have never seen directed towards me... Just when Katharine was regretting her impulsive invitation, and beginning to long for the end of the supper interval, a diversion occurred.

'Adam! I've found you at last! And Miss Payne, too.' It was Ivo Trenchard. 'I see you have a spare place at the table—you weren't by some miracle saving it for me, were you?' He smiled engagingly at the rest of the company.

All three ladies were delighted to make the numbers even with such a handsome and distinguished addition to the party. More introductions were performed and Ivo sat down next to Katharine. 'I've been hearing so much about the ravishing Miss Payne, that I was very much afraid I would never get near you. You haven't forgotten your promise to dance with me, I hope?'

'No, indeed,' said Katharine warmly. 'You were my first supporter, sir, I don't forget such things.'

'Wonderful! Do you dance the waltz? And, if so, would you delight me by saying you will dance it with me? I believe it follows the next set of country dances.'

'I would love to dance the waltz with you, Lord Trenchard,' said Katharine, casting a glance at Adam. He was frowning slightly, but at his friend, not at her.

'Adam! *You* must dance the waltz with *me!*' cried Lady Balmenny. She turned to the company. 'I was such a *child* when I knew Adam last that we would *never* have been able to waltz together. Indeed, I don't believe I knew how! Miss Payne, you must have made *lots* of progress since last Christmas, if you can manage the waltz. When Mama last wrote, you appeared not to be having a great deal of success with your dancing. I understand that Monsieur Edouard gave up in *despair!*'

'Ah, but since then I have had the best of teachers, Lady Balmenny,' said Katharine demurely.

'What? Better than Monsieur Edouard? Who was that, pray? We always considered Monsieur Edouard *outstandingly* good, even with the most *inept*. Who was this wonder?'

Ivo had been regarding Lady Balmenny with appreciation. He said now, 'My dear ma'am, do not ask! Mrs Calthorpe produced him, just at the right time.'

'But what was he called?'

'Er… He had a very curious name,' said Lord Trenchard with a grin. 'Twinkletoes… Twinkletoes… What was the rest?'

'Smith!' said Katharine promptly. 'Twinkletoes Smith. An excellent fellow. But I understand he has retired from the art of giving instruction. At least, I hope he has.'

Lord Trenchard gazed at Katharine in laughing admiration. 'Why did I wait so long before returning to London? You're even better than your brother said!' he exclaimed.

'What *are* they talking about, Adam?' asked Lady Balmenny, looking bewildered.

'Don't waste time trying to understand them, Julia. Lord Trenchard often talks nonsense and he has infected Kate,' said Adam, with a glare at his former fellow officer.

The sound of music came from the ballroom. Walter, thinking it was time he made a mark, stood up and reminded Katharine that she had promised him the set of dances after the interval. Adam had already asked Catherine Payne. With a look on his face which Adam had seen countless times in ballrooms all over Europe, Ivo Trenchard bowed to Lady Balmenny.

'May I have the pleasure of dancing this set with one of the most beautiful ladies in London?' he asked. Julia looked at him sharply. Had there been a touch of cynicism in Lord Trenchard's tone? But then he smiled, as he took her by the hand and led her to the ballroom, and she was reassured.

* * *

Walter had been much encouraged by Katharine's spontaneous invitation to join her at supper. Now, dancing the long set of country dances with her, he allowed himself to become more personal again. He spoke more boldly of his hopes for the future, of how much she really meant to him…

Katharine hardly heard him. Whenever the dance permitted she watched Adam's tall figure out of the corner of her eye. As he danced with her cousin Catherine, his face, which in repose was normally rather severe, was softened by an indulgent smile. Her heart twisted. It seemed to Katharine that she had been watching that smile for weeks, while Adam talked, danced or walked with her cousin Catherine. He seemed to handle the girl as gently as he would a piece of the delicate porcelain she so much resembled. Was this what Adam wanted? Someone to cherish, to protect? Was he about to ask Catherine Payne to marry him, thinking he would find in her, not an equal, but someone who would let him make the decisions, without argument or protest? Or was she merely a reflection of his lost love—a younger, available, substitute for Julia Redshaw?

For all the smiles Katharine directed at Walter as she made her way up the set with him, her heart was heavy. Julia would never have made Adam happy, and nor would Catherine. Catherine might be young, but she was just as selfish, and, in spite of her submissive appearance, just as determined to have her own way as the lovely Lady Balmenny. They neither of them regarded men as partners, as possible friends, but as trophies, to be coaxed with smiles and threatened with tears into giving them whatever they wanted at the time.

What a waste it would be! Life with Adam Cal-thorpe could be wonderful! What a strong, loving, tender husband he would make for the right woman! He might be a touch autocratic, and his self-control was such that Katharine couldn't imagine him ever falling desperately in love again. But there was no one in the world that she, Kate Payne, would rather marry…

Her heart missed a beat and she came to a sudden halt. *No one she would rather marry?* Was she really in love with Adam Calthorpe! Yes! It seemed to her that she had always really been in love with him, ever since the beginning, ever since he had knocked her over in the churchyard. Though she had only just real-ised it, she had fallen in love with him then, and had loved him ever since!

'Kate? Kate! Are you unwell?'

Katharine came to with a start. Walter was looking at her in concern. The set round them was in some confusion.

'I…I'm sorry,' she said. 'Please excuse me… No, no, I am perfectly well—pray carry on.'

Fortunately the set came to an end shortly after and they returned to the table in the supper room. Walter, still full of concern, went away to fetch Katherine a drink of water, and Adam came to sit by her almost immediately.

'What was the trouble?' he asked.

'Nothing!' For the life of her she could not speak naturally. She knew her tone was too detached, almost rude, but the revelation on the ballroom floor had been too great a shock.

'You're ill!'

'No! No, I'm not ill.' She gave a little laugh. 'I must have missed my entry, Adam. For some reason I was totally confused. I'm glad you were not my partner. You would have been less understanding than Walter.' He started to argue, but she put out her hand. 'Please don't make any more fuss. I am perfectly well. And I don't want to miss my waltz with Lord Trenchard.'

He looked sternly at her. 'I don't like it,' he said severely.

The Kate which the world never saw wanted to cry, 'Please, please, Adam, don't look at me like that! Look at me as you look at my cousin, tenderly, warmly. Take my hand as you take hers, as if it might break in your grasp... Tell me you care for me...!'

But what Katharine Payne rather coldly said was, 'Don't be tiresome, Adam! Ivo Trenchard is one of your oldest friends. You've always told me what an excellent dancer he is. He'll see that I manage.'

'That's not what I was worried about—' He could say no more. Walter Payne was coming back with the water, and at the same time Ivo Trenchard returned to the table with a laughing Lady Balmenny. His skilled compliments seemed to have restored her good humour.

She said as they sat down, 'So. Your Signor Twinkletoes doesn't seem to have taught you *everything*, Miss Payne. What confusion you brought to your set! And in such a *simple* dance, too.'

'Miss Payne was ill,' said Walter, putting a solicitous hand on Kate's shoulder.

Adam's gaze rested on it for a moment, then he said coldly, 'Payne, I expect your sister will be looking for you. I took her back to your friends in the small saloon.'

Walter looked as if he wished to demur, whereupon Adam added very firmly, 'I promised her I would send you to her.' Walter could hardly disagree without challenging Adam, so he shrugged his shoulders, gave Katharine a warm smile, bowed to the rest, and left.

Adam said to the others, 'I think Kate needs a breath of fresh air. Excuse us. We'll be back in a moment. Kate?' He held out his arm and Katharine, still in something of a daze, took it. They went through the hall into the small garden which lay behind the Marchmonts' house.

Here Adam stopped and turned to Katharine. 'I should have thought you had seen enough of that fellow, Kate.'

'By "fellow" you mean Walter Payne, I suppose? Unfortunately he is my cousin. I think tongues would wag if I refused to recognise him. Besides, I really think he has changed. He says he is sorry for his behaviour at Herriards.'

'Leopards don't change their spots. I've known a good few like Payne in my time. They're not to be trusted. Don't spend so much time with him.'

Katharine exclaimed, 'I wish you would not always try to dictate to me, Adam! What business is it of yours what I do? I don't need your permission to talk to my cousin. It nearly always concerns Herriards and the people down there.'

'Don't you think this nostalgia for Herriards is a mistake?' said Adam coldly. 'You might remember that it is no longer your affair. Or are you now re-gretting your decision to leave there?'

His coldness, his indifference, cut Katharine to the quick. Without stopping to consider, she said defiantly, 'I could go back there any time I liked! Walter said so.'

Adam's frown grew. 'Don't be such a fool! You would never stand it! While your Uncle Henry is in charge, Herriards would be the last place you would wish to live!'

Some perverse demon caused Katharine to carry on. 'But afterwards? If I were mistress there? I dare say I could be if I wanted to, you know.'

She had succeeded in surprising him. He said at last, 'You mean you might marry Walter? You? I refuse to believe it! What a waste of all our efforts that would be!'

So much for my hopes, thought Katharine. I'd just represent a waste of effort! That's all.

Sounds of music came through the windows. 'We'd better return,' she said wearily. 'This breath of fresh air doesn't seem to be doing either of us much good.'

They returned to the ballroom in silence. The waltz was just about to begin. Ivo Trenchard swept Katha-rine up and they launched straight away into the swirl of figures circling the room. Adam watched them grimly. He didn't believe for one minute that Katha-rine Payne had the slightest intention of returning to Herriards! She had only said it to provoke him. It must be that! What a perverse creature she was!

'Adam!' Julia was standing a yard away, tapping her foot angrily. He pulled himself together.

'Please forgive me, Julia! Someone caught me as I

came through the hall and I was held up. Shall we dance?'

Julia Redshaw was having quite a difficult time. She was not accustomed to being kept waiting. In fact, the whole evening was turning out to be far less agreeable than she had thought. It had been a blow to find that her throne as London's queen of hearts was being threatened by a chit of seventeen! Several misguided friends had raved about Catherine Payne, had even thought they were complimenting her when they said the girl was so like Julia at her age. And when she had glanced into the small saloon—just to see if Adam and the other Payne girl were there—she had been annoyed to see Catherine Payne surrounded by a bevy of gentlemen, among whom were several of her former lovers, gentlemen who not long ago had sworn undying devotion to her, Julia Redshaw! She could get them back, of course, any moment she chose! But it was irritating, all the same.

Then there was the question of Adam. He seemed quite unnecessarily concerned with the other Katharine Payne, his friend's sister! What a burden that girl was to him! His mother was behind it, of course. Mrs Calthorpe had never liked Julia, and she was using the girl as a shield to keep her son from falling in love all over again with his childhood sweetheart. Well, Mrs Calthorpe would fail! The Adam of today was a prize worth having and Julia fully intended to conquer him again. She was sure it wouldn't have been difficult except for the presence of those wretched girls—Walter Payne's sister, who looked so like her, and Tom Payne's sister who was just always there!

These thoughts and others like them caused Julia to sound more ill-tempered than was her custom in public when she answered Adam's question.

'And where is Miss Kate Payne now? Better, I hope?' she snapped.

Chapter Twelve

Julia looked quite shrewish, thought Adam. A genuine shrew, as opposed to the shrew he had found in the churchyard, a shrew who was really a girl at her wits' end, trying to cope with the loss of everything she loved and hitting out at the world... His heart gave a thump. What if Kate wasn't teasing? What if she really did consider Herriards worth a marriage to Walter Payne? No! That mustn't happen. She *mustn't* go back to Herriards! He would have to stop it somehow...

'Well?' said Julia impatiently. 'Have you managed to get rid of her?'

Adam looked at Julia again and said coolly, 'She's dancing with Lord Trenchard. Over there. See? Shall we join in?'

He had been offended at her tone. Julia took a breath and told herself to be careful. The Adam of ten years before would have fallen over himself to explain, to make excuses, done anything to win back her smiles. The Adam of today was a distinguished man of the world. He was less easy to deal with—though, she had to admit, infinitely more interesting. But a crowded ballroom was not the place to deal with him.

'Adam, I don't feel like dancing. We've had so little time to talk. Will you take me, too, into the garden for a breath of fresh air?' She smiled sweetly and a little sadly at him. There was a touch of moisture in her deep blue eyes.

Adam bowed and said, 'Of course. If you think it is wise?'

'Balmenny isn't here,' she said, taking his arm. It wasn't quite what Adam had meant, but, though he frowned, he accompanied her into the garden.

Once outside Julia said softly, 'Forgive me if I sounded impatient before. It's just that…I dreamed so often of meeting you again. When I heard you were going to be in Surrey at Christmas I was determined to be there, too. Balmenny doesn't like travelling in winter, but I made him bring me to visit my parents. And we met again on Christmas Eve. It was just like old times, didn't you feel it, too?'

'Hardly. In old times we had to meet in secret,' said Adam drily.

'Oh, yes—and it was so romantic! Oh, those summer days! We were so in love… I didn't forget you, Adam. After you left England I was quite desolate, you know. And then I heard of your success, and of all those balls and parties you would be attending, and I longed to be there with you. How I envied those foreign ladies who were your partners. You once said that I was just as high as your heart. Were there many who made you feel the same?'

Adam looked down at her. 'I forget,' he said easily. 'It all seems so long ago. I remember the fighting better. But, Julia—surely you didn't pine for long? I thought I heard that you married Balmenny that same year?'

'Oh, Balmenny!' she said pettishly. 'Don't let us talk of him! I wish I had never met him!'

Adam took a step back and examined her, letting his eyes wander over her dress of silk and lace, and the clusters of diamonds at her throat and in her hair. 'He's been very good to you,' he said a little cynically.

'He's dull! And old! Adam! Please, don't be unkind! Surely you haven't forgotten how much we loved one another! Confess! I don't believe you have. I've watched you with Catherine Payne, and you look at her as if you're looking at a ghost. As if you were seeing me. Isn't that true? Everyone says how like me she is.'

'It is certainly true that she is very like you.'

'Tell me that I'm right. That when you're with her, you don't see *her* at all. You only see *me*. Isn't that so? You imagine that we are together again.' She drew a little nearer. 'But why make do with the imitation? I'm here! I'm real! And, Adam—I now have so much more to offer…'

Adam's face was in shadow. Disconcerted by his silence she went on, her voice full of pathos, 'You can't have forgotten how much you loved me!'

Adam hesitated. Then he said, 'That was a long time ago, Julia. We've both changed since then.'

'It isn't so long! And I won't let you say we've changed! Please, Adam, can't we at least be…friends again?' She gave a small sob. 'I'm so lonely. My marriage was a mistake. And I'm not hard and independent like that other girl—the one you've been saddled with. Katharine Payne. I need someone to fight my battles for me. I need help. I need love.'

Julia moved even closer. Her tiny hands were against Adam's chest. She raised her face to look at him, her beauty unaffected by the tears now rolling down her cheeks...

Adam had a sudden vision of Kate standing back, angrily refusing to accept sympathy from anyone. He remembered the detached tone she adopted when most moved, her refusal to parade her emotions. And as he regarded Julia now he was surprised to feel nothing but a slight distaste. He took a step back and said as gently as he could, 'I don't believe I am the right person for that, my dear. And Kate is not as invulnerable as you think. Kate needs me more than you do. You see, she has no husband to guard her interests.'

Julia looked at him in disbelief. He had rejected her! The tears stopped and a tide of colour swept over her cheeks. Her tone was venomous as she echoed his words. '*"Kate needs me more than you do!"* That lump of a girl? Needing help? Of course she hasn't a husband! Who would marry *her*? How dare you compare her with me! But don't worry! I understand what you really wanted to say. Adam Calthorpe is too much of a gentleman, too *noble* to make love to a married woman—isn't that it? My God! You always were a prig, Adam Calthorpe! I wonder why I ever tolerated you. Well, that's all over. I don't care which of the Paynes you marry. Marry the simpering miss if you wish—you won't find *her* as innocent as you think! But it's my belief you'll end up with the overgrown beanpole! That's what your mother intends! As for me, I wish you joy of neither!'

She ran to the door which led into the hall, but remembered to stop for a minute or two while she carefully dabbed the marks of tears from her face. Then she shook out her fan, took a breath and walked into the house, smiling right and left at her acquaintance, waving her fan gracefully, as beautiful and as charming as ever.

Adam watched her go with nothing but relief. The old dream had been shattered. For the first time he had seen Julia Redshaw as his mother saw her, and he marvelled at his former blindness. What an escape he had had all those years ago! But it wasn't long before his thoughts turned again to Katharine, and he followed Julia inside. The waltz was still in train, and she and Ivo Trenchard were dipping and turning with the rest. What the devil had Julia meant? Kate was no lump, no beanpole, she moved like a queen! Hardly knowing it, he walked down the room, watching the pair from a distance. Kate seemed to have recovered her spirits. She was laughing up into Ivo's face, saying something which made him laugh in turn. It worried Adam. Someone ought to warn her. Ivo was the best of fellows, but not one to be trusted as far as the ladies were concerned. He left a trail of broken hearts wherever he went. True, they usually belonged to ladies who should have known better—Ivo seldom spent his time on débutantes. In fact, this was the first time Adam had seen him do so. One might have thought that Ivo's friendship with Tom would protect Kate, but it apparently didn't…

There they went again, Ivo pulling Kate closer to avoid a collision with another couple! Adam had a sudden memory of Kate dancing with him in the saloon at Bridge House, how she had seemed to float in his arms. He had kissed her…

This really wasn't good enough! Something had to be done about Katharine Payne! She was too inexperienced, too green to be out alone! First it was Walter, and now here was Ivo! They could say anything they liked to the girl and she believed them! Well, it wasn't going to continue. Tom had extracted a promise from him to look after his sister. He had even wanted Adam to marry the girl! And if that was the only way Kate Payne would be safe, then it ought to be considered at least!

The following day Katharine was out visiting some friends and Adam and his mother were alone. A previous engagement had prevented Mrs Calthorpe from attending the Marchmont ball and she wanted to hear all about it. At the end of Adam's carefully edited account of the people who had been there and who had danced with whom, Mrs Calthorpe put her head on one side and asked, 'And what happened, my dear?'

'I've told you.'

'No, I mean what happened to make you so uneasy?'

Adam started to deny that he was uneasy, then he stopped and thought. His mother waited in silence.

'It's Kate,' her son said finally. 'I'm not sure she is always very wise.'

Mrs Calthorpe looked serious. 'I knew I should have gone with her last night. It was my duty to do so. I should have made my apologies to the Carterets and accompanied her. But tell me what happened? I can't believe she behaved badly.'

'No, no, no! Nothing like that. You needn't reproach yourself. And you couldn't possibly have disappointed your other friends. Kate was perfectly safe and perfectly well-behaved.' He stopped and thought. 'Except with me. She seems to enjoy provoking me. I don't know why—she is always charming with everyone else.'

'Could it be that you provoke her?'

'If offering perfectly good advice can be called provoking, I suppose I do. She refused to listen to it, of course.'

'You can sound a little peremptory, my dear. Kate is a girl of spirit.'

'Too much so for her own good! It made me uneasy about the future.'

With a touch of anxiety Mrs Calthorpe asked, 'She hasn't found someone else—?' She stopped short and then began again. 'She hasn't found someone in whom she is interested, has she?'

'That's just it! Ivo Trenchard was in one of his frivolous moods, and Kate seemed quite taken with him. They spent half the evening laughing and making jokes... And then he danced the waltz with her.... I must confess I was surprised at him. I hope he isn't setting up one of his flirtations with Kate, Mama!'

'That's a relief. I was worried for a moment. There's no harm in Ivo, Adam! I am quite sure Kate would come to no mischief with him. You can be easy on that score.'

'But Kate doesn't know the rules—she could be hurt!'

'Is that all that makes you anxious?' Mrs Calthorpe was clearly not anxious herself.

'No. Walter Payne is working hard to persuade Kate that he is a reformed character. I think she almost believes him.'

'Oh, dear! Now that is a far more serious matter, I admit. But Kate is surely too intelligent to be in any danger from him?'

'One would think so. But he tempts her with talk of Herriards, and of course she is more than ready to listen. It meant a lot to her. Does she still pine for the place, do you know?'

'She never mentions it.'

'That means nothing,' Adam said gloomily. 'The more Kate feels, the less likely she is to talk about it.'

'It might mean that she is enjoying herself too much, that she has too many other things to talk about, you know. Don't be too depressed, Adam.'

'But Payne tempts her with Herriards! He tells her she can return there at any time, that she could one day be mistress of it! What if she is persuaded?'

Mrs Calthorpe, who had her own suspicions what Kate's real feelings were, said, 'Most unlikely. But what can you do about it if she is?'

'We must stop her! Look, Mama, I should be betraying my promise to Tom if I let her go back to that place! Especially if it meant marriage to that tricky character.' He walked restlessly about the room. 'That girl is more trouble than she is worth!'

'You don't mean that, Adam.'

'It would all have been much simpler if I had married her when Tom asked me. There wouldn't be any of this nonsense then! And Ivo wouldn't be a risk, either.'

'Well, why don't you?'

'What? Marry Kate after all?'

'It would seem to be the only solution.'

'You'd like that, I know,' Adam said, with a rueful smile.

'Yes, I would. I like Kate. I think she would make you an excellent wife. But I don't want her made unhappy. It wouldn't be any use if you were still hankering after Julia Redshaw or that ninny that looks so like her, Kate's cousin.' There was a question in her voice.

Adam said decisively, 'There's no question of that. Julia is in the past and will stay there. Catherine Payne is lovely to look at, but after ten minutes in her company I'm bored.' He moved restlessly. 'When I was in the Army I had such a clear idea of the sort of wife I wanted, but now... To tell the truth, Mama, I haven't found anyone that fits.'

'That's a pity,' said his mother with a satisfied smile.

'So we come back to Kate. She can be very provoking, but I like her better than I did. We should quarrel, of course. I can't think marriage to me would tame her. But we usually come about in the end. And she is never boring. Yes, I'm of the opinion that marriage to me would be the best solution.' He came back to his mother. 'I'll speak to her today.'

'Be careful, Adam! Kate is not an ordinary girl. She won't fall over with gratitude just because such a handsome, lordly creature as yourself has asked her to marry him. Don't take too much for granted.' Adam bent over and kissed his mother.

'You make me sound such a coxcomb! I don't take anything for granted—not with Kate Payne. But, as far as I can tell, there isn't yet anyone else. And on the whole she is fairly open to reason. I think she likes me, and she is certainly very fond of you. Have no fear, Mama—I think I can persuade her.'

Later that day three things happened. The first was that Walter Payne was riding in the park when he saw Lady Balmenny being driven along in her elegant barouche. He felt he had made a good impression on the lady the night before, and since he was a man who was always ready to improve his stock in the eyes of the world, he rode up to enquire of the Viscountess how she was. Julia was not deceived by his attention. She was still resentful of his interest in Katharine Payne. But it didn't do any harm for the world to see that Julia Redshaw could still hold a handsome young man in conversation, and they talked for several minutes.

Just before they parted company, Julia said sweetly, 'I do hope you are going to wish your cousin happy, Mr Payne.'

Walter looked puzzled. 'I'm afraid I don't perfectly understand you. Why should I wish her happy?'

'Oh, am I betraying a secret? I shall say no more.'

'No, please! Tell me!'

'Well, Lord Calthorpe and I are old friends, you know. He confides in me. And from something that was said last night, it seems that he is intending to ask your cousin Katharine to marry him. I gather it was a choice between your sister and your cousin, and your cousin won. Intriguing, is it not? I hope your sister is not too disappointed. Goodbye, Mr Payne.' And, well satisfied with that little piece of revenge, Julia drove off. She had no idea which girl Adam Calthorpe would choose. But Walter Payne's hopes had been dashed for a little while, at least!

The next thing that happened was that Adam caught Kate as she came in from her visits and asked her to join him in the library in a few minutes. He sounded rather serious, and Kate wondered what she had done. She hurried upstairs and tidied herself, then came down and entered the library. Adam was standing in front of the fireplace looking grave.

'Sit down, Kate.'

Somewhat nervously Kate sat in one of the chairs nearby.

Adam cleared his throat. 'Kate, am I right in supposing that you have not yet found anyone you would like for a husband?'

Now there's a difficult question to answer, thought Katharine. What should I say? That I discovered last night that *you* are the only man I could bear to marry? No, I don't think I want to tell you that, Adam. After a slight hesitation she replied, 'Why do you ask?'

'You may confide in me, you know. Though if you have a liking for Ivo Trenchard I ought to warn you—'

'I like Lord Trenchard very much, but I would never think of him as a possible husband.'

'Good. Good! And…what about Walter Payne?'

'Walter Payne? Why on earth should you suddenly think that I want to marry Walter Payne?'

'It might be because you almost said as much last night,' said Adam, slightly nettled at her tone.

'I did? Well, I didn't mean it.' When Adam looked unconvinced she said firmly, 'Of course I didn't, Adam! You should know me better than that! It was just because you were being more than usually dictatorial and I resented it. I wouldn't marry Walter Payne—'

'Not for Herriards?'

A shadow passed over her face, but she said firmly, 'Not even for Herriards.'

Adam started to lose his temper. 'Do you mean to say that I have been worrying quite unnecessarily? That you told me you were tempted to marry Payne, merely for *amusement?*'

'You needn't sound so annoyed. You deserved it. And I didn't think you would take me seriously, anyway. Not for long.'

'You really are the most provoking girl it has been my misfortune to meet!' he exclaimed angrily. 'To think that I worried half the night about you! I was even going to ask you to marry me!'

Katharine went pale. 'Ask me…to…to marry you!'

'Yes, dammit!'

'And…and…now?' she said breathlessly.

'It's not necessary now!'

'N…not necessary?' Shock and disappointment had almost taken Katharine's breath away. She paused, swallowed, then said, 'What a strange word to choose—necessary.' Her voice rose as she went on, 'Of *course* it isn't necessary! Why should you think it was?'

'I wanted to prevent you from making a mistake. To protect you, as I promised Tom I would.'

'Protect me? From what?'

Adam was feeling distinctly off balance. The decision to ask Kate to marry him had been taken almost in a spirit of sacrifice. Now that he had discovered that she was in no danger from either Ivo or Walter Payne, he ought to be feeling relief. But it wasn't so. He seemed overnight to have become accustomed to the thought of Kate as his wife. It was disconcerting, not comforting, to find that he needn't marry her after all.

'I was worried when Ivo started to flirt with you— I was afraid you might take him seriously.'

'And why shouldn't I? Had it occurred to you that he might mean what he said? Do you find it so unlikely?'

'What did he say?' demanded Adam. 'By God, if he has—'

'Stop being so possessive, Adam! I've told you— I'm not interested in Lord Trenchard, any more than he is interested in me. Except as a friend who knew Tom.'

'I'm not possessive! What have I to be possessive about?'

'Exactly!' said Katharine with a snap. 'So why were you worried?'

'Because I consider I have a responsibility towards you! And then when you started saying you would marry Payne—'

'I did not, I did not!'

'Well, I thought you had! So I decided the best thing would be if I married you myself. It's not perhaps what either of us would have planned, but I thought it would work.'

Katharine got up. 'How very *noble* of you,' she said sarcastically. 'You can have no idea how *obliged* I am to have someone who was prepared to sacrifice *so much,* just to protect *me!*' Her tone carried little in-dication of obligation—indeed, it was positively vit-riolic. She went on, 'But what a narrow escape you've had, Adam!'

'I don't think of it as an escape. In fact, I'd—'

Katharine swept on, growing angrier by the minute. 'Oh, I don't mean from the necessity of marrying me. I meant from loss of face! For, if you had brought yourself to the point of *actually* asking me to marry you, I'm afraid I would have had to decline the offer, however overwhelmingly generous you might have thought it!'

'Why on earth would you do that?' asked Adam in genuine astonishment. 'You've said there's no one else. Didn't you?'

'If and when I do marry, it will be because someone wants me for myself! Not because of some *stu-pid…senseless…*promise made to my dead brother!'

Adam, offended at the scorn in these last words, said icily, 'If I remember correctly, ma'am, you did not regard my actions in rescuing you from your un-cle's clutches as either stupid or senseless!'

After a brief pause Katharine managed to calm down enough to say, 'No. I was and am grateful to you for that. But you may now regard all obligation to my brother at an end. You have done enough.'

Adam was not sure exactly what he did want, but it was not this. 'It *isn't* enough,' he exclaimed. 'You can't dismiss the matter like this. Tom wanted me to do more than look after you—he asked me to marry you.'

Katharine found this more humiliating than all the rest put together. 'How thoughtful of him! How very kind!' she said bitterly. 'After leaving me to cope with Grandfather, and with Herriards for years, he finally delegates his responsibilities to his commanding officer. As if I were a…a puppet or…or a doll, to be disposed of at will. You must have been highly embarrassed, sir! Dare I ask how you responded?'

'I…I said I would see that you were safe,' said Adam uncomfortably.

'But you didn't wish to offer marriage. Of course you didn't!'

'Dammit, I hadn't even seen you!'

'And when you did? Ah, yes! I remember now. You thought my cousin was Tom's sister. I remember you looked quite besotted!'

'Beso— I was not besotted!'

'How disappointing it must have been to discover that it was the plain Miss Payne who was to be your bride! I'm not surprised it has taken all this time for you to bring yourself to the sticking point!'

'I wasn't going to marry you! Not at first. I thought it would be enough if I made sure you were safe… That's why I saw your guardian. That's why I rescued you from Henry Payne.'

'But it was your mother who pushed you into bringing me to London. Wasn't it? And you were prepared to make the final sacrifice. Noble Major Calthorpe, rushing to rescue this innocent girl from the enemy, and prepared even to marry her! Thank you, but I don't want your empty gallantry!'

Adam was incensed. 'By God, Kate, you *are* the shrew I first thought you! Empty gallantry, is it?' He pulled her towards him and kissed her hard. She fought to escape, wriggling in his grip, stamping on his toes and kicking him in the shins, but her delicate sandals made little impact and she only succeeded in hurting her feet. He laughed at her efforts and kissed her again, more lingeringly. Kate's struggles lessened and died. She was in a daze. How had she ever believed Adam incapable of passion? These kisses were a world away from the kiss at the end of the waltz in Bridge House. Under no circumstances could they be called brotherly and, though she resisted them, they roused in her a desperate longing to respond. She had never before been in greater danger of losing control. The discipline she had exercised for so many difficult years, refusing to give way to her emotions, refusing to let the world see what she felt, was in danger of melting away in the magic, the heat of this moment. For the first time in her life Katharine experienced overwhelming desire.

Adam held her away from him and laughed again. 'You'll marry me,' he said with satisfaction.

For a moment she was still, gazing into Adam's laughing face. Then shame and anger overcame her at this final betrayal and she swung her arm to give him a ringing slap on the cheek. He bit back an exclamation and grabbed her arms. 'You little termagant!' he said. 'I've told you before that it's dangerous to hit a man when he's aroused.'

Katharine glared back at him unafraid. 'What am I

supposed to do?' she hissed. 'Lie back and allow you to rape me? Who can I call on for help? My uncle? Walter Payne?'

'*Rape* you! Kate!'

'Let me go!' she said frantically. 'I won't marry you any more than I would marry my cousin. You're the same, both of you! Animals.'

Adam stood back and stared at her, shocked. He was pale except for the scarlet mark on his cheek. 'How could you think…? And yet…I suppose it was natural…' Then he turned and walked to the window. 'I am…deeply sorry for what occurred just now, Kate,' he said, his back to her. 'I…I don't quite know what happened. I didn't realise…'

Katharine gazed at his back. She would not give in to tears, she would not! Now, more than ever before, she had to be strong. She must suppress the desire to go over to him, to beg him to ignore what she had just said, to beg him to love her, to tell him that she would marry him whatever his reasons for asking her. That she had enough love for both of them…

But some instinct which was wiser than her rioting emotions told her that this was not the way to happiness. Unless Adam Calthorpe fell in love with her she could not marry him. She would be happier alone.

He turned back. 'I hadn't realised how strongly you felt about me,' he said. 'I knew you were often angry at me, of course. But I believed…I believed we were friends. Sometimes. So I thought…. But it's obvious you dislike me too much even to contemplate marrying me. Don't look like that, Kate. I won't bother you again. But before I go…promise me you will be on your guard with Walter Payne. He is a villain.' Adam gave a twisted smile. 'Much worse than me. You mustn't trust him, Kate. And now, if you will excuse me…'

He bowed and went out of the room.

Katharine, left to herself, sat like a stone. She would not cry! Adam Calthorpe was not worth it. No man was worth it! How could he believe that she disliked him? How could he be so blind? Stupid, stupid man! As if she could even *look* at Walter Payne after getting to know Adam Calthorpe! And now he had gone, believing she disliked him. Oh, why had she been so cruel to him? He might be blind, but he had done so much for her…more than he realised. He had caused her to fall in love for the first time in her life, with a man who merely wanted to be sure she was safe!

Why was it that all the men she loved only succeeded in hurting her?

At that point the day's third event—one which was to have a profound effect on the weeks that followed—took place. The footman came in to say that a Mr Payne wished to see her. Katharine was still hastily denying him access when Walter Payne came striding in.

'I'm sorry. But I had to see you!' he said.

Katharine hesitated, then gave a nod to the footman, who left the room. 'What can I do for you?' she asked.

'Tell me it isn't true! Tell me that you're not going to marry Calthorpe!'

For the second time that day Katharine's breath was taken away. Her inner turmoil was masked with anger. 'Whatever do you mean by bursting in here and asking such an impertinent question?' she exclaimed. 'I think the world has gone mad!'

'I demand that you tell me!'

'I shall do no such thing! What right do you think you have to demand anything of me?' said Katharine even more angrily.

'Because I love you! Because I want you to marry *me!* Because you have encouraged me to think that you would!'

'I encouraged you?' asked Katharine, fighting off an attack of hysterical laughter. 'Whenever did I encourage you, sir?'

'Don't try to pretend. It won't do! Last night, when we were dancing together we talked of Herriards. You said you would like to be mistress of it one day. That must mean that you wish to marry me, after all. Don't deny it, Katharine!'

Katharine began to regret bitterly her behaviour at the ball. It had seemed so harmless at the time, but it was having such disastrous consequences! 'I'm sorry if I gave you the wrong impression, Walter,' she said carefully. 'But I assure you—'

'But you must marry me! You must! You don't realise what it means—'

'I will not, sir!' Katharine's hysteria was even more imminent. Fighting off two importunate suitors in one afternoon was more than her nerves would stand! But this one was less of a gentleman. Walter took hold of her without warning or provocation, but panic gave Katharine strength. She pushed him away and fled behind the table out of his reach. He pursued her, desperate with frustration and rage, calling her names, telling her she must love him and threatening dire punishment all at the same time. At last she managed to dodge round to the fireplace and take hold of the bell pull.

'If you lay a finger on me I will call the servants and have you thrown out,' she said fiercely. 'I made you no promises, Walter Payne. I listened to your stories of Herriards, though I only half believed most of them. And I may have tried to be pleasant to you and the rest of your family. But even that was sometimes more than I could stomach. As for marrying you… *You?*' Katharine stopped as fury almost choked her. 'Heaven knows I have no particular cause to admire the male of the species, but *you* are beyond contempt! I would never even *consider* marrying a worm like you! Now leave this house! I wish never to speak to you again!'

Walter's face was suffused with rage. A vain man, he could hardly bear the biting scorn in Katharine's voice, and, even worse, the collapse of all his hopes. 'I'll go,' he snarled. 'And I won't bother you again. But I'll find other ways to solve my difficulties. You'll pay for this, Katharine Payne.' He went out, slamming the door behind him.

Chapter Thirteen

Katharine sank back on to her chair. Her knees were trembling and she was perilously close to crying. She sat there for some time, trying to get calm, the thoughts churning in her head. None of them concerned Walter. The interview with him had been unpleasant, but neither Walter nor his family could affect her very deeply, and his threats had not seriously disturbed her. The cause of her distress was not with him.

For the scene with Adam was still vividly in her mind. Apart from the occasional sign of irritation he had always before been so cool in her presence. She had always found the very qualities which had made him such a successful Army commander—a strong sense of duty, a cool head and an iron will—at the same time admirable and irritating. And she realised now that, during that last scene with him, consciously or unconsciously, she had been goading Adam throughout until his self-control had finally snapped. What sort of a girl was she? And what had she gained? She already knew that Adam Calthorpe would never be ready to risk all for love. For honour, for a promise made to a dead man, to protect the weak—for all of these Adam Calthorpe would fight to the death. But not for love. That had gone with Julia Redshaw.

However, Katharine had begun to hope that Adam might one day ask her to be his wife because he wanted to, because he liked her for herself. So, when he made it so clear that he would marry her simply to satisfy his obligation to Tom, simply to save her from making idiotic mistakes, never because he wanted to, she had been left with a desire to hurt him, to make him angry. As she had. And what had been the result? Adam was convinced that she disliked him, and she…? She had been left not only with the sadness of love which was not returned, but also with an aching desire for more of Adam's kisses, more of Adam's embraces—a desire which was most unlikely ever to be satisfied.

The tears could not be held back. They rolled slowly down her cheeks, and because she fought them ugly red blotches appeared on her face. She couldn't even cry as beautifully as that wretched woman!

'Kate! Oh, my dear child, what is it?' Mrs Calthorpe had slipped into the room unnoticed.

'Nothing!' said Katharine, frantically scrubbing her face with her sleeve.

'Don't be ridiculous! Look at you! I've never seen you in such a state. Come with me. We can't have you sitting here in the library looking like that. Adam went out some time ago, but he might be back at any moment. We'll go to my dressing room.'

Once installed in the little room which she had made into her private chamber, Mrs Calthorpe bathed Katharine's face and gave her a clean handkerchief.

She ordered some tea to be sent up and told the servant they were not to be disturbed.

'Now,' she said. 'Was it Walter Payne? I was on my way down to see you when he arrived. So I waited. And just when I was thinking you might need support, I heard him leave. Was he…importunate?' Katharine was still coping with sobs and couldn't answer, but she shook her head.

Mrs Calthorpe said with sudden anxiety, 'You haven't said you will marry him, have you?'

'No, no!'

There was a silence. Then Mrs Calthorpe said slowly, 'It was Adam, wasn't it? What did Adam say to you?'

The tears broke out afresh. 'He…he didn't ask me to marry him!' sobbed Katharine.

Mrs Calthorpe looked completely bewildered. 'I don't understand,' she said. 'He fully intended to. What stopped him?'

'He s…s…aid it wasn't necessary!'

Mrs Calthorpe waited till Katharine was calmer again, then said, 'Kate, I'm sorry to press you, but…did he explain what he meant? Dear child, I think you had better tell me the whole. For when Adam left me he was fully determined to make you an offer.'

Katharine now had better control of herself. She said, 'I don't know why Adam thought I would really want to marry Walter Payne. And even less why he brought Lord Trenchard into it. I told him that I liked Lord Trenchard, but was never in any danger from him… And then I said that I had never had any intention whatever of marrying Walter. That was when

Adam became quite angry.' She stopped and looked slightly guilty.

Mrs Calthorpe waited until Katharine went on, 'You see, last night Adam had annoyed me and I wanted to worry him. I…I pretended to be more tempted by Walter's offer than I was… I think it did worry him.'

'Yes, I think it did, too!'

'I thought he knew me better than that! But it seems that I had made him really anxious. So when I told him today that I had never had any intention of marrying Walter, he grew angry and called me the most provoking girl he had ever met. That was when he said that he had been going to ask me to marry him.' She paused, then said forlornly, 'But then he said that it wasn't necessary any longer.'

'I wouldn't have believed that a son of mine could be so stupid! What did you say to that?'

'I got angry, too, and said that that was just as well, for if he had asked me I would have refused him!'

Mrs Calthorpe bit her lip. There was a slight quiver in her voice as she said, 'So the situation is this… My son nearly asked you to marry him, but didn't, and you would have refused him, but didn't have the chance. Is that right?' When Katharine nodded she continued, 'And that is why he has gone out in the worst temper I have seen him in for years, and you have been crying your eyes out?'

Katharine looked down. 'It's not as simple as that,' she said unhappily. 'I made Adam really angry after that. Something I said… He…he…'

'Adam kissed you?'

'Yes. Because he wanted to punish me, I think.'

'My dear girl, I have never subscribed to the ridiculous idea that men kiss us to punish us! They wouldn't do it if they didn't enjoy it! And Adam is not the sort of man—at least I don't think he is—who would hurt someone for pleasure. Don't deceive yourself—if Adam kissed you it was because he wanted to. May I ask—did you respond?'

'Not more than I could help,' said Katharine earnestly.

Mrs Calthorpe nodded. 'I remember the feeling,' she said sympathetically.

'But then he laughed at me! He was so…so sure of himself! He was so sure I would marry him after all.'

'The stupid fellow,' exclaimed Mrs Calthorpe. 'Really, I could lose patience with my son! What did you do?'

'I slapped him.'

'Quite right! He deserved it. Did he kiss you again?'

'No.'

'That's a pity!'

'And now he thinks I dislike him,' wailed Katharine, bursting into tears again.

'I can see that he might,' agreed Adam's mother. 'My dear, forgive me if I seem impertinent, but am I right in thinking that you do, in fact, love my son?'

Katharine nodded her head. 'I didn't realise it myself till last night,' she said miserably.

'Well, it is my opinion that he is very likely in love with you.'

'Oh, no! I am not at all the kind of woman he admires. I know that. He likes my cousin. Or…or Lady Balmenny.'

'I think you are wrong. He is no longer in love with Julia, certainly. And I think he is just beginning to realise that he needs to look for something more than a pretty face. But he is sometimes so blind… Now, may I suggest that you put yourself in Kendrick's hands? Get her to make you pretty again, and wear one of your new dresses for dinner tonight. You mustn't let Adam think you are unhappy.'

The new dress suited Katharine very well and Kendrick's ministrations removed all traces of the afternoon's distress. But Adam was not in to dinner to see her. He left a message to tell his mother that he would be out for the evening. And from then on they saw rather less of him, as he appeared to lose interest in the social scene. His mother noted, however, that he always seemed to know where she and Katharine were going each night, and that he often appeared wherever it was for a while before leaving again, apparently in pursuit of his own pleasures. And she knew that the servants all had strict instructions to accompany either of the ladies whenever they went out. Adam had not abandoned his obligations.

The supper parties, the balls, the evenings at Almack's continued as the London season entered its last few weeks. Katharine had at first enjoyed life in town more than she had expected, but she was now heartily sick of it. She smiled, conversed, danced as charmingly as ever, but without Adam's attention the evenings had lost their zest. Even when he escorted them he avoided her company, and when he was forced to dance with her his touch, like his conversation, remained impersonal. The Adam who had tried to dominate, who had quarrelled with her, taught her to dance, forbidden her to ride Sholto, bought her Cintra instead, that Adam had vanished and in his place was Major Calthorpe, the complete officer and gentleman, a perfect member of the Duke of Wellington's staff. It was sometimes almost more than she could bear. As the weather grew warmer and the streets dustier Katharine began to long for the fresh air and cool breezes of the countryside. She grew pale and listless, and that special smile of hers, the one which transformed her into a beauty, was seen less and less often.

Mrs Calthorpe looked on in concern. She had tried several times to talk to her son, but he was as courteously unresponsive as she had ever known him. Using the expertise gained in the Duke's service, he fended off all her careful attempts to discover the state of his mind with an easy switch in the conversation, or some skilful diversion of her attention. She suspected that he was every bit as unhappy as Katharine, but could never get near enough to him to find out.

In fact, Adam was more miserable than he had ever been in his life—even including the dreadful months after Julia Redshaw had rejected him. His youthful despair then had given way surprisingly quickly to enjoyment of his new life, and the new lands and people he was getting to know. But now nothing seemed worth the effort. He went through the motions of life in London, and pretended an interest he did not feel in the people round him. It seemed to him as he watched Katharine Payne that she continued to charm everyone around her as much as ever. Sooner or later she would find among her many admirers someone to love, someone who wouldn't annoy her, who might even be willing to let her have her own way as often as she wanted it. And the poor idiot would be completely wrong for her! Why the devil couldn't she have accepted his own offer of friendship and care? He and Kate would have had a good life together, he was sure of that.

Whenever he remembered the scene in the library he was filled with regret. He had been a fool—so certain that Kate would accept his offer of marriage in the spirit it was meant. Perhaps if he had taken more trouble to explain... Had managed to keep his temper... But then he hadn't realised himself until it was too late just how important Kate was to him. Though his behaviour at the end had been unforgivable, he couldn't forget how sweet it had been to hold Kate in his arms, to feel her slender body pressed close to his, and, when he had sensed a response in her, he had suddenly felt like a king! He had laughed in sheer happiness at the thought of marrying her... How wrong he had been! She hadn't felt the same. She had felt ashamed, had believed he was laughing at her. It wasn't surprising that she disliked him. And now here he was, tied to a London which was like a desert, waiting for the season to end and his release. He could go then to Calthorpe and work this misery out of his system.

Katharine had been in regular correspondence with Tilly ever since she had left Herriards. A little while ago she had been worried to receive a shakily written letter from her governess in which Tilly said she had a cold, but making light of it and assuring Katharine that she would soon be her normal healthy self. When Katharine didn't hear for some time after she sent a note to Tilly's neighbour, Mr Cruikshank, the surgeon, with an anxious enquiry about her friend. The reply was not reassuring. Tilly seemed to be unable to shake her illness off.

Katharine went to Mrs Calthorpe straight away and showed her the letter.

'I expect you would like to see for yourself how Miss Tillyard does, Kate. I'm sure something could be arranged.'

'As soon as possible,' said Katharine gratefully. 'But I can't ask you to leave London in the middle of the season. I can go alone.'

'Of course you can't! Sir James would never forgive me!'

'But there really isn't room for more than one visitor in Tilly's little cottage, ma'am! And no suitable accommodation in the village for you. I wouldn't dream of going anywhere near Herriards, even though the Paynes are here in London.'

'Not so, my dear! They left London yesterday but not for Herriards—for Bedfordshire. Catherine and her family have accepted Lord Acheson's kind invitation to stay with him at Souldrop. I rather think your cousin is about to announce her engagement to a most eligible *parti*.'

'I didn't know Lord Acheson had a son!'

'He hasn't. The *parti* in question is the noble lord himself.'

'But my cousin is only seventeen and he's forty if he is a day!'

'And rather rich,' added Mrs Calthorpe dryly.

'Poor Catherine!'

'Not at all—from what I have heard, she is delighted. But it means that your uncle and his family are all to be in Bedfordshire throughout July and August. You would be quite safe in your old home, if you wished to stay there.'

Katharine instantly rejected the idea. 'No! I wouldn't dream of going back! Never!' she said, sounding almost desperate. 'I'll stay with Tilly.'

Mrs Calthorpe smiled sympathetically. 'I quite understand. We must think of something else.' She thought for a moment. 'How would it be if I stayed with the Quentins once again? It isn't so far away. I could come over whenever you needed me, and I'm sure they would be pleased to see me—I had a letter from Marjorie Quentin just the other day repeating her invitation.'

'What would your son say to this?'

'Ah, yes! Adam. I think he could quite easily be persuaded to agree. I have the impression that he is no longer enjoying life in London—any more than you are!'

'You...you think Adam is unhappy?'

'Yes, I do. But don't ask me more, because I couldn't tell you. When he wishes, Adam is even more successful than you at disguising his feelings.'

As a result of these plans Katharine spoke to Adam at some length for the first time since their argument. She naturally wished to leave London immediately, and tried hard to persuade the Calthorpes to let her go without them.

'I should be perfectly safe,' she said desperately. 'And Tilly needs me now, not next week!'

'If all goes well, we can leave quite soon,' Adam said decisively. 'I've already sent to the Quentins to tell them of our plans, and the groom will go on to

Herriard Stoke to find out the present state of Miss Tillyard's health. You surely don't wish to arrive on Tilly's doorstep before anyone knows you are coming?'

'Adam is right, Kate dear. You mustn't travel alone to Hampshire. What would Sir James do if something happened to you?'

'I think you know very well what Sir James would do! He'd express his sorrow for a minute or two, grumble about the extra work my death would cause him for the next half-hour, then take to his bed.'

'There's something I've been intending to ask you,' said Adam slowly. 'Would you mind telling me the terms of the Frampton-Payne trust? For instance, what would happen to it if you *should* die?'

'Adam!'

'I'm not asking out of idle curiosity, Mama!'

Katharine said reluctantly, 'In that event, if I haven't married, it returns to the Herriards estate.'

There was a curious silence. Then Mrs Calthorpe said briskly, 'This is a gloomy subject and, moreover, it is not one that will ever need to be discussed. Kate is not going to die, she is going to marry and be very happy. Now, Adam, stop asking unnecessary questions and tell us how soon we can travel.'

'I should think before the end of the week. I have one or two things to see to, and we shall then be off.'

Adam did not tell them that one of the things he was determined to do was to find out exactly when and where Henry Payne and his family were planning to be, in particular Henry's son, Walter. But it seemed perfectly safe. The Paynes were all quite certainly staying with Lord Acheson at Souldrop Court, a full seventy miles from Tilly's cottage. They would stay there at least six weeks, and it would be late August at the earliest before they would return to Hampshire. There was no risk that Katharine would meet them at Herriard Stoke. Not for some time, at least.

The one matter which was not discussed was what Katharine would do when she eventually left Herriard Stoke again, though it was a question which had occurred to all three of them. It was as if they were all waiting to see what the future would bring, for events to run their course.

All arrangements were complete even before the day Adam had promised. Letters were sent and acknowledged, the London house shut up and the keys returned to the agent, the luggage packed, and Miss Kendrick given two months' paid leave. There would be no place for her in Herriard Stoke, and Mrs Calthorpe had her own maid to go with her to the Quentins. Katharine was reluctant to dismiss Miss Kendrick altogether. She hoped that her own future would be clearer after two months, and she could decide then whether there was a role for Miss Kendrick in it.

The Calthorpe party left London for Basingstoke early on Thursday morning. It was a bright, sunny day and they had an easy journey, the two ladies in the carriage and Adam riding alongside. All the same, though she put on a brave face, Katharine's spirits were low. Tilly's illness, her own uncertain future, and, most of all, the change in the man accompanying them made it impossible to stay cheerful. Adam Calthorpe seemed to have withdrawn into himself. An invisible barrier surrounded him that Katharine found impossible to cross, however much she wished she could. He remained courteous, helpful, concerned for her comfort, but the easy, natural companionship, which had become a feature of their acquaintance, had disappeared. Adam Calthorpe was not in any way an enemy, but he was no longer a friend.

They arrived at the Quentins in the early afternoon. Mrs Quentin insisted on serving them a delicious meal before Katharine could leave again. But at last she set off in the middle of the afternoon on the last stage of her journey. Adam accompanied her.

'Really!' she had protested. 'I don't need your escort, Adam. It isn't far, and I'm sure your men are trustworthy!'

'I would rather come with you, all the same,' he had replied, still in that coolly courteous voice. 'I am sorry if you find the situation difficult if I do, but we don't know what is waiting for you in Herriard Stoke. You cannot go alone, and my mother is too tired to come with us. But I assure you I will not bother you more than I have to. I'm afraid I must ride with you inside the carriage, if you don't mind.'

Katharine wasn't sure whether to be delighted or appalled at the thought of sitting next to Adam for a journey of an hour or more. She hesitated, the colour rising in her cheeks, before saying in a restricted tone, 'Of course not.' His expression grew even more remote.

Promising to see her very soon, Mrs Calthorpe kissed Katharine and hoped that she had good news at the other end of her journey. 'Remember, my love, that you can send for me at any time! Adam and I will be here for you whenever you want us.' Then she whispered, 'And try to be kind to my poor son.'

Katharine pulled a face and whispered back, 'I doubt he'll allow me! But I'll try.'

They drove in silence for a while, then Adam seemed to make up his mind. He sat up and said, 'I wonder if we might talk a little about your future?'

Katharine's heart missed a beat. 'Of course!' she said as calmly as she could.

'Since you don't as yet seem to have formed any attachment—' He stopped and asked, 'Am I right to assume so?'

Katharine had difficulty in finding her voice. 'Yes,' she whispered.

Adam showed neither approval or disapproval. He simply nodded and went on, 'And since you have also rejected the solution I put forward a week or two ago—'

'Adam, I—'

'Please! The last thing I want is to cause you embarrassment. I don't intend to go further into that. But…since that is so, would you like me to talk to Sir James while I am here?'

'To say what?'

'To support your original plan of setting up house with Miss Tillyard. You are obviously very attached to her, and, from what her neighbour says, Miss Tillyard will find it difficult to live by herself much longer. You could provide her with a more comfortable home, and servants to look after her. Now that you have established yourself in the eyes of Society, I think it would no longer damage your social position.

You could…you could look for somewhere with some life in it, where you might make new…friends. You would be wrong to cut yourself off from the possibility of a future marriage. I would suggest that you remove from Hampshire, however.'

To hear Adam talking of her future in this impersonal manner was painful in the extreme. The plan, which had seemed so desirable just a few months before, now seemed sterile. But what else was there for her? It was most unlikely that she would ever marry, and it seemed that Tilly needed her. More than anyone else did. But she was reluctant to shut the door completely. She said, 'Can we wait a day or two, Adam? I must first see how Tilly is. But I agree with you. Whatever I decide, I don't wish to stay anywhere near Herriards.'

'Agreement at last!' said Adam with a wry smile.

'I have never wished to disagree with you,' Katharine said in a low voice.

'Haven't you? I'm disappointed. I found it one of your most refreshing characteristics.'

'How can you say that? You always seemed impatient when I did.'

'Perhaps. But I still enjoyed it.'

Katharine hardly dared to breathe. Adam was at last talking almost normally once again. He sat back against the squabs of the carriage and mused, almost as if he was talking to himself, working things out as he went.

'You see, I spent almost ten years in the Army, and, except for the first year or two, nearly always in a position of command. I hope I had a good relationship with the men under me, but they didn't answer back.

Or, if they did, I soon saw to it that they stopped. I never thought of myself as a tyrant, merely as someone who worked out the best strategy and saw that it was carried out. I gave the orders. And then I met you.' He looked at her. 'I didn't like you at first, you know.'

'Any more than I liked you,' said Katharine.

'I know. But I changed my mind.'

'So did I.'

'Did you? Did you, Kate? Never wholly, I think.'

'You made it so clear that I was not the sort of woman you admired. My cousin—'

'Kate, you've seen Julia Redshaw. I am aware that you don't like her, but, just for one moment, forget the way she acts, just think of the way she looks. She was and is still exquisitely beautiful—can you not agree?'

'Perfectly.'

'Your cousin is just like her. At twenty I idolised Julia Redshaw. To me she was the epitome of female beauty. For years I judged all other women by her. And though I no longer loved her, I still thought I would one day marry someone who looked something like her. I knew exactly what I sought—Julia's looks, small, perhaps a little clinging, delightfully dependent on me, in need of my protection... After all the years of dirt and noise and warfare, I wanted a peaceful life. I wanted someone who wouldn't argue...and then I met you.'

'Why did you take so much trouble with me?'

'I had given my word to Tom.'

'I don't think that is the whole story at all. You saw

I was desperate. If Tilly had been in the same straits you would have done the same for her.'

'Some of it. But not all. You became a thorn in my flesh, an ever-present source of irritation, someone I had to do something about before I was driven mad. You became, not Tom's responsibility, but mine.'

'I didn't want to be anyone's responsibility!'

'I know. That was what made it all so intriguing. I had intended to look for a beautiful, delicate clinging vine, and what did I find? A girl who is fiercely independent, a girl who has a spirit like Sholto's, and is as tricky to handle.'

'You don't handle—'

'Shh! I haven't finished.' Adam settled himself more comfortably and went on, 'The lady of my choice was to be a soothing influence in the home, full of patience and forbearance, an example to our children. And what was I presented with? A girl who plays tricks, who would rather fight than give in, who becomes belligerent when she is nervous, or thinks she might be in the wrong, who is even prepared to use her fists when she is angry enough.'

'I wonder you spent any time at all on such a virago,' said Katharine sourly.

'Ah, but this same girl has such courage! Such a determination not to evoke anyone's sympathy by a parade of feeling when she is hurt. I have met many courageous men in my time, but she is as courageous as any of them, and as loyal. She is intelligent, too. And when she smiles she can charm the world. Do you want me to go on?'

'Why are you saying these things?'

'I'm trying to explain why I've made so many mistakes. How it is that I have made you dislike me so?'

'I don't dislike you.'

'Not even...after the way I treated you when we were together in the library.'

'It was partly my own fault. You're right. I do play tricks, I do get belligerent. I must take some of the blame for what happened. Adam, if you only knew how I've reproached myself for the way I goaded you, gave you and Walter Payne an entirely false impression on the night of Lady Marchmont's ball. So much evil came of it.'

'I know what I did. What did Payne do?'

'He came that same day, just after...after you had gone. He asked me to marry him, said I had encouraged him.' She turned to the man beside her. 'That was not so, Adam! But I had invited him to join us at the table...'

'Why did you?'

'Oh, I wanted company. Lord Trenchard hadn't yet appeared and...and you and Julia Redshaw seemed to want a tête-à-tête.'

'I remember feeling annoyed with Julia. And later I saw for the first time what she was really like. But go on. Payne thought you had encouraged him and was disappointed when his hopes were dashed...'

'He wasn't just disappointed. He was beside himself. He...he raved like a madman.'

'What did he say?' Adam, who had been leaning back, now sat up sharply. 'What did he say?' he repeated urgently.

'I really don't remember. I was still...still upset. He threatened me, I think. Nothing specific. He said some-

thing about making new plans. Something like that…
I really can't remember.'

'Kate, if Walter Payne ever comes near you, you
must send for me, do you understand? No independence, no thinking you can deal with him alone.'

'Very well.' She paused, then said hesitantly, 'Will
you be there, Adam?'

'Whether you want me or not.'

They were entering Herriard Stoke. Speaking rapidly Adam said, 'Kate, you say you don't dislike me.
If that is indeed so, won't you at least consider my
proposal? I still think we could have a happy life together. You need a home, and I need a wife. And we
have neither of us found anyone else we should wish
to marry. It isn't a question of necessity or otherwise.
I'm asking you to marry me.'

Chapter Fourteen

Katharine was torn. It was far from a declaration of love, but Adam had come closer in the last hour to showing genuine admiration for her. Was it enough? She looked at him, her doubts and anxieties clearly revealed.

Adam shook his head. 'I'm a fool! Of course you're upset at the moment. This isn't the time to make important decisions, and I shouldn't have asked you. But may I hope that while you're here you'll consider what I've just said?'

'I…I will, Adam. And I am very happy that we are…friends again.'

'Friends?' he said with a smile. The carriage was drawing up at Tilly's gate. Adam took her hand and kissed it, then leapt out. He helped her out of the carriage and they went up the path together. Tilly's little maidservant showed them in.

Tilly was lying on a day bed, but her eyes were bright and she had colour in her cheeks. Katharine went over and hugged her, then plied her with questions about her health.

'I'm better for seeing you, Katharine. And Lord Calthorpe, too! Good evening, sir. How kind you are!'

The next half-hour was engaged in bringing Katharine's luggage in from the chaise, and discussing plans for the next few days. Tilly had clearly been more seriously ill than Katharine had realised, but it looked as if she might at last be on the mend.

Adam went next door to spend a few minutes with the surgeon, who assured him that Miss Tillyard was no longer in any danger, but would benefit from company. He finished by saying, 'That servant of hers is a good, sensible little girl, but Miss Tillyard sometimes gets bored with her chatter, and that's when she gets up and tries to do too much. Miss Payne will keep her in order. It's very pleasant to see her again. I'm afraid things here aren't quite the same as they were when her grandfather was alive.'

When Adam returned they had some of Tilly's favourite cordial, then it was time for him to go.

Katharine went to the gate with him. 'After we had met for the first time, I looked back from here and saw you waiting at the corner,' she said. 'I thought you overbearing even then.'

'And later I went back to the Quentins and described how I had met a shrew.'

'We make a fine pair,' Katharine said, smiling ruefully.

'I think we do,' Adam replied, looking serious. He took her hand in his. 'Let go of the past, Kate. Think of the future.'

Katharine sighed. 'I know you're right. Whatever happens, Tilly and I will leave Herriard Stoke when she is well enough, and we shan't come back. I shall use the time I'm here now to visit all the places I knew with Tom—and bid them a final farewell.'

'Ah! I almost forgot. Cintra and her groom will arrive tomorrow. I've arranged for her to be stabled at the inn down the road. But…' He seemed to be at a loss. 'I hardly dare say this! You'll take care, won't you?'

Katharine's face lit up with laughter. 'You needn't look so worried, Adam. I promise not to snap at you any more when you try to look after me. But, in any case, I know this place and its people like the back of my hand. I won't come to any harm round Herriards.'

Adam was driven off, and Katharine went back into the cottage. She was still smiling.

'You're looking cheerful, Katharine.'

'Tilly, Lord Calthorpe has taken the trouble to have Cintra delivered to Herriard Stoke for me to use while I'm here. Isn't that thoughtful?'

'I think he's a very thoughtful man. You seem to be on better terms with him than when I last saw you together?'

'It varies, it varies!' Katharine found herself unwilling to discuss her relationship with Adam Calthorpe, even with Tilly. She was still confused about it herself. 'We seem to be friends at the moment. Now, how shall we set about making you absolutely well again?'

In the days that followed Katharine looked after Tilly and caught up with the news of the district. It wasn't all good. The Paynes had till now had a reputation for looking after their own, but Henry Payne was failing to live up to it. The good impression he had created on his arrival had been dissipated by broken promises and blatant neglect of his obligations. He was no longer as popular in the area as he had been, even among the gentry. Katharine could only commiserate and try to comfort. She was powerless to help.

After two days Adam brought Mrs Calthorpe over to see Tilly. They came laden with gifts and good wishes and stayed for several hours. Adam made no attempt to have private conversation with Katharine. It would have been difficult in any case, but she felt it was more than that. He was deliberately giving her time to think things through, and she was grateful. Just occasionally she had to chide herself for being idiotic enough to daydream, foolishly imagining a day when Adam would appear and demand her answer, swear undying devotion, tell her that he was desperate, he could wait no longer for her reply... Of course, that would never, never happen. Adam *liked* her, they were *friends.* Not lovers.

Cintra was regularly exercised, but at first Katharine did not go very far, because she did not like to leave Tilly alone for too long at a time. But then, as Tilly progressed, she took to riding further afield, doing as she had said she would, bidding the scenes of her childhood farewell. Now, after a year of freedom from the stress his death had caused her, she could remember Tom with a love free of resentment, could look back on their adventures and games in and around Herriards with fond amusement.

She returned regularly to their favourite haunt—the remnants of the old castle which had been the first dwelling of the Paynes of Herriards. She and Tom had been whipped more than once for climbing among its ruins, for the masonry was unstable, and the ground was dangerously uneven. Her grandfather had had its old well partially filled up and covered over after twelve-year-old Tom had climbed down and found himself stuck. It had taken a team of farm hands several hours to bring him out, and there had been moments when rescue had seemed impossible. Tom had boasted of it afterwards. He claimed he could have saved himself by climbing up the series of rungs on the side, which had once formed part of the ladder that went all the way down. But it was as well he hadn't tried. The rungs were rusted and brittle. It wouldn't have taken much for them to give way, and Tom would have fallen all the way to the bottom.

They had both kept clear of the place for a long time afterwards. And now, Katharine tied Cintra to a tree well clear of the castle, and herself walked with caution along the paths through the ruins. Dangerous it might be, but the place was beautiful. The air was full of herby fragrances, birds and small animals of all kinds had their homes in the ruined chimney stacks, in the scrub, in the thick ivy which covered the walls left standing, and summer flowers were beginning to appear in the overgrown heaps of stone. She sat here, remembering the past, thinking of the future, trying to come to terms with the reality of her relationship with Adam. And after a while she reached a decision. She would marry him. Life with him had so much to offer. She must learn to be happy with what there was, and not to dream of having the moon.

Meanwhile Catherine Payne, up in Bedfordshire with the rest of her family, was being fêted, complimented and admired to her heart's content. Lord Acheson was a gregarious character and, moreover, he wished to show off his latest acquisition, his future bride—lovely, young and fresh as a rose. So the house party at Souldrop Court was a large one, and numbers of visitors came and went. Some of the guests envied Catherine the match, for Lord Acheson was a very rich man. Very few dared to express doubts about its suitability, for he was also a bad-tempered one.

Henry Payne and his wife basked in their daughter's reflected glory, and enjoyed the luxury of life at Souldrop. For a while at least they could forget their financial embarrassments and join in the many entertainments offered by their prospective son-in-law. Only Walter was finding it less than enjoyable. His sister's success made his own failure the more obvious. In private his father lost no opportunity to rail at him, to remind him of his boastful promise to marry Katharine Payne and her fortune.

'But why do I expect anything of you, Walter? You always were a great talker, but a poor doer! You're a fine fellow with the housemaids and farm girls from what I've heard, but you don't seem to be such a success where it matters! I warn you, if you don't do something about this money, I shall be sunk! And you along with me! We've spent far more than we ought in impressing Acheson. What do you suppose he'll do when his betrothed's father is declared bankrupt? I can't see that bag of conceit sticking to Catherine when the family is in disgrace, can you?'

Walter, still smarting at Katharine's contemptuous rejection, had not yet told his father how hopeless his case was. He said with as much bravado as he could muster, 'Don't worry, Pa! I'll see that Kate comes round. Something will come of it yet.'

'I'll be glad to see some evidence of that! Perhaps you'd better get back to town. You're wasting your time here when Kate Payne is in London! For God's sake go and do what you said you would!'

Or more, said Walter to himself. He was in a dangerously vindictive state, furious with himself, furious with his father, but chiefly furious with Katharine Payne. He would go to London, he would find her, he would make her listen…or… He had said she would pay for his humiliation, and it was time to see that she did!

But at dinner that night, one of the guests newly arrived from London mentioned that the capital was remarkably thin of decent company and listed several families who had recently left.

With a significant glance at Walter, Henry Payne said, 'However, I suppose my niece is still in town? She is staying with the Calthorpes.'

'They left last week, the three of them! I was surprised—we all were. One day they were there, and practically the next they were gone! I wonder what can have caused such haste—do you know, sir? Not a family crisis, I hope?'

'Not as far as I know. Strange. I find that worrying. Walter, I think you had better look into it. I could not be easy if I thought dear little Kate was in trouble and we were doing nothing about it.'

Walter left the next morning and made straight for Dorking. This was where the Calthorpes had taken

Katharine before Christmas, and he had decided it was the most likely place to which they would return. But Bridge House proved to be closed, the only activity being round the farm buildings and the stables. Questioning the stable hand only produced a scratching of the head.

'Has your mistress gone to Lord Calthorpe's estate near Bath, perhaps?' asked Walter impatiently.

'I don't rightly know, sir… But wait a minute! Jem,' he shouted to a lad nearby. 'Where were they to take Miss Payne's mare?'

'Quite a distance. Somewhere near Basingstoke, I think. Would it be Herod…Stone? Stoke? Something like that.'

'Thank you. I think I know where you mean.'

'But his lordship's horse didn't go there,' said the lad, anxious to be helpful. 'I think his lordship and the mistress are staying at friends of theirs. It's nearer still to Basingstoke.'

'Thank you, again,' said Walter slowly. He threw the lad a few coins and rode off. What he had just learned was deeply interesting! Katharine Payne was at Herriards, was she? Taking advantage of his family's absence, no doubt. And Calthorpe and his interfering hag of a mother were not with her! How very interesting! Herriards had been shut up and most of the servants sent away while his family were in London. It looked as if he might have that girl all to himself… Walter continued on his journey, almost cheerfully.

He was disappointed therefore to find that Katharine was not, after all, at Herriards, but staying with her old governess in the village nearby. But he didn't give up his hopes of catching her. He kept his own presence quiet by staying in one of the deserted outbuildings, and paying one of the farm girls to fetch him food and drink. He was pleased to see that he hadn't lost his touch with farm girls, at least! The girl, a friend of Miss Tillyard's Meg, quite innocently informed him of Katharine's habits, prattling away, in response to some clever questioning, about Master Tom and Miss Kate and their games in the past, wondering at Miss Kate's present wish to visit her old haunts, and asking if it meant Miss Kate was soon to leave them forever. Walter listened, reassured her and sent her on her way. He soon picked up Kate's trail, and by following her, always at a safe distance, discovered that she was particularly attached to the old castle and often to be found there. Now here was an opportunity! The castle was some distance from any other buildings, and it was so dangerous that the local people avoided it. Surely he could approach Katharine here, and make her listen to reason—or force her to consent! He might even enjoy that. Walter laid his plans and waited.

And eventually he was rewarded. After only a couple of days of lying in wait Walter heard Kate arrive, tie her horse up to one of the trees at the edge of the clearing, and walk slowly into the castle precinct. She sat on the edge of the old well, lost in thought. Walter took his chance.

'Good afternoon, Kate!'

Katharine swung round, startled. 'Walter! What are you doing here?'

'I live here now. Had you forgotten? No, don't get

up! You look charming there.' He smiled at her engagingly.

'What do you want?'

'I said, don't get up! Why are you so suspicious of me?'

Katharine clutched her riding crop more firmly. 'I suppose because the last time we met, we didn't part on the best of terms. And now I must go—I feel I'm trespassing.'

'Trespassing? That's a harsh word. I'm sure no one would hold it against you, Kate. What is it that brings you here? A touch of nostalgia?'

Katharine looked at him suspiciously. Walter was being too friendly. 'I'm…I'm saying goodbye,' she said, trying to edge round him.

He stood firmly in her way. 'Why should you do that? When you'll be living here.'

'I won't. You were right. I've decided to marry Lord Calthorpe.'

'That isn't so, Kate, my dear,' he said, still calmly, still with that hatefully false smile on his face. 'You're going to marry me! *Me,* do you hear!'

'Let me pass!' He shook his head, and put his hand on her arm.

'Kate, listen to me! I'm ready to make a bargain with you. And I'm afraid you won't be going anywhere until you've heard what it is.'

'Take your hand off me first.'

Walter took his hand away and held it up. 'You see? You've no need to be frightened. I'm harmless, really.'

'I'm not frightened, Walter.'

'Well, you should be!' he said with sudden viciousness. The change in his manner was so abrupt that

Katharine was shocked. This was more like the Walter she knew, but there was such an added venom in his tone that she began to think he might be a little mad.

She said cautiously, 'Well? What is this bargain, Walter?'

'I've seen you and Calthorpe together. You're not in love with him any more than he is with you. I don't know why you want to marry him. It's not as if you need his money, and he certainly doesn't need yours!' His voice rose. 'But *I* do! I need the Payne money. So does my father. We'll go bankrupt without it. And it's *our* money! Ours by *right!*' He almost shouted the last words at her.

Katharine moved back nervously. Walter saw it, and made a visible effort to speak more calmly again. 'If marriage is all you want,' he said, trying to smile, 'you can marry me and have Herriards, too. My father won't last forever, and I'll see to it that you are not bothered with either of my parents.'

When Katharine began to shake her head, Walter said quickly, 'You needn't be bothered by me, either. As a husband, I mean. All I want is for you to marry me. I swear I'll leave you alone afterwards. If that is what you want.'

For the life of her she could not control a gesture of distaste. Walter saw it and his expression changed. He suddenly became a very dangerous man.

She swallowed and said placatingly, 'Walter, I need to think over what you've said. I understand about the Payne money. I agree, it isn't really fair. And Herriards is a tempting prize, believe me. Give me some time. Let me go back to Tilly's and I promise I'll consider—'

'What sort of a fool do you take me for? I saw the way you looked at me just now. You don't want to think things over, you want to get away! Well, I'm not having any of your tricks! I'm not letting you go! I want an answer! Now! And if I have to take you by force right here on the spot to make sure of you, I'll do it! Do you understand?' He took hold of her arm again and pulled her roughly towards him.

Katharine raised her riding crop and struck him across the mouth.

Walter was consumed with white-hot anger. He grabbed a piece of wood which was lying on the ground next to him and struck her hard on the head. She gave a little gasp and dropped to the ground like a stone.

Walter stared at her in horror. Katharine lay quite still, and her face was colourless, except for a scarlet trickle of blood down the side. What had he done? The thought of getting rid of Katharine Payne was not new, but this reality was terrifying! Frantically he knelt down beside her and pulled open her riding habit, but there was no sign of life. He had killed her! For a moment he was overcome with remorse and fright, but then the instinct for self-preservation took control. He looked around. Except for her horse cropping the grass by the edge of the trees, the woods were silent. No one was about. By the time Katharine was missed there would only be a couple of hours' daylight left—three at the most. It would be morning before anyone could possibly search properly. If he concealed the body well enough, they wouldn't find her for hours. He could be miles away before it was discovered. No one would suspect him—no one in the village knew he had ever been at Herriards. The girl from the farm knew, but he would see to it that she didn't talk.

Walter looked at the figure on the ground and panic rose in him again. Oh, God! What had he done? What would happen to him if anyone found out that he was a murderer? He must hide the body, put it out of sight, quickly, quickly! Where? Walter gazed round wildly. The well! He dragged the cover away, hauled Katharine's limp form up on to the parapet, then tipped it over. He didn't wait to hear it land, but picked up the whip and ran to the horse in the trees. His own horse was back at Herriards, where he had left it deliberately in order to lie in wait for Katharine unobserved. Hers would do to take him away from here. He would turn it loose later. That was all that mattered, to get away! He untied the horse and mounted it, kicked his heels hard into its flanks and gave it a slash with Kate's whip…

Cintra, all her instincts at war with the terror emanating from this stranger, and thrown into a panic by his rough treatment, reared up violently, then took off in a mad dash to rid herself of the unwelcome burden. Walter was powerless to stop her. He held on desperately for a minute or two, but then was knocked flying by an overhanging branch, and was thrown into the undergrowth, where he lay half-hidden. He didn't move. He would never move again. His neck was broken.

Instinct eventually took Cintra back to the stables, where she created chaos as the groom tried to catch her. The alarm was raised, one of the lads ran round to Tilly's cottage, and Lord Calthorpe was sent for straight away. But it was too late in the day to wait till he arrived before taking any action. It would be almost three hours before he could possibly be at Herriard Stoke, leaving little daylight for a search. All the inhabitants of the village knew Miss Kate, and they were all anxious to do what they could. Jem Banks, the landlord of the inn, organised search parties and they were sent off along all the bridle paths, over the fields, along the lanes. With no result. Unfortunately, they were all working on the assumption that Cintra had thrown Kate, and that she was lying injured somewhere near a path or road of some kind. It never entered their minds to go into the castle grounds. Nobody would ever take a horse there, and very few would venture there themselves.

Adam arrived far sooner than anyone had a right to expect, but even so the daylight was just beginning to fade. He questioned the men as they returned, asked Tilly for anything Kate might have said about her plans for the afternoon, went to have a look at Cintra, and demanded an explanation from the groom as to why the man had not accompanied Miss Payne on her ride. The servant was worried and distressed and it took him a minute or two to tell a coherent story.

'Miss Kate told me she wasn't going for a ride this afternoon,' he said. 'She hasn't been what you might call riding out properly for a few days now. She's been exploring more. She said she didn't need me. In fact, she said she didn't want me!' he said aggrievedly.

Adam was too fair a man to blame the groom. He knew how insistent Kate could be. 'Tell me where she used to go on these explorations,' he said brusquely. 'No! Don't bother! You don't know the district.'

He went back to Tilly. 'What has Kate been doing these past days? The groom says she hasn't taken him because she didn't need him. Where would she go?' he asked.

'Adam, she's been saying goodbye. She's been to all the old places where Tom and she used to play. They're not usually very far away… The castle! She might have gone to the castle! She's been there more than once.'

Jem Banks had accompanied Adam back to Tilly's. He shook his head. 'She wouldn't go there!' he protested. 'It's dangerous!'

'We're going to look all the same,' said Adam peremptorily. 'You say you've looked everywhere else.'

They gathered together some lanthorns and sticks and rode in the direction of Payne Castle. It was gloomy under the trees, and the men were distinctly uneasy. It didn't help when one of the horses shied and nearly threw his rider. They stopped.

'What's that?' exclaimed one of the men. He pointed to a figure lying in the undergrowth a short distance away. Adam leapt off his horse and ran over to it.

'It's a man!' he shouted. 'And he's dead—his neck is broken.' He rolled the body over. 'Oh, my God!'

'It's Walter Payne!' said someone. 'What's he doin' 'ere?'

'You mean what was he doing here,' said Adam grimly. 'And my guess is nothing good. Come on! We'll deal with this on our way back.'

They left the body lying where it was, and picked their way cautiously through the trees to the castle.

'You'd best not take your 'orse any further, your lordship,' said Jem Banks. 'The ground is mortal bad for 'orses.'

They dismounted and advanced into the clearing. It was very nearly dark. 'Kate!' shouted Adam. 'Kate!' He turned. 'All of you! Shout!'

They shouted and waited, but when the echoes died the place was silent.

Adam took a step forward. 'I'm going to look round,' he said.

'My lord, it isn't safe!' Jem protested. 'You'd end up with a broken neck yourself! This is a dangerous place even in daylight. It's impossible in the dark. We'll have to come back tomorrow morning. Unless Miss Kate is found somewhere else before that.'

Adam said, 'She's here. Somewhere. I know it.' He thought for a moment. 'I'll stay here,' he said. 'I...I can't leave.'

'It's madness!'

'I'll stay here,' Adam repeated. 'I won't do anything foolish. I just...I just don't want to leave. Understood?' He looked at Jem's disapproving face. 'She might be lying unconscious somewhere round here. And if she comes to during the night and manages to call, I'll hear her. I don't want anyone else to stay—you can come back tomorrow.'

'Er...what about Mr Payne, my lord?'

'Who? Oh, yes. We must do something about him. From the way he was lying it looks very much as if he has been thrown. But where's the horse? You'd better ask someone to look into that. I can't do anything about it at the moment.'

'Would he have been riding Miss Kate's mare? She turned up without a rider.'

'In that case, what has happened to Miss Kate?'

The men shook their heads and looked grave. Adam said, 'It's all such a confounded *mystery!* But I am still certain that she is somewhere here...' His eyes searched the darkness ahead. The men waited. Adam turned and said, 'What are you waiting for?'

'Mr Payne, my lord. What to do about him.'

'Oh, yes. Yes. I'd be obliged if two or three of you could deal with him. He should be taken to Herriards. Is anyone there?'

'A caretaker, that's all. The Paynes took one or two of the old staff to London, and let the rest go for the summer.' There were some murmurs. This was obviously a matter for resentment.

'Well, something has to be done with him. And a message must be sent to his family. What a mess this is! Look, take him to Herriards and help the caretaker to find somewhere suitable to lay him. Inform Mr Cruikshank. I'll see to the rest later, when...when...I have time. Good night.'

'Very good. We'll be here tomorrow first light.'

'And bring some equipment with you—ropes, that sort of thing. We might need them.'

'You're sure you'll be all right, my lord?'

'Quite certain. Goodnight.'

Adam was left to himself. He took Sholto to a nearby stream and rubbed him down with some grass. The stallion wouldn't suffer from staying out on such a warm night. Then he came back into the clearing and surveyed the scene. The men were right—searching the ruins tonight was impossible. But it was equally impossible that he should leave this place. Not while he was so convinced that he would find Kate here. The night was warm and he was used to camping out. He wouldn't come to any harm. He sat down on a fallen boulder.

What had happened today? What had Walter Payne been doing in Herriard Stoke? Adam was sure it had something to do with Kate, and his heart was heavy. Walter had probably known where Kate was now, but he wasn't going to tell anyone. He was silenced forever. When would they find Kate? What in God's name had happened to her? Unable to sit still, Adam got up and shouted again.

'Kate! Kate! Where are you?' He waited, but there was no answering cry. He slammed one hand into the other in a gesture of frustration and despair. What would he do if Kate…if Kate… No! It was impossible! Kate couldn't be dead! She couldn't be! Not when she meant so much. He gazed around again. The moon was rising, casting slanting shadows of silver over the ruins of the castle. Black and silver everywhere. No colour, no life. He threw himself down again, his head bowed, resting his elbows on his knees, gazing down at his loosely clasped hands. To lose Kate was unthinkable. She was the other half of himself, his companion, his friend… He looked up, startled, at the moon. Kate was more than all of these! Kate was the love of his life! The centre of his existence. He sat staring at the moon like a lunatic as this thought gradually filled his consciousness. Then he closed his eyes. What a stupidly complacent fool he had been! Thinking his desire to marry Kate was merely for her good, merely to protect her. He, who had always prided himself on his clearsightedness, on the power of his reason. How could he have believed it? Why had he not identified his own feelings sooner? He wanted to marry Kate because no other woman would do! He jumped up impatiently. 'Kate!' he called, louder than ever, his voice echoing through the ruins. 'Ka-a-a-ate!'

Katharine blinked as reflected moonlight fell on her face. Where was she? Wherever it was it was not very comfortable... She gasped as she tried to move. White hot pain lanced up her arm. She felt sick...dizzy... faint...

When she next noticed anything she saw that it was dark. The moonlight had gone. She must have been asleep, though how that was possible with a head like hers was difficult to see. It was pounding. What had woken her? Had she heard something? There it was again! *'Kate!'* She tried to shout back, but the sound wouldn't come. She couldn't speak! She became agitated, tried to shift her arm, and this time the pain was even greater. Kate fainted again.

The next time she came to, she was shivering. It was cold and dark here...walls all around... She was down a hole! With her good hand she felt behind her. Stones. Metal. How was this *possible?* She was down the well at the castle! Frightened, she called as loudly as she could. 'Adam! Help me!' It came out as a mere whisper. Katharine slumped in despair. No one would ever hear that! She was chilled to the bone...she was going to die! She would never see Adam again, never be able to tell him that she loved him...never marry him…live with him…love him… But then she set her jaw and roused herself. She was not going to die! She must live, must get out of this dreadful prison! How on earth had she got here in the first place? She must concentrate, but it was difficult with this hammer beating in her head… Half-dozing, half-waking, she pieced together the events of the day before. Walter's face swam before her eyes, contorted with rage, a red slash running diagonally across his mouth. She had hit him with her riding crop… Why? He had attacked her… Then what had happened? But memory wouldn't come back… She gave a silent little whimper. She couldn't remember…

When Katharine next opened her eyes she felt a little more wide awake. The piece of sky she could see was less dark. This was better! Daylight was coming again. Surely someone would come to look for her? She struggled to stand up, sweat pouring down her face as her head throbbed and her arm was a searing pain. But pain was forgotten as she heard Adam's voice shouting.

'Kate! Kate! Where are you?'

'I'm here, Adam. I'm here! Help me! Oh, Adam, help me! I'm down the well!'

More voices. Adam talking again. 'Be quiet! I thought I heard something, but it got lost in your talk. Listen!'

Katharine's knees could hardly hold her. She clung on to an iron support with her good hand. 'I'm here!' she screamed. 'Help me! Adam, help me!'

Chapter Fifteen

The patch of daylight disappeared as heads leant over the parapet of the well. A chorus of exclamations, 'She's there!', 'Look!', 'It's Miss Kate!', 'She's standing!', 'God be praised!' and then Adam's voice again.

'Move away! Let's have some daylight. Get the ropes!' Then, leaning over, he called, 'Kate, how badly are you hurt?'

Kate took a deep breath. It was really extraordinarily difficult to do the simplest things—to talk, for example. That scream had taken her last bit of strength.

'Come on, Kate! I need to know, so that we can get you out safely.'

How practical he is, thought Katharine hazily. How very *rational,* not to waste time on exclamations of relief or gratitude. Even the men were more enthusiastic! Come on, Kate! Answer him! She took another breath. 'I think…I must have broken…my arm. Nothing…else.' She started to feel faint again, and held on fiercely to her support.

'Good!' Adam wiped the sweat from his brow with his sleeve. Without comment one of the men passed him a drink. He nodded his thanks, drank some of it and felt better. 'I'll go down,' he said, taking his coat off. 'Put the rope round me for a standby, but I think I can climb down.'

Jem Banks, looking at Adam's pale face, said, 'One of the others could—'

'Save your breath! I'm fetching Miss Payne up. But—thank you. You'll have plenty to do, Jem. Hard work. Do you know how it's done—pulling two people up by rope? Or do you want me to demonstrate?'

'I can do it, my lord. You leave that to me. Now, are you ready?'

'I think so.' He leant over the parapet. 'Kate, listen to me!'

'I'm…listening, Adam.' Her voice seemed weaker.

He said urgently, 'Hold on! One more minute and I'll be with you. Just make sure you're to one side. Can you do that? I don't want to crash into you.'

'I think so.'

'Right!'

Adam nodded at the men who were now preparing the ropes, and climbed over the side. The well was not in fact very deep—it had been partially filled in—and the remnants of the iron ladder gave him a few footholds. He had done many a more difficult descent in his Army career. But never before in circumstances like these. Kate was weakening—he had heard it in her voice. She might well be more badly injured than she knew—or had admitted. Shock would have taken its toll, too… How could he manage to get her out without making things worse for her? If Kate was really badly injured…

Adam swore silently and told himself to concentrate. It wouldn't do Kate any good if he gave way to his fears. He made his way down slowly, carefully, till, looking down, he could see her face just below his feet.

'Now for the most difficult bit,' he said. He edged his way past her, and with a sense of enormous relief felt his feet touch the base. 'My good girl!' he said approvingly as she held herself back to let him pass. But he was a long way from happy. Kate's knuckles were white where she was clinging to the bar. Her other arm was hanging uselessly at her side. Her face was dirty, but underneath it was chalk white—except for a dark blue bruise on her temple. There was some dried blood on her cheek...

Adam took a deep breath. Now was not the time to hug Kate tightly, to give way to his overwhelming relief. First he had to check her for any other broken bones before he moved her, and then Kate had to be taken out of this hell-hole as quickly and as safely as possible. Gently he felt her all over. No other breaks as far as he could tell. He looked at her again. She was, if possible, even whiter. Her lips were trembling, and though she had winced as he had touched her, she hadn't said anything. Kate was really at the end of her tether. Adam allowed himself the luxury of a short, swift, featherlight kiss.

'You'll soon be safe, Kate!' he whispered. 'I've got you now. And I shall never let you go again.' He wasn't sure that she had even heard him. Her head was falling forward, and the hand holding the bar was slipping... Adam worked as quickly as he could in the restricted space. He used a strap one of the men had given him to bind the broken arm close to her body, and at this point Kate passed out completely. He caught her as she fell and held her wrapped in his arms for a moment, consoling himself with the thought that it was just as well she was unconscious—she would not enjoy the next few minutes. Then he wound the ropes round the two of them and shouted to the men to pull them up. Slowly, painfully the double burden was raised to the surface. Willing hands, surprisingly gentle for such big men, lifted Kate over the parapet and put her down on the grass. Adam climbed out after her. He covered her carefully with his coat, then stood, breathing fast, waiting to get his strength back. The men were already replacing the cover on the well, and winding up the ropes. Then Adam lifted Kate into his arms and walked to where the horses were tethered. He asked one of the men to hold her for a moment, then mounted and took her back. Sholto moved restlessly, but calmed down again when Adam spoke. Kate's eyelids fluttered open for a moment. A smile appeared on her worn face.

'Adam!' she said contentedly. 'Adam!'

The little procession made its way slowly back to the village. Some of the men had ridden on ahead to warn Tilly and the surgeon of their arrival, and by the time they reached Tilly's cottage, a bed had been prepared for Katharine, and Mr Cruikshank was waiting. The broken bone was soon set and the surgeon thought there was no reason for it not to heal perfectly well. He was more concerned about the bruise on her head, and the fact that she had spent the night in a state of shock in such uncomfortable circumstances.

After that moment of lucidity Kate had lapsed into

semi-consciousness. As the day wore on she grew quieter and stiller. When Mrs Calthorpe arrived Adam was at Kate's bedside, looking himself like death, but fiercely rejecting all offers of help.

'Adam, be reasonable,' his mother said. 'Go and get some sleep. Kate doesn't even know you're here! I'll look after her for the moment. Mr Cruikshank will find a nurse tomorrow if he thinks one is necessary.'

'What are we going to do?'

'Mr Cruikshank has offered us rooms in his house. If you will go and get some sleep now while I keep watch, then you can sit with Kate this evening. Miss Tillyard is not yet well enough to do much, but she will fill in. She can fetch one of us if there's any change. Do as I say, my dear! You'll do Kate no good at all if you collapse, too! Be reasonable.'

Adam reluctantly gave way. In his time he had given so much good advice to others to be reasonable, to be patient, not to worry... How totally worthless it all seemed now!

However, he did manage a couple of hours' rest and returned to Kate's room refreshed and ready to deal with whatever was necessary. His mother greeted him at the door with relief.

'She's very restless. I can't keep her quiet, Adam. I've given her some drops, but they don't seem to have done much good, and the surgeon says we mustn't give her any more until he calls again. I'm so glad you're back. She's asking for you all the time, though I'm not sure she knows what she's saying.'

Adam went to the bed.

Kate's arm prevented her from moving a great deal,

but she was twisting her head from side to side, murmuring impatiently, moaning, then calling out in a cracked voice, 'Adam! Help me, Adam! You said you'd be there! Where are you?'

'I'm here,' said Adam calmly. He sat down close to the bed and took Kate's good hand in his. 'I'm here, Kate. You can rest now.'

The sound of his voice seemed to calm her for a moment. Then she began again, turning her head restlessly. 'Adam, don't go away from me! Don't go!'

He reassured her once more, and she was quiet, but only briefly. The cracked voice soon began again.

'You look at her so fondly, Adam. I'd like you to look at me like that... Why can't you look at me like that? Such a loving smile... You don't love me, that's why, isn't it? Adam! You like me, that's all.' The hand in his moved convulsively. 'It will be enough, Adam, I'll make sure it's enough. But please, please don't leave me! Please don't go away!'

To hear strong, independent Katharine crying out such an urgent need of anyone almost overset both her watchers. Adam's mother had tears in her eyes.

'I knew she loved you. I didn't realise how much. You mustn't let her down, Adam.'

He shook his head. 'I won't let her down. You go and get some rest. I'll stay here for now.' He turned back to the figure in the bed, talking to her softly, reassuringly until she was quiet again.

The daylight slowly faded. Tilly came in with a lamp which she placed on a table shaded from the bed. She stayed for a short while, then went back to rest. Her maidservant came in with a tray for Adam and fresh barley water for Katharine. Later on Mrs Calthorpe came back and, after taking a look at Katharine, insisted that Adam go out for some air.

'You say she's been quiet for some time? I actually think she's asleep. That's a good sign. Come back in half an hour.'

As soon as Adam appeared outside in the street he was swamped with enquiries about Katharine. He said what he could to reassure them, and thanked them all once again for their help.

'It was a bad day for us when Master Tom was killed, your lordship,' said one grizzled farmer, heavily. 'Herriards will never be the same without Miss Kate.'

Adam nodded. His world would never be the same without Miss Kate, either.

When he returned to the sick room his mother assured him that Katharine had not stirred. 'Don't look so worried, my dear! I truly think she is on the mend. The surgeon called in and gave her some more drops, so she is sleepy again, but he was very hopeful. We are to see that she drinks plenty of the barley water. You can sit with her here, if that is what you want. I'll rest on the couch.'

Mrs Calthorpe made herself comfortable on the couch by the window, and Adam sat down by the bed again. Kate's colour was better, and she was breathing more peacefully. The room was quiet, as the world settled down for the night. He sat lost in thought by Katharine's bedside, thinking of Tom, of how the death of one young man could make such a difference to so many lives, wondering what would happen to Herriards and its people now that Henry Payne's heir was dead, even feeling some pity for Walter's family. But most of all he was content to sit by Katharine and feel profoundly grateful that she had survived.

Katharine's hand stirred. Adam got up and bent over her. Her eyes opened.

'Are you thirsty?' he whispered. She nodded drowsily, and he took the glass of barley water and supported her while she sipped. When he started to withdraw his arm she gave a little moan of protest.

'Don't go!' she whispered. 'Stay with me. I need you here, Adam. I think I'll always need you. I don't think I can face life without you.'

He was deeply moved. 'I've told you. I won't go away,' he said softly, putting the glass back on the table and settling her more comfortably on his arm. 'But you mustn't talk.'

She smiled at him sleepily. 'I want to! I have to tell you. All I could think of during the night…was that…I wouldn't be able to tell you if I…if I died down there…I love you, Adam. I was wrong to say I wouldn't marry you. I love you so much that it doesn't matter…' Her voice faded away.

'What doesn't matter?'

'That you don't love me the way I wanted you to love me. The way you loved Julia.'

'I *do* love you, Kate!'

'I know you do, really. And it would be stupid of me to want more, wouldn't it? I love you enough for both of us. It's enough that we would be together. But…but don't ever leave me—I couldn't bear that. I couldn't bear it, Adam…' Tears rolled slowly down her cheeks and she moved restlessly.

'Kate, you're sick, you need to sleep. I shan't leave you, I promise. I promise you, I'll never leave you. But rest now. We'll talk when you're better. Go back to sleep, my darling.' Adam settled her down on her pillows, wiped her tears and kissed her lingeringly on the cheek. She gave a little sigh of contentment and fell asleep again.

Adam got up and stretched himself. His arm was stiff, but that was of no importance. It really looked as if Kate was almost herself again. But what *was* Kate's self? He felt as if he had never really known her. He studied the sleeping form in the bed. She had always been so careful to conceal the vulnerable, passionate woman that was the real Katharine Payne. Did she even know herself that such a Kate existed? His own discovery of how much, how comprehensively, he loved her, had been so recent, that he hadn't had time to think about her feelings towards him. The last ten minutes had been a revelation. Detached, independent Kate had wept, had pleaded, had revealed her soul to him. Kate loved him almost as much as he loved her! He looked back at the bed. My darling, he thought, I will never feel prouder or more humble than I do at this moment. I adore you! And I will never, as long as I have breath in my body, knowingly hurt or disappoint you!

Mrs Calthorpe stirred. 'I'm sorry, Adam. I must have fallen asleep. Has there been any change?'

'A slight one, I think,' he said, trying not to smile. 'Kate seems much better, Mama. She's sleeping very peacefully. I think we're almost out of the wood.'

His mother regarded him closely. 'Adam, I haven't

seen you look like this since you were a little boy, and your father gave you your first pony. Remember? You were ecstatic with delight.' She came and kissed him. 'I think something *has* changed. And I think you and Kate are going to be very happy.'

Adam hugged her. 'I think we shall be, Mama. You were right about Kate Payne, all the time. She is the one for me. The only one. But how did you know?'

'I just *did!*' said Mrs Calthorpe.

But the next day it looked as if all was not to be such plain sailing.

Katharine slept the night through and in the morning was, except for her arm and the bruise on the head, almost her old self. Mr Cruikshank said she could get up for a few hours, and sit in the garden. Adam came to see her as soon as she was dressed and proposed carrying her downstairs.

'I'm sure that isn't necessary,' she said coolly. 'I can walk perfectly well.'

He looked at her warily. This was the Kate he had known in the churchyard last year. Kate the shrew. A slow bubble of amusement grew inside him, till he thought it would burst out into delighted laughter. But he was careful to let no sign of this appear in his face. Kate was suffering from reaction. The emotional scenes of the day before had horrified her. He should have known this would happen!

He said calmly, 'In that case, let me go ahead of you down the stairs. It would be a pity if you damaged the arm further. Come!'

She walked unsteadily across the room, stopped at

the door and leaned against the post. Then she said, 'I think I'll stay here. It will be too hot in the garden.'

'Kate, my darling shrew, my sweet virago, let me carry you downstairs! To please me. I badly want to talk to you, and I can't here.'

'You talked enough last night,' she said.

'I rather thought you did, too.'

'I was ill. I didn't know what I was saying.'

'Didn't you? Didn't you, Kate?' He held her eye.

After a moment she looked away. 'Perhaps I did. But you needn't pay any attention to it,' she said in her old detached manner.

'Oh, no, you can't use that tone with me—not any more. I've seen the real Kate Payne.'

Katharine looked at him with desperation in her eyes. 'Can't you forget what I said last night, Adam? It's so humiliating!'

'Let me take you downstairs. There's something I want to say to you. We shan't be disturbed. Mama has taken Miss Tillyard for a drive in the country.'

'What do you want to say?'

'I'll tell you in the garden.'

She gave a little gesture of resignation and allowed him to pick her up and carry her downstairs.

In the garden she sat under the apple tree, gazing at her fingers, refusing to meet Adam's eyes. He took her hand.

'Don't shut me out, Kate. Don't ever shut me out.'

'What do you mean?'

'I mean,' he said deliberately, 'that it would hurt me, more than I have ever been hurt before, if you were to deny me the girl I saw last night. Let the rest of the world be happy to know the Katharine Payne it saw in Bridge House, and in the London ballrooms. But you mustn't deprive me of the real Kate Payne. I fell in love with her before I really knew she existed, but now that I've seen her, I will never be content with less. I love you, Katharine. Never doubt that. Passionately and forever.'

'You…you said you wanted us to marry because I needed a home and you needed a wife.'

'I was mad! I need *you!* No other woman will do. And making a home with you, living at Calthorpe, building our future together, is everything I want. Can you forgive me for being so blind before?'

'I suppose you *did* call me your darling,' she said slowly.

'I thought you were asleep!'

She smiled. 'I heard that,' she said. 'So perhaps you do mean what you said. Perhaps it's not just because you feel sorry for me—'

'*Sorry* for you! Are you mad? Just wait till you're stronger. I'll show you what I feel for you!'

'It's only my *arm,* Adam…' Kate gave him a sideways look. He found he couldn't stop the laughter. It came out, joyful, jubilant, triumphant. When Kate began to look offended, he drew her from her seat, put his arm carefully round her good shoulder, and pulled her slowly to him. The kiss that followed began gently—almost a brotherly kiss, thought Katharine, disappointed. But then she decided she had been too quick to judge. The kiss grew in depth, in feeling, in passion. The sensation was like nothing she had ever before experienced. She was whirling round like a leaf in a storm, floating like thistledown, the blood coursed through her veins with a singing joy, yet all the time she felt safe, held close, held in a lover's arms. When he released her she had to hold on to him—she would otherwise have fallen. He held her with trembling hands for a while. Through her own tumultuous heart-beats she could feel his. They were just as uneven.

'I'm so sorry,' he said. 'I meant to treat you so carefully… And then…you're like wine, Katharine! Champagne! You go to my head. I could have hurt you! I shouldn't have—'

'No! Don't say that! It wasn't weakness. If I held on to you it wasn't because I was ill, Adam. And you mustn't say you shouldn't have kissed me like that. I…I liked it. I want more! Indeed, I think I could become addicted!'

Adam shook his head. 'I shouldn't have done it, all the same. This isn't the time or the place for such things. Talking of which…'

He sat her down again. 'Now we've sorted our-selves out—'

'Is that what you call it?' murmured Katharine. 'I've seldom felt more unsorted, myself.'

Adam ignored this interruption. 'I'll tell you what I really brought you down here to say. And I'm not afraid you'll misunderstand me. Not now. I want you to marry me—'

'Well, I should hope so!'

'Be quiet and let me finish! I want us to marry al-most immediately. Apart from a very natural desire to have you to myself, I want to see you absolutely safe. Let's have no more nonsense about the Frampton in-heritance. Until you're married you will be in danger.'

'I don't think Walter will try any more tricks,

Adam. He will be so shocked to hear I am still alive that he wouldn't dare.'

'Do you remember what happened in the castle grounds?'

'Walter came. He wanted to talk, he said. He said he was going to marry me whether I liked it or not. I tried to get away... Then he attacked me.'

'Did he hurt you?'

'Not then. I...I hit him. With my crop. There was blood on his face.'

'What happened next?'

She frowned. 'I'm not sure. I think he hit me with something heavy... And when I woke up I was in the well.'

Adam hesitated. 'He was a villain. Thank God we found you in time.' He grasped her hands firmly in his. 'But, Kate, I have to tell you this. Walter got his desserts. He's dead.'

'Dead! How? You didn't—'

'No. He was dead when we found him. He'd been thrown.'

'How could he have been thrown? He didn't have a horse with him! I'd have seen it.'

'Where was Cintra?'

'I tethered her under the trees. I didn't want to risk taking her into the castle grounds.'

'That's how Walter died. He tried to get away on Cintra. He was probably in a panic.'

'And Cintra threw him? I think she might if he treated her badly.'

Adam nodded his head slowly. 'That was probably the way of it.'

'I can't help feeling sorry for him, Adam. That

wretched inheritance! If only he hadn't been so obsessed by it…'

They sat in silence for a moment. Then he said, 'I still want to marry you as soon as possible.'

She gave him a glance. 'It's not *necessary* now, is it?'

'More than ever! And you will marry me here in Herriard Stoke, as soon as you are well enough! It will be a quiet wedding, of course. Your cousin's death, to say the least—'

'Are you ordering me what to do, Adam?'

'Yes!'

'In that case, and for this once, I submit. I think it's a wonderful idea!'

'Good. I'll put things in motion straight away. I must get in touch with Ivo, too. I'd like him to be there.'

'I'm so glad.'

'Why?'

'Why not? He's your friend. I like him. He dances the waltz *so* well. And he talks so charmingly, too,' said Katharine with an innocent look.

Adam took her chin in his hand. He said with a mock-threatening look, 'If I ever see you flirting with *any*one, best friend or anyone else, I shall run him through with my sabre, then cut out his heart. Do you understand?'

'Perfectly! And if I ever see you looking besotted at Julia Redsh—'

'I was not besotted! I have never been besotted in my life!' He stopped short. 'I *am* besotted,' he said in tones of disgust. 'I'm besotted with my future wife!'

Epilogue

July 1817

One year later, more or less to the day, Lord Calthorpe came into his lady's bedchamber with a letter in his hand. Lady Calthorpe was sitting up looking slightly wan.

'Are you feeling more the thing, my love?' he asked, bending over to kiss her.

She caught his hand. 'I expect I will soon,' she said. 'Give me another quarter of an hour. Is the letter from your mother? It's not to say she can't come this month, is it? I hope not! I can't wait to show her all the things we've done at Calthorpe since she was last here.'

'My darling girl, I can't imagine what could possibly arise to keep my mother away!'

'Good! It's time we told her that she's to be a grandmother in six months' time, as well.' Katharine looked worried. 'She won't mind, will she?'

'Not in the slightest. That's why she was so anxious to have me married! She wants grandchildren.'

'Oh? And I thought it was because she liked me,' said Katharine mournfully.

Adam kissed the fingers twined round his hand. 'She adores you,' he said. 'But not as much as I do.'

After a short interval Katharine said, 'Tell me who sent the letter.'

'Ivo. He's going down to visit his father at Sudiham, and he would like to call in on his way.'

'That's very good news! When?'

'Tomorrow fortnight. Do you agree?'

'Of course! But I don't think I'll try the waltz with him this time!'

Lord Trenchard arrived to the warmest of welcomes from both the Calthorpes. Katharine had felt at ease with him from the start, even though she had never had the slightest desire to flirt with him. Adam, of course, still counted him among his closest friends.

After dinner that night Ivo gave them the latest news from town. Towards the end he said carefully, 'I hear Henry Payne is back at Herriards, but I doubt he'll hold on to it for long. Rumour has it that he is trying to break the entail. Have you heard anything about it?'

'We haven't been away from Calthorpe since we first came down here last year. We haven't heard a thing. What is being said, if anything, about Walter?'

'There were rumours, of course. But nothing substantial. Nothing the scandalmongers could get their teeth into. Acheson married Catherine Payne, in spite of her father's difficulties. And now the world doesn't know whom to pity more—the bad-tempered husband or his flighty wife.' They all laughed. Ivo went on with a comic look, 'Talking of which, Balmenny has kept his lady firmly at home in Ireland. London hasn't seen her this season. I think he's trying to set up a family before it's too late.'

'Wise man!' said Adam idly, filling his guest's glass. Then he sat back. 'So, Ivo, what brings you to Somerset? Your father?'

'First, yes. I'll spend some time with him. Since we became reconciled he seems to need to see me quite often. He's getting old, Adam. I'm sorry now for the years we spent apart. Still, there's nothing I can do about that—it's water under the bridge...' He paused. 'I saw Colonel Ancroft in town, by the way. He has sold out of the Army, and has leased a house in Mount Street. He lives there alone. To tell the truth, I thought he looked a little lost. Has he no family?'

'It's a long story, Ivo,' Adam said. His tone indicated that he wasn't about to say any more.

'And not a story for publication, I take it?'

'Well, not mine to tell, at least,' agreed Adam a touch apologetically. 'It would be good to see the Colonel, though. Kate, sweetheart, would you mind if I invited him down? I'd like you to meet him.'

'Er...it'll have to be soon, won't it?' asked Ivo with a wicked look. 'Or is he to be the godfather? I was rather hoping that would be my assignment.'

'Be quiet, Ivo!' said Katharine, blushing.

Adam raised his eyebrows. 'What? Burden our child with a rake for a godfather?'

'I'll reform! I'll take the cloth! I'll do whatever you say! What do you wish me to do?'

'Nothing so drastic. But we'll talk of it nearer Christmas,' said Adam with a grin. 'I expect when the time comes we'll consider it. Will you be ready to report for duty?'

'Try to stop me!'

'Ivo, it sounded almost as if you had another reason to be down here,' Katharine said, thinking it time to change the subject. Though her husband laughed at her, she was childishly superstitious about tempting fate.

'Well, there is another reason—'

'A lady! A lady! Tell us!' cried Katharine gleefully.

'Not exactly a lady, Kate. A girl. Or better still, half-boy, half-girl.'

'What? This doesn't sound like your normal quarry, Ivo!'

'Oh, I'm not pursuing her. She's far too young. She pursued me. With a pistol. She was a jolly fine shot, too.'

Katharine looked at him in disbelief. 'You're making this up!'

'I swear I'm not.'

'My dear chap, why are you planning to seek her out again?' asked Adam. 'I should have thought you would want to steer well clear. So why?'

'I'm curious. I want to see what happened to her... It's an intriguing situation...would you like to know more about her?'

The Calthorpes demanded to know the whole story immediately.

'I don't know the *whole* story. I suspect it hasn't yet come to an end.' Ivo sipped his wine, thought a moment, then began.

'It all started when I was on leave in the spring of '15. I tried to visit my father, to make my peace with him before rejoining the regiment, but he refused to see me. So, since I was at something of a loss, I decided to stay with my aunt who lived not far away…'

The night was warm and, after their guest had gone to his room, Lord and Lady Calthorpe took a walk in the garden.

'What do you think of Ivo's story?' asked Adam.

'I think that this may be the best thing that has ever happened to him,' Katharine said slowly.

'What on earth do you mean?'

'He may not be very complimentary about the girl. But she intrigues him. And you know, Adam, Ivo would never be happy with your conventional débutante. She would bore him in no time. Yes, I predict some interesting times ahead for your friend.'

'You may be right,' said Adam, losing interest as he turned to take Kate in his arms. 'But there are more interesting times ahead for us, my love. My very… dearest…love.'

They kissed. Ivo caught sight of them from his window, and felt, just for a moment, that there was something he had not yet found… Something that could be wonderful.

* * * * *

Look for Ivo Trenchard's story.
Coming soon from Sylvia Andrew in
Mills & Boon Historical Romance

Modern Romance™
...seduction and
passion guaranteed

Tender Romance™
...love affairs that
last a lifetime

Sensual Romance™
...sassy, sexy and
seductive

Blaze
...sultry days and
steamy nights

Medical Romance™
...medical drama on
the pulse

Historical Romance™
...rich, vivid and
passionate

27 new titles every month.

With all kinds of Romance for every kind of mood...

MILLS & BOON®

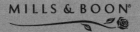

MILLS & BOON®

Historical Romance™

RINALDI'S REVENGE by Paula Marshall

Renaissance Italy
...condottiere, conspiracy, passionate conquest...

As ruler of a small but wealthy Italian duchy,
Elena de' Carisendi fears her land will be taken
from her by force. Her only chance of survival is
to hire an army – and mercenary Marco Rinaldi is
the best soldier money can buy. He awakes the
sensual woman in her, but it appears he harbours
a dark secret...

LADY LAVINIA'S MATCH by Mary Nichols

When their parents married, James, Earl of
Corringham, and Lady Lavinia Stanmore became
as close as brother and sister. Now, years later,
James has outgrown his rakish ways and is burning
with a love for her that he longs to reveal.
However, he faces a mysterious rival and Lavinia is
torn between the two. Can James persuade her to
look for love a little closer to home?

Regency

On sale 5th July 2002

FREE

2 BOOKS
AND A SURPRISE GIFT!

We would like to take this opportunity to thank you for reading this Mills & Boon® book by offering you the chance to take TWO more specially selected titles from the Historical Romance™ series absolutely FREE! We're also making this offer to introduce you to the benefits of the Reader Service™—

- ★ FREE home delivery
- ★ FREE monthly Newsletter
- ★ FREE gifts and competitions
- ★ Exclusive Reader Service discount
- ★ Books available before they're in the shops

Accepting these FREE books and gift places you under no obligation to buy; you may cancel at any time, even after receiving your free shipment. Simply complete your details below and return the entire page to the address below. *You don't even need a stamp!*

YES! Please send me 2 free Historical Romance books and a surprise gift. I understand that unless you hear from me, I will receive 4 superb new titles every month for just £3.49 each, postage and packing free. I am under no obligation to purchase any books and may cancel my subscription at any time. The free books and gift will be mine to keep in any case.

H2ZEC

Ms/Mrs/Miss/Mr ....Initials ....

BLOCK CAPITALS PLEASE

Surname ....

Address ....

....

....Postcode ....

Send this whole page to:
UK: FREEPOST CN81, Croydon, CR9 3WZ
EIRE: PO Box 4546, Kilcock, County Kildare (stamp required)